chick Lit

SACRED TEARS

A Novel

CLAUDIA TERRY PEMBERTON

SACRED TEARS
A NOVEL

iUniverse books may be ordered through booksellers or by contacting:

iUniverse
1663 Liberty Drive
Bloomington, IN 47403
www.iuniverse.com
844-349-9409

ISBN: 978-1-6632-1513-0 (sc)
ISBN: 978-1-6632-1512-3 (e)

Library of Congress Control Number: 2021904329

Print information available on the last page.

iUniverse rev. date: 03/22/2021

To my beloved daddy and sister—gone but not forgotten.
I love and miss you both every single day.

This book is dedicated to personnel in all areas of public service. From doctors and nurses to police officers, firefighters, paramedics, and the heroic military men and women who safeguard this great nation of ours, all of you have my utmost admiration, love, and respect. I thank you from the bottom of my heart. Thank you for your healing, your service, and your protection.

ACKNOWLEDGMENTS

I have many people to recognize and thank for generously sharing their expertise and knowledge with me in order to make my work of fiction as realistic as possible.

I would like to thank David C. Borgstrom, MD, MBA, FACS, Program Director, General Surgery Residency Chief, Division of General Surgery, Professor of Surgery at the West Virginia School of Medicine, for taking time out of his busy schedule to help me authenticate my character and her medical training and profession. Thank you, Dr. Borgstrom, for your kindness, sharing spirit, and input.

I would like to thank Amanda Pauley, MD, FACOG, for helping me to accurately portray the miracle of childbirth. Thank you, Dr. Pauley, for generously sharing your time and knowledge with me.

I would like to thank Emily Vore, MD, with Marshall Surgery, for her insight into the life of a third-year surgical resident. Thank you, Dr. Vore, for giving me a glimpse into the daily routine of my character.

I would also like to thank Julie Watson, midwife and author of *Born for Life: A Midwife's Story*. Thank you, Julie, for sharing with me your expertise in helping to bring a new life into the world.

To my editors and proofreaders—Allyson, Gloria, Hannah, Karen, Keri, and Pam—thank you all for your hard work on my behalf. As always, I appreciate your keen eyes and incredible insight. You are an author's dream team.

If only life didn't pass by so quickly. If only there were some way to slow it down or, better yet, enjoy every single moment of it as it comes.

Even the horrible, heartbreaking things that happen to us bring with them life lessons. They bring tears—sacred tears—that, if embraced, will bring about acceptance, healing, and, eventually, a smile.

1

FIRST CONTACT

While on her annual vacation with her family at Virginia Beach, one of Evie Edwards's favorite things to do was to get up before sunrise in order to enjoy a long jog on the beach. Dressed in a blue bikini top and a pair of black running shorts, Evie stealthily slipped out the back door of their first-floor condo. Not wanting to wake the rest of her family, she cringed as she slowly closed the creaky door.

Evie walked down the short path to the boardwalk and then down the ramp and onto the sand. She could see the first rays of the morning sun beginning to penetrate the horizon—not deep out to sea, as on most beaches on the eastern seaboard, but far to the left. The gentle curve of the land created this phenomenon. Gazing at the coral-and-turquoise predawn sky, Evie found the landscape breathtaking. She couldn't wait to get back to her canvas and oil paints to try to capture the beauty before her.

With not a cloud in sight, the first day of their two-week vacation promised to be glorious.

After pulling her nearly waist-length blonde hair back into a ponytail, Evie did her stretches and walked toward the surf. Facing east, she wanted a bird's-eye view of the rising sun as she jogged.

Mature beyond her nearly eighteen years, Evie merely smiled at the small group of construction workers who watched her and whistled at her as she approached.

It appeared they were building some sort of addition to the boardwalk. She was unsure what it was going to be.

As she continued walking toward the surf, she saw and heard one of the men tell the other males to be quiet and leave her alone. Looking at him, she smiled her thanks. He smiled back. He had short dark hair and a hint of a beard. Evie estimated he was in his early twenties. She found him ruggedly handsome.

Evie began her run. She liked running at the edge of the water, where the tide had rolled in and cleared a pristine path before her. The compacted sand provided the perfect running surface. She didn't have to worry about sidewalk cracks or gravel that might cause her to trip or roll an ankle, which meant she could keep her eyes trained on the spectacular horizon and the slowly rising sun.

Starting with a slow jog, she sped up as she went along. She adored the way an early morning run cleared her head. The tension in her body seemed to melt away with each pound of her foot against the solid, wet sand.

She had so much on her mind these days. She'd just graduated high school, and her parents wanted her to follow in their footsteps and pursue a career in medicine. Although Evie was certainly intelligent enough to follow that route, she had no desire to do so. She aspired to become an artist and study art history in college back home in Huntington, West Virginia. Once she graduated college, she wanted to travel abroad to Paris to immerse herself in her passion. That was her dream—a dream her parents did not support.

Evie was not the rebellious type, so it broke her heart to be torn between the life her parents wanted for her and the life she wanted for herself. Surely there had to be a common ground.

Checking her fitness watch, she saw she had jogged three miles down the beach. She stopped and walked up to the boardwalk. Slightly winded, she purchased a bottle of water from a small bait-and-tackle shop. After thanking the cashier, she walked back to the beach and sat down for a moment in the soft sand. She took several sips of the ice-cold water as she watched the rolling surf. The powerful ocean crashing ashore was music to Evie's ears. She could have watched and listened to the waves for hours on end, but right now, she had jogging to do.

She stood up, made her way down to the water's edge, and started sprinting back toward the condo.

By the time she finished her six-mile run, she had been gone for nearly an hour. As she stood staring out at the majestic Atlantic Ocean, it held her spellbound. She stretched her legs and body as she admired the endless water.

A male voice behind her startled her slightly. She jumped in response.

"I'm sorry. I didn't mean to frighten you," he said.

She turned around to find a young man smiling at her. It was the attractive dark-haired construction worker who had spoken up for her earlier that morning before her run.

His voice had a gentle, calming tone as he approached Evie along the water's edge. He kept a comfortable distance, as if waiting for her to invite him closer. Looking out at the ocean, he said, "It's beautiful, isn't it?"

Evie followed his eyes to the sea. "Yes, it is absolutely enchanting."

"I'm Sam," he said as he stepped forward and stuck out his hand. "Sam Wright."

Evie received his hand. "Hi Sam. I'm Evie Edwards."

"It's nice to meet you, Evie. I hope I'm not interrupting you, but I just wanted to apologize for my guys' behavior this morning. They didn't mean any disrespect, although they should have better manners. After you left, I made sure to set them straight, so it won't happen again."

She smiled at him. "Thank you. I appreciate that."

"How far did you jog?" he asked.

"Six miles, and it felt fantastic," Evie answered.

He grinned and nodded as if impressed. "Are you here on vacation?"

"Yes, I'm here with my family from West Virginia. We'll be here for two weeks."

Just then, Evie heard her little twin sisters calling to her from the back door. "Mom says it's time for breakfast!" they yelled.

Evie smiled. "Those are my sisters, Cloe and Clarissa. They're five years old and think they can tell me what to do. Truth is, they pretty much can." She laughed. "They're precious." She waved to her sisters and watched them turn and walk back into the condo.

Sam smiled again. He had a nice smile—the corners of his eyes crinkled up when he grinned.

"Well, it was nice meeting you, Evie," he said. "I hope you have a wonderful family vacation. May I walk you back up to the boardwalk?"

"Sure," Evie said. "I would like that."

As they walked side by side in the sand, Evie had an almost irresistible urge to reach out and take hold of Sam's hand.

"Who was that man you were talking to on the beach?" Evie's father asked as soon as she walked through the back door. Holding a tablet in his hands, he tilted his head downward and looked at her over the top of his glasses.

"Oh, Dan, don't give her the third degree," Evie's mother said as she busied herself at the kitchen stove.

"Lorretta, she's seventeen years old, and that guy looked to be in his twenties. I think I have a right to ask who he was."

"He's nobody—just a construction worker who's doing some kind of addition to the boardwalk. His name is Sam. That's all I know," Evie said as she bent down and kissed her dad on the cheek. The graying at her father's temples caused him to look a bit older than his thirty-nine years.

"Well, he's too old for you," her father said.

Evie giggled. "Shoot! I guess that means I can't accept his marriage proposal then, can I?"

Her father laughed too. "Now, don't be a smart aleck, Evie Marie, or I'll ground you for two weeks."

"Is everybody hungry?" Evie's mother asked as she carried a platter of pancakes into the dining area.

"I am," Evie said. "Let me help you with the food, Mom." She followed her mother back to the kitchen to retrieve a large platter of scrambled eggs and bacon. Her mother carried a pitcher of orange juice in one hand and a container of milk in the other. Evie hoped to be as beautiful as her mother when she got to be her age. Her mom was tall and slender, with short blonde hair and dazzling blue eyes. Evie was glad she had inherited her mother's thin frame and amazing eyes.

Once the food was on the table and all were seated around, they joined hands while Evie's father said grace over their meal. They then served themselves and began to eat.

"This is delicious, Mom," Evie said. "I was starving."

"I don't doubt it," her father said with a half-hearted-looking grin. "What time did you sneak out this morning anyway?"

Evie laughed. "I didn't sneak out. I was merely being quiet so as not to wake up everybody in the house. Just because I like to get up at the crack of dawn on vacation doesn't mean everybody else does." Recalling the beautiful scenery she had seen that morning, she said, "The sunrise was absolutely astonishing. I'm going to try to paint it this afternoon."

At the mention of her painting, a cross expression formed on her father's face. He would have preferred she stick her nose in some medical journal than sit in front of a blank canvas, doing what she knew God had created her to do.

As if changing the subject on purpose, her father asked, "What are we going to do today?"

"Swimming!" the twins exclaimed in unison with their mouths full of food. Cloe and Clarissa were identical twins who, unlike Evie, had the physical characteristics of their father more so than their mother. They had shoulder-length light brown hair and captivating, large brown eyes.

Evie furrowed her brow in a mock serious expression. "I think I'll just stay in and watch TV," she said, trying to bait the twins.

Both girls' eyes widened as if in heartbroken disbelief. They began to plead with her.

"Please come swimming with us," Cloe begged.

Clarissa joined in. "Yeah, it won't be no fun unless you come too."

Evie looked at her two baby sisters. No longer able to maintain her serious expression, she broke into a wide smile. "I'm just kidding. Of course I'm coming swimming with you."

Their faces lit up. "Yea!" they shouted as they clapped their hands.

"Nobody's going anywhere until they finish their breakfast," Lorretta said. "And that includes you, Dan. Put that tablet down, and enjoy your food with your girls."

He grinned and laid the tablet aside. "I guess the world news can wait," he said as his voice softened. "Besides, my world is right here in front of me."

The family of five stepped out into the bright sunshine. Being a dermatologist, Evie's mother had made certain that everyone was covered in sunscreen.

The twins looked adorable in their matching blue polka-dot bikinis. Most people couldn't tell the identical twins apart, but Evie could. Cloe's eyes were slightly closer set, while Clarissa's eyes were the slightest bit lighter brown in color. Personality-wise, Cloe was a bit more outgoing, while Clarissa was more on the shy side.

Dressed in a pink bikini, Evie walked down the path with a sister on either side. Off to her right, she spotted Sam working on the boardwalk with his crew. He looked at her and waved. She waved back. Had her dad not been around, she might have walked over and said hello, but that was not the case. She glanced at her father, who was looking at her disapprovingly.

Once they had found the perfect spot on the beach to make their camp, her dad set up the umbrella and began blowing up the inflatable canoe that the twins could not wait to take a ride in.

"Hurry up, Daddy," Clarissa said.

Dan chuckled. "I'm blowing as hard as I can."

Once their ride was fully inflated, Evie led her giggling sisters down to the water. After placing the little red-and-yellow canoe into the surf, she said, "Climb in, girls."

Evie watched and listened as her sisters scrambled into the canoe. Cloe jockeyed to the front with the promise that Clarissa could take the lead the next time.

Evie waded out into the ocean, pulling a length of cord tethered to the canoe. Each time a small wave lifted them into the air, the girls laughed and begged Evie to take them out farther. When Evie was about waist deep in the water, she saw a good-sized wave coming. "Hold on, girls!" she shouted as the wave picked up the small canoe and carried it swiftly to the shore. Evie could hear the girls giggling loudly as she walked back to the shoreline to get them for another ride.

The three sisters played tirelessly in the water until their mother motioned them in.

Evie picked up the canoe out of the surf and walked her sisters back to her parents and the shade of the large umbrella.

"You girls need to rest," Lorretta said. She laughed as she examined their hands and feet. "Your little fingers and toes are pruned. Besides, I don't want you to get a sunburn on our first day here. How about we head back to the house for lunch?"

The twins protested to the point where their daddy had to get firm with them. "Now, you heard what your mother said, girls. It's way past lunchtime; plus, you all need a rest, especially from the sun."

"Would it be all right if I take one quick swim in the ocean before I come in?" Evie asked.

"Sure you can," her father said. "But your mom and I will have lunch ready soon, so make it a fast one."

"Okay, Dad," Evie said happily as she turned to walk back toward the ocean.

The early afternoon sun was brilliant and felt warm and delightful on Evie's skin. Their area of the beach was located at the end of the boardwalk and was relatively remote. Evie appreciated the smaller crowd of people milling around. Walking out into the water and the rolling waves, she loved the feeling of unbalance that the declining surf caused. When she had walked out to her waist in the water, she duck-dived the larger waves. She marveled at the strength and majesty of the ocean.

She swam out to the point where her feet could no longer touch sand. She paddled there erect for a few moments, enjoying the cooler water against her toes.

Now that she was out past the break, she could swim without being pummeled by waves. Swimming perpendicular to the shore, she swam as if she were in a race. Cutting swiftly through the water with her hands felt invigorating. She had always been a fast swimmer, but the salt water made swimming even easier.

She swam for about a mile or so down the beach before she stopped and turned back for home.

Slicing through the water, she paddled with her feet. She couldn't help but grin each time she turned her head to gasp a gulp of air. She was having the time of her life.

Looking ahead, she could see that she was back to where she had started. Stopping the forward propulsion of her body, she softly treaded water. Being in the vast ocean felt incredible—she felt utterly small, as if barely existent. She allowed herself a few moments to be lost in the glorious sensation.

Just as she was about to swim for shore, she felt it: something huge brushed up against her side. It felt like sandpaper being rubbed roughly against her tender skin.

She didn't mean to, but out of instant fright, she released a loud scream and immediately began swimming for the beach. When the water was about knee deep, she was able to stop and catch her breath. Looking up, she saw Sam walking hurriedly toward her. She walked out of the water to meet him.

"I heard you scream and saw you frantically swimming to shore. Are you okay?" he asked, appearing concerned.

Breathlessly, Evie looked down at her right side. Her skin was red and scraped. "Something brushed up against me. It was big and rough—like sandpaper."

Sam bent down to examine her wound. "I bet it was just a sandbar shark," he said. "He was probably just curious. Sandbars don't generally attack humans unless they're provoked. You didn't provoke him, did you?" he asked with a smile.

Evie giggled. "No, I did not provoke him in the slightest."

"Put something on that when you get in the house," Sam said, pointing to the scrape on her side as they walked.

"Oh, don't worry about me," she said. "Both of my parents are doctors."

Sam appeared impressed. "I bet that comes in handy, doesn't it?"

"Sometimes," she replied, suddenly weighed down by their expectations of her to follow in their formidable footsteps.

When they reached the ramp to the boardwalk, he said, "Well, this is my stop."

Evie laughed. She liked his witty sense of humor.

"I'm glad you weren't badly hurt. This isn't going to keep you out of the water, is it?"

Turning back, Evie looked out at the enormity of the bewitching sea. "Not on your life," she answered.

Between the boardwalk and the condo, Evie changed her mind about having her parents tend to her superficial wound. She was fearful that if she told them about the shark, they wouldn't let her and the twins go back into the ocean.

Hiding the scrape on her side would be no problem in a one-piece swimsuit. She felt slightly guilty for keeping a secret from her mom and dad but was able to convince herself it wasn't that big of a deal.

2

ON THE BOARDWALK

After a delicious dinner of a variety of fresh seafood, baby red potatoes, and corn on the cob, Evie felt like getting out into the fresh ocean air. "Who wants to go for a walk with me down the boardwalk?" she asked.

The twins' eyes lit up, and their arms shot up in the air. "We do!" they shouted as they jumped up from the floor, where they had been playing with their dolls.

Tickled by her sisters' enthusiasm, Evie asked her parents if it would be all right if she took them out for a little while.

"I guess," her mother answered hesitantly. "Is it okay with you, Dan?"

"I suppose," he said. "Just be careful and hold hands, and be home before dark."

"We will," Evie said. In her opinion, her parents tended to worry too much, but she would do as they asked.

With a sister on either side, she headed for the boardwalk, holding their hands. Judging by the sun's position in the sky, Evie estimated it to be about seven o'clock in the evening. It wouldn't get dark until after nine, so they had plenty of time for a nice walk and maybe even a surprise ride on the Ferris wheel. That would make her sisters happy, and Evie adored putting smiles on their precious little faces.

She looked down at them. Dressed in matching pink outfits, they looked so cute that Evie couldn't help but grin. She loved them more than she ever had thought possible. There were times when she felt more like a mother than just an older sister. There was a bond with them that would never be broken.

The twins chattered with each other as Evie looked out at the immense ocean. She wouldn't mind living next to the sea someday, she thought. She didn't know why, but it seemed to beckon to her.

Before Evie knew it, the towering Ferris wheel was looming up ahead.

"Can we take a ride on the Ferris wheel, Evie?" Cloe asked.

"Please, can we?" Clarissa pleaded.

Evie laughed. "Of course we can."

After paying for the tickets, with her baby sisters clinging to her hands, Evie boarded the ride with the twins.

"You guys aren't scared, are you?" Evie asked as the wheel began to turn.

Her question was met with giggles. "No, we're not scared," Clarissa said. "We're not scared of anything."

Evie wished she could have said that. She was afraid of many things, mostly her future. She didn't know what to do. Should she do as her parents wished and become a doctor, or should she follow her heart and become an artist? She was at a major crossroad in her life, and she had no clue as to which road to take.

"Evie, why aren't you having fun?" Clarissa asked.

Evie grinned at her observant little sister. "Oh, but I am having fun. I always have a good time with the two of you." She put her arms around them and pulled them in for a sisterly hug. "I love you guys very much," she said. Unexpectedly, her eyes filled with tears. Her love for her siblings was almost too much for her heart to contain.

When they reached the top of the ride, it stopped.

"Oh my gosh!" Cloe said while pointing. "The water is so pretty from up here."

"Are you going to take us back out into the ocean in the morning, Evie?" Clarissa asked.

"I sure am. Playing with you guys in the waves is the best part of my day."

Both girls smiled their apparent approval.

When the ride came to an end, they walked back out onto the boardwalk.

"Do you all wanna walk out onto the pier?" Evie asked.

"Can we?" Cloe asked excitedly as Clarissa bounced up and down.

"Sure we can. Just hold tight to my hands," Evie replied.

Evie felt their little fingers gripping her hands. She appreciated that they were such thoughtful and obedient little girls.

They walked down the pier, closer to the left side so they could look out at the water. There were men and women fishing on both sides of them.

They watched as a young man in a blue baseball cap reeled in a fish. Evie readily recognized that it was a flounder—a large one.

"What kind of fish is that?" Clarissa asked the man.

"It's a flounder. Some people call it a fluke," he answered politely.

He turned around in their direction, and to Evie's surprise, it was Sam Wright. He smiled, and his eyes did that crinkly thing.

Evie smiled back. "Hi, Sam," she said.

"Hey, Evie." He looked at the twins and asked, "Now, who might you two be?"

"I'm Cloe Ann."

"I'm Clarissa Ann."

Sam grinned at them. "Well, you two look a lot alike. You must be sisters."

The girls giggled and told him they were twins.

"Oh, I see," he said, appearing shocked. "No wonder you look alike."

The fish lay flopping on the dry, weathered boards of the dock.

"What are you going to do with that fish?" Clarissa asked as a tear rolled down her cheek.

Sam reached out and touched the tip of her nose. "I'm going to take the hook out of its mouth and set it free. Would you like that?" he asked.

Clarissa nodded.

They watched as he did what he had said. He dropped the fish back into the ocean.

"Are you girls going to fish?" he asked.

"No, we're just out for a walk. We took a ride on the Ferris wheel, and now we gotta head back. I promised I'd have the twins back before dark," Evie said.

"Well, I'm all finished here. Would you gals mind if I walked back with you?"

"I wouldn't mind," Evie said. "How about you girls? Would you mind?"

"No. We don't care," Cloe said.

Clarissa nodded approvingly.

Sam smiled and gathered his fishing gear. The four then started walking back down the pier. Once they reached the boardwalk, Sam said, "Just let me run and put this stuff in my truck. I'll be right back."

"Okay," Evie said.

"On second thought," he said, "do you girls have your hearts set on walking the boardwalk, or would you rather go over on the boulevard to get some ice cream?"

The twins began to jump up and down. "Can we, Evie?" they begged.

Evie thought about what her dad would think, but what would some ice cream hurt? It was still daylight outside, and they would be home before dark. After giving it only a moment's thought, she replied, "We would love some ice cream, if you don't mind."

"Of course I don't mind. Let's go, girls," he said, grinning.

With Cloe on one side and Clarissa on the other, Evie held tightly to their hands as they crossed the busy street. It was only about half a block to the ice cream shop.

"Do you have to hold our hands?" Clarissa asked. "I wanna hold Cloe's hand."

"You know what Dad said. I gotta hold your hands. Maybe after we get our ice cream cones, you two can hold hands while you eat them. Okay?"

"Okay," Clarissa replied.

As they walked inside the ice cream shop, the unmistakable sweet aroma of homemade waffle cones hung heavy in the air. "I love that smell," Evie said.

"Me too," Sam replied. Smiling, he bent down and asked the girls what flavor of ice cream they wanted. Without giving them time to answer, he said, "Let me guess. I bet you want chocolate."

Evie laughed. "How did you know?"

He pretended to be insulted. "I was a kid once, you know."

"Chocolate!" Cloe and Clarissa shouted out.

"And for you?" he asked Evie.

"Chocolate, of course."

After ordering four cones of ice cream, Sam pulled out his wallet.

"I can pay for ours," Evie said.

"No way. This was my invitation, and it's my treat."

As Sam handed the twins their cones, Evie said, "What do you say to Sam, girls?"

"Thank you," they said in unison as they took the ice cream from his hands.

Evie could see the happiness in her sisters' large brown eyes. She felt blessed to have this time with them. Life would change soon when she started college. There would be less time to spend with her treasured siblings.

"Here ya go," Sam said as he handed Evie her cone.

"Thank you," she said.

As they walked out of the ice cream shop, Evie looked at the busy street. "Would you mind if we crossed back over to the boardwalk? I'd feel safer with the girls. I don't trust them with this much traffic."

"I think that's a good idea," Sam said. "Want me to hold your ice cream until we get them across the street?"

"Please," Evie answered as she handed him her cone. "No stealing licks off of mine," she added teasingly.

After they were safely across the street and onto the boardwalk again, Evie allowed Cloe and Clarissa to walk in front of her and Sam. They looked lovable walking hand in hand while eating their ice cream.

Sam must have been reading her mind. "Your little sisters sure are cute," he said. "I don't have any brothers or sisters."

"I'm sorry," Evie said. She couldn't imagine life without her sisters.

"My mom always said that after she had me, she saw no need for any more children," Sam said, smiling. "She always told me, 'Why mess with perfection?'"

Evie laughed. "Sounds like your mother loves you very much."

"She did," Sam said, sounding suddenly sad. "I lost her about two years ago. She passed away from breast cancer."

Evie's heart went out to him. "I'm so sorry to hear that," she said.

"I'm sorry too, but I had twenty-one great years with her, so I consider myself blessed."

"So that means you're twenty-three years old," Evie said.

"Yep. I'm an old man." He laughed. "How old are you, if you don't mind me asking?"

Evie licked her ice cream cone. "I'll be eighteen next month."

Sam appeared shocked. "Oh my gosh! I thought you were older. I mean, not that you look old or anything." He laughed again. "I'm digging myself into a hole, aren't I?"

"It's okay," Evie replied. "I've been told that I look older than I am. I take it as a compliment. It makes me feel mature."

"Well, either way, you sure are beautiful," he said.

She appreciated the way his flattering comment made her feel. She felt pretty and like a woman. "Thank you very much, Sam."

By the time the girls had finished their ice cream, they were almost back to the condo, and the sun was beginning to set.

"Looks like you got back just in time," Sam told her. "Just before dark. I guess I'll say good night here."

"I'm glad we ran into you on the pier. And thank you again for the treats," Evie said as she grasped the twins by their sticky hands.

"Maybe I'll see you again before you leave," Sam said as he backed away.

Evie smiled. "I hope so. Good night, Sam."

"Night, Evie."

"Well, from the look of your faces, you two had some chocolate ice cream," Lorretta said when Cloe and Clarissa ran into the living room.

"We did! Sam bought it for us," Cloe said.

Dan, who had been watching television, turned his head in Evie's direction. She had his full attention. "What's this about Sam? Didn't I tell you that he was too old for you?"

"Yes, you did, Dad," Evie said with a playful roll of her eyes. "But we saw him on the pier, and he took us across the street for ice cream. That's all—just ice cream." She bent down and kissed her father on the cheek. "You worry too much, Dad."

"I worry when I see a reason to worry, and from what I can see, that boy—that man—is bad news."

Evie was glad when her mother came to her defense. "She said it was just ice cream, Dan. Except for some sugar and empty calories, what harm could that possibly do? Besides, the twins were there the whole time," Lorretta said.

"Sam's nice," Clarissa said. "I like him."

"Well, I can see I'm outnumbered here. I concede defeat," Dan said with a sly grin.

"Good," Evie said. "Now, I'm going to go to my room and try to paint that awesome sunrise I saw this morning."

Her father's grin quickly faded.

3

RAINY DAY

It was warm outside, even though there was a misty rain falling. Evie didn't mind; she was going for her morning jog anyway.

Dressed in a yellow T-shirt and cutoff jeans, she stood on the boardwalk, doing her stretches. She looked in the direction of Sam's construction site, but there was no one milling about. Supposing they weren't working because of the rain, she headed toward the beach for her run.

Although she knew her father wouldn't approve, Evie found herself thinking about Sam. She liked him. He was older than she, but she didn't mind.

As she jogged along the beach in the misty rain, she thought about what his home life might be like. He hadn't mentioned his father, and she knew he was an only child who had lost his mother. She felt bad for him. She didn't know what she would do without her family. They were her world. Her sweet sisters had laid claim to her heart the moment they were born. She would lay down her life for them and her parents. Even though her mom and dad didn't support her dream of becoming an artist, she loved them dearly. She knew they had her best interest at heart.

Before Evie knew it, she reached the end of her first three miles. It was time to turn back and head for the condo.

She looked toward the eastern sky one last time. The sun couldn't seem to break through the heavy cloud cover. Slightly disappointed at not being able to see another spectacular sunrise, Evie started her run back home.

She derived much pleasure from jogging, especially on the beach. It felt refreshing to her body, mind, and soul. Smiling to herself, she wished she could jog on for hours and hours.

As she ran, the misty rain slowly evolved into a downpour that cooled her warm body. When she arrived in front of their condo, she stood there in the rain. With her head back, facing the heavens, she let the refreshing water beat down onto her flushed face. It felt exhilarating. She just stood there grinning.

She heard a male voice yell out, "Hey! Don't you know it's raining?"

She lowered her head and looked in the direction of the familiar voice. It was Sam. He was alone, sitting in the sand underneath his construction site.

Walking toward him, Evie answered, "Yes, I know it's raining. I love the rain. Don't you?" She held her arms out and twirled around.

When she stopped and looked at him, he appeared amused. "Yes, I do, but it doesn't make for a very good workday."

"Oh, I'm sorry about that," Evie said, still standing out in the downpour.

"You're welcome to come in out of the rain if you want. There's plenty of room under here," he said, motioning with his arm.

Evie appreciated his invitation. "Sure. If you don't mind some company, I'd be glad to."

"Don't mind at all. I called the crew off work for the day, so I'm just waiting for a lull in the rain to make a run for my truck." He looked up at the sky. "I was hoping the mist this morning would give way to the sun, but it doesn't look like that's going to happen until maybe this afternoon." He looked at Evie and laughed. "You're soaked to the bone. Are you chilly?"

"No, I'm just fine." She wiped the rainwater off her face. "I guess my jog kept me warm. I feel good."

"Do you jog every morning or just while you're here at the beach?"

"I jog every morning, rain or shine. I love running."

He grinned. "I mostly only run when someone is chasing me."

Evie laughed at his corny joke. "Well, you should try it for fun sometime. I think you'd enjoy it."

"So what are your plans for the future, Miss Evie Edwards? I assume that since you'll be eighteen next month, you have just graduated from high school."

"Yes, I did just graduate, but ..." Evie paused, unsure how much personal information she wanted to divulge to someone she had just met.

"But what?" he asked, seeming genuinely interested.

After thinking about it for a moment, she told Sam about her dream to study art history in college and then go abroad to Paris after she graduated. She wondered if he would laugh at her lofty ambition. She looked over at him. He wasn't laughing. He appeared impressed.

"Gosh, that sounds like a wonderful and fulfilling aspiration, but if you don't mind me saying so, you don't look very happy about it. As a matter of fact, you seem rather sad."

"Well, my parents don't approve of my plans," she said glumly. "They want me to follow in their footsteps and become a doctor."

"Oh, I see," he said. "That must be tough. That sure does put you between a rock and a hard place, doesn't it?"

"You have no idea," Evie replied. "Not to sound prideful, but I've always done what my parents told me to do. I just don't think I can go against their wishes—not even if it costs me my dream."

To Evie's surprise, Sam reached out and took her hand. "I would hate for you to give up on your dream."

His hand felt nice. His skin was rough, but his grip was gentle. She squeezed his fingers and smiled. "Thank you for saying that."

"I mean it. You seem like a sweet girl. You deserve to be happy." Looking into her eyes, he said, "We have to be careful. The choices we make can change our entire lifetime."

She wanted to ask him more about himself, but she knew her parents must be worried and would come looking for her at any minute.

"I wish we had more time to talk," she told him. "But I'd better get back now."

"I understand," he said. "The rain is letting up. I think I can get to my truck now without getting soaked."

"I wish we could talk like this every day," Evie said shyly while staring down at their hands, which were still locked together.

"Well, let's hope for rain again tomorrow," he said. Smiling at her, he slowly released her hand.

"Okay then," she said, returning his smile. "I'll be praying for rain."

They crawled out from under the shelter of the construction site, and Sam ran toward the parking lot, while Evie slowly walked back to the condo, thoroughly enjoying the sensation of the rain on her skin.

Evie entered the back door to find her parents awake and going about their usual morning routine. Her father was staring down at his tablet while sipping a cup of coffee. Her mother was preparing breakfast, and the twins were apparently still sleeping.

"Did you have a nice run in the rain, Evie?" her mother asked.

"Oddly enough, yes, I did. It felt wonderful," Evie replied as she removed her wet shoes and socks.

"If you don't mind, sweetie, please put those shoes out on the deck so they can dry. You're dripping all over the floor," her mother said.

"Sorry," Evie said as she opened the door and placed her wet shoes outside. "I'm going to go get a quick shower before breakfast."

"Okay, but don't dawdle. The food will be ready in about thirty minutes."

"Got it, Mom," Evie said as she ran up to her room to get her clothes. She figured that since it was raining, they would be going shopping for the day instead of playing in the ocean, so she chose a blue sundress to wear. Blue was her favorite color.

After a refreshing shower, she was dressed and ready for breakfast. By the time she got to the kitchen, the girls were up. Still barefoot and dressed in their pajamas, they looked cute sitting on the floor, playing with their baby dolls.

"Good morning, girls," Evie said.

"Good morning, Evie," the girls echoed.

"You look nice," Cloe said, appearing disappointed. "Aren't we going to play in the ocean today?"

Before Evie could answer, her father spoke up. "You can't play in the ocean today. It's raining and starting to lightning out there. You can play in the water tomorrow. The weather is supposed to clear up tonight."

Evie could see the disappointment on her sweet sisters' faces. She walked over to where they sat playing. "It's okay. We'll play in the waves tomorrow. I promise."

The girls beamed. "Thanks, Evie."

"You're welcome," she said as she tapped them on their little noses.

"Breakfast is ready," Lorretta announced. "Evie, will you help me get it on the table?"

"Of course, Mom."

Her mother had outdone herself with the food. She had prepared waffles, sausage patties, and scrambled eggs.

"Gosh, Mom, this looks and smells divine," Evie said as she picked up the platter of waffles. The sweet aroma of warm maple syrup mixed with the spicy scent of the sausage tempted Evie's nose.

Her mother appeared pleased with the compliment. "Thank you, sweetie. Can you go back and get the butter, please? I forgot it."

"Sure," Evie replied. "I can't wait to eat. I must have jogged up an appetite."

After they were all seated around the table, Dan said grace over their wonderful-smelling meal, and they began to serve themselves.

The waffles were crispy and warm as Evie put her first bite into her mouth. Her mother was a fantastic cook. Evie hoped to cook half as well as she did someday.

"This is scrumptious, Mom," Evie said.

"It's good," Clarissa said with her mouth full.

Evie smiled at her little sister with syrup on her chin. She reached over with her napkin and wiped it off. Clarissa smiled up at her.

Evie made a heart sign with her hands. Clarissa giggled and did the same, and then Cloe followed suit.

"You girls stop playing, and eat your food," their father said.

"Don't be so gruff with them, Dan. They're just having fun," Lorretta said. "After all, we are on vacation." She got up and walked to his side of the table. Taking the tablet out of his hand, she bent down and kissed him.

"Well, if you can't beat 'em, join 'em," Dan said as he took a bite of his breakfast. "So what would my girls like to get into today?"

"Swimming!" the twins shouted.

"Now, we already talked about that, girls. What about shopping? Would you like for me to take you to the mall and the outlet stores?"

"Yes!" Evie exclaimed. "Shopping is what I was hoping for."

"Me too," her mom added.

"Okay," the twins said with unenthusiastic frowns on their faces.

Evie couldn't help but grin at her ocean-loving sisters.

4

A PATTERN

Evie got up extra early the next morning for her jog. She secretly hoped she would catch Sam alone again at the end of her run. She enjoyed talking with him. He was mature, and for some reason, she trusted him.

It was a few minutes into her jog before the sun started to illuminate the horizon. Evie kept her eyes trained straight ahead as it slowly made its magnificent appearance. It changed with every step she took. The colors were deep and dark at first and slowly evolved into bright and vibrant hues that took Evie's breath away. She wished she could stop right then and there to paint the glorious scene before her. She knew she could never have truly captured the beauty, but she would have loved to try.

Oh, how she wished her parents, especially her father, could have understood what art meant to her—what painting meant to her—and how deeply it touched her soul.

As the sun made its full appearance, it was time for Evie to turn around. She had more than crossed her three-mile mark.

The sun felt warm on her back as she sprinted toward home. She ran next to the water's edge, watching the foamy waves roll in close to her feet.

Before she knew it, she was back, and Sam was there, sitting alone on a bench on the boardwalk. Evie smiled when she saw him.

"What are you doing here so early?" she asked as she approached him.

"I wanted to enjoy the view for a few minutes before the crew got here," he answered.

Walking up to him, Evie asked, "May I sit down and soak up the view with you?"

"I was hoping you would."

Evie grinned again as she sat down next to him on the wooden bench. The seagulls were flying low and cawing as if announcing the dawn of a wonderful brand-new day.

"I can't believe you get to look at this breathtaking scenery every single day," Evie said. "I'm so jealous. I hope one day to live near the ocean."

Sam looked over at her. He had an expression of contentment on his suntanned face. "I have to admit it is pretty nice, although I don't always have jobs right on the oceanfront," he said.

Evie looked in the direction of the obvious soon-to-be concert stage that Sam and his crew were working on. "How soon will this job be finished?" she asked.

"Oh, about ten more days, I'd say—give or take a day or two, depending on the weather."

Evie was glad to hear he would be around for the remainder of her vacation. "How did you come to do construction work? Do you enjoy it?"

Sam's smile revealed his satisfaction. "Much like what you were telling me about following in your parents' footsteps, that's what

I did. I work with my dad. We're partners. We are Stan and Sam Contractors Inc."

Evie was impressed. "I like the name of your company. That's very catchy."

"Thank you," Sam said. "I like it too, and to answer your question, yes, I do enjoy my work. I get great satisfaction from creating something lasting and hopefully beautiful to the eye."

"That's the way I feel about my painting," Evie said.

Sam looked over at her. "What are you going to do about your future? Are you going to pursue medicine like your parents want you to?"

Evie shook her head. "I have no earthly idea."

"Well, you'd better hurry up and make up your mind."

"I know. I'm starting college in the fall back home at Marshall University."

"Hey, I know that school!" Sam exclaimed. "I loved that movie about your inspirational school and your heroic little town."

Evie nodded. "I loved it too. That movie was a very accurate portrayal and very well made. It captured the spirit of our community."

"You have a nice spirit too, Evie," Sam said. "I would hate to see you give up your dream of becoming an artist. I know I don't know you well, but I can see how your eyes light up when you talk about your painting. Your passion shows."

"Thank you, Sam." Evie grinned at him.

"And you have a beautiful smile too," he said.

"Thank you again, Sam. So do you. I love to see people smile. I think it changes their entire appearance. I know it sounds cliché, but I think everyone is beautiful when they smile."

"I couldn't agree more."

Evie thought about her precious sisters. "When Cloe and Clarissa giggle, it makes my heart happy."

"It makes me smile to see that you are so much in love with those two adorable little girls. I always thought siblings were supposed to be at each other's throats all the time. I guess that's not always the case, is it?"

"Not at all. They have me wrapped tightly around their cute little fingers—that's for sure," Evie said. "I don't know what I'd do without them."

"It's good that you'll be staying at home for college. That way, you'll still be close to them."

Evie sighed deeply. "Yes, and if I do decide to go to medical school, hopefully I can get accepted at Marshall for that too."

To Evie's surprise, Sam reached out and took her hand again. "I don't mean to overstep my bounds here, but don't let your parents bulldoze you into a career you don't want. It's your life, you know?" He shrugged.

"I know," she answered while staring into his hazel eyes. "I just can't bear the thought of disappointing them."

"Better to disappoint them temporarily than to make yourself miserable permanently. But like I said, I'm overstepping my bounds."

"No, you're not. You're just giving me your opinion, and I'm happy you are. I feel like ..." She paused.

"You feel what?" he asked.

"I feel like you're my friend," she replied, shaking her head. "That makes me sound silly, doesn't it?"

"Not at all. I think we would make great friends."

Evie was shocked at his response. "You do?"

"Yes, I do."

"Can I give you my number so we can talk after I go back home?" Evie asked, hoping he would say yes.

He let go of her hand and took his cell phone out of his pocket. "What is it?" he asked.

She recited her number and watched as he typed it in. Within seconds, she heard a familiar ping from her own phone in her pocket, indicating she had received a text.

"There," he said. "I texted you, so you'll have my number too. Now we're officially friends."

"Are you making fun of me?" Evie asked, feeling herself blush a little.

"No, not at all," he answered seriously as he gently nudged her shoulder with his. "I'm happy to have met you and made a new friend—a pretty one at that."

"Thank you very much," she said, liking the way he treated her like a grown-up instead of a silly teenager. With bravery overruling her brains, she asked, "If my parents say it's okay, would you like to come have dinner with us this evening?" Her heart pounded in her chest. Part of her was fearful he would accept her invitation. What was her daddy going to say?

"Oh, darlin', I don't think that would be a very good idea. I've seen the way your father looks at me. He looks like he wants to punch my lights out." Sam laughed. "I can't say I blame him. I'm too old for you."

"No, you're not. It's just five years."

He looked seriously at her. The way he gazed into her eyes caused goose bumps to form on her skin.

"Yeah, but you're only seventeen."

Evie immediately felt perturbed. She would be eighteen—an adult—in just one short month. She was tired of people treating her as if that weren't a fact. It was as if they would forever see her as a child. It made her want to throw a temper tantrum and prove their point.

"I've made you mad at me, haven't I?" he asked.

She grinned slightly. "Yeah, a little." She paused. "Are you coming to dinner if my parents say it's okay?"

He shook his head as if surrendering. "Sure. If your parents say it's all right, I'll come. Needless to say, I'm not planning on it, and neither should you." He gave her another playful shove with his shoulder.

Evie pretended to be slightly winded when she ran through the open back door of the condo. Her parents were having coffee at the kitchen table. They were laughing about something her father was reading aloud to her mother from his tablet. They seemed to be in good spirits. Evie thought about it for a moment and decided that it was as good a time as any to ask if Sam could come to dinner.

She drew in a deep breath to gather her courage. "Mom, Dad, I have a favor to ask you." They looked up at her expectantly. Evie wrung her hands nervously. "I was wondering if it would be all right if Sam came over to have dinner with us tonight."

Instantly, her parents' smiles disappeared, especially her father's. With a scornful look on his face, he stared at Evie. She could feel herself shrink beneath his disapproving gaze.

"I told you that man was too old for you, Evie," her father said.

"Only five years," Evie replied. "And I'll be eighteen next month, so what difference does it make?"

Her father laid his tablet down on the table. "I'll tell you what difference it makes: prison. That's the difference in an older man dating a young girl of seventeen. Is that plain enough for you to understand?"

Evie's eyes began to sting. Her father's harsh words hurt her feelings. He seldom spoke hatefully to his family, so Evie took his words to heart.

"You don't have to be so condescending, Dan," her mother said as she stood up by her daughter's side.

With her mother's arm around her, Evie began to cry.

"Now come the tears," her father said as he threw his hands up in the air.

"Honestly, Dan. I don't see what having the boy over for dinner is going to hurt. We'll be right here with them," Lorretta said.

"I can't believe it. Now you're taking her side against me," Dan said. "What happened to always having each other's back when it comes to decisions and discipline?"

Her mother sat back down in the chair. "You're right, Dan. I'm sorry. It's just that we're on vacation, and Evie asks us for so very little. I just ..." She trailed off.

Evie watched as her father looked from one of them to the other. She wiped away her tears. She was disappointed but conceded defeat. "I'm going to go get a shower and get dressed for breakfast," she said softly as she walked past her mother.

Her father let out a deep breath. "Oh, all right," he said dolefully. "If your mother agrees, I don't suppose it would hurt if the man comes for dinner—but only because your mother and I will be right here with you. There will be no sneaking off for any solitary walks on the beach. You got that, young lady?"

Evie squealed and ran to her father. She hugged him around his neck. "Thank you, Daddy," she said happily. "Thank you, Mom."

"You're welcome, honey," her mother said.

"Just don't make us regret this decision," her father said, wagging his finger at her.

"I won't," Evie said as she ran toward the back door.

"Where are you running off to now?" her mother asked.

"I'll be right back. I gotta go tell Sam he's invited to dinner."

After a fun-filled morning of playing with the twins in the ocean and then shopping and eating lunch at an outdoor café with her family, it was time for Evie to get ready for her dinner date. She felt excited and nervous at the same time. Smiling to herself, she recalled the look on Sam's face when she'd told him her parents had invited him over for dinner. He had seemed shocked but pleased. It had taken him a moment, but he finally had accepted the invitation.

Evie hadn't brought many dresses with her. She hadn't thought she would need them. Now she wished she had more to choose from. It came down to a pink one, a yellow one, or the blue one she had worn shopping with her family. Finally, she chose the blue one because it matched her eye color. She slipped into the spaghetti-strapped sundress and began to fidget with her hair. Sam had only seen it pulled back into a ponytail, so she decided to wear it down. After she ran a flat iron through it, it looked like blonde silk. She applied some black mascara to her long lashes and some pink lipstick to her full lips. She was dressed and ready but felt uneasy. She hoped her parents would be nice to Sam, especially her father.

Walking into the kitchen, she was greeted by a delicious aroma. "Something smells great, Mom. What are you cooking?"

"I'm making my world-famous bouillabaisse," her mother answered with a smile. Cooking was Evie's mother's hobby and one she did well.

"It smells divine. I can't wait to have a taste."

"Well, come over here, and I'll give you a spoonful. It's ready. It's just simmering now until our guest arrives."

Evie walked over to the stove.

Her mother took a spoon and dipped it into the pot of seafood stew. After blowing on the spoon, she placed it into Evie's open mouth. "Now, tell me what you taste."

Evie thought for a second. "I taste onions and garlic for sure, and there is something else. It tastes kind of like ..." She paused and licked her lips. "It tastes like licorice."

"Bingo!" her mother exclaimed happily. "That's fresh fennel. You're developing quite the palate, my dear." She wrapped her arms around Evie and gave her a heartwarming hug. "We're having a garden salad and crusty bread to go with it. How does that sound?"

"Sounds absolutely wonderful. Thank you, Mom, for going to so much trouble for Sam."

"It's okay, sweetie. I was a young woman once too, ya know." She winked. "I can see how you would be smitten with Sam. He's a very good-looking young man."

Evie couldn't have agreed more. She found Sam irresistibly attractive.

Her mother continued. Her smile of seconds before had melted into a concerned expression. "I just don't want you to go falling in love with Sam. We're only going to be here for a short time, and I don't want to see you hurt."

Evie hugged her loving mother. "I won't fall for him, Mom," she said, knowing in her heart that it was already too late.

Suddenly realizing how quiet the condo was, Evie asked, "Where are Dad and the girls?"

"They went out to find something good at the market for dessert. I didn't have time to bake anything, and I forgot to pick up something this morning when I shopped for the bouillabaisse ingredients. They should be back any minute."

Evie walked over to the back door. It was open, and a cool, refreshing ocean breeze was blowing in. The sound of the pounding surf was mesmerizing. With her arms crossed in front of her, she stood there taking in the sights and sounds of the awesome scene before her.

"You love this place, don't you, sweetie?" her mother asked.

"Oh my gosh, yes!" Evie replied. "I absolutely adore the ocean. I would love to live in an oceanfront home someday." She turned around to face her mother. "The sea inspires me like nothing else. It makes me feel like I could fly." She giggled.

Her mother laughed too. "Well, I would hate for you to live so far away from me someday, but if you have your heart set on it, then that is what I want for you."

Evie's smile faded at the thought of being away from her family. She couldn't imagine living every day without them close. "Perhaps a summer oceanfront vacation home would be a great compromise," she said.

"Now, that sounds like just the ticket." Her beautiful mother beamed.

Evie hoped to be even half as lovely as her mom when she got older.

Hearing the opening of the front door and the melodious chatter of her twin baby sisters brought an instant grin to Evie's face. Stooping down, she opened her arms. "Where have you been, girls? I've missed you."

Cloe and Clarissa ran into her arms, sending them all toppling over onto the floor into a heap of laughing sisters. "We went to the store for dessert," Clarissa answered happily. "Sam's coming to dinner," she added as if Evie didn't know.

"He is?" Evie asked. Clapping her hand over her mouth, she pretended to be shocked.

"Yes, silly," Cloe said.

"What did you guys pick out for dessert?"

"Chocolate ice cream!" they exclaimed in unison.

Evie laughed. "I figured that much."

"And a fresh two-layer coconut cake from the bakery around the corner," her father added.

"Yum! That sounds delicious," Evie said as she tickled her cackling siblings.

Evie looked up from the floor to see a smiling Sam standing at the open back door. He was dressed in jeans and a short-sleeved white shirt and was holding a large bouquet of pink roses in a glass vase.

"Hi, Sam," Evie said as she rose to her feet. Walking to the door, she invited him in.

"Thank you," he said. Extending the flowers, he added, "These are for your mom. My mother always taught me to bring a gift for the cook when invited to dinner."

Evie was glad he had brought her mother a present. She admired his manners and thoughtfulness.

"My goodness!" her mother exclaimed as she took the roses from Sam's offered hands. "They're absolutely stunning. Pink roses are my favorite. They'll look lovely on the dinner table."

"Something sure does smell good," Sam said. He seemed slightly nervous but congenial.

"Bouillabaisse," her mother said. "I hope you like it."

"That's one of my favorite dishes," he replied.

Sitting at the kitchen table, Evie's father cleared his throat.

"Oh," Evie said, "I almost forgot. Sam, this is my father, Dan. Dad, this is Sam."

Sam walked over to her father and stuck out his right hand. Her father received it and shook it. "It's nice to meet you, Mr. Edwards. Thank you for the invitation to dinner."

"You can call me Dan, and you're welcome for the invite. My eldest daughter seems to be infatuated with you."

Evie could feel her face immediately turn red. "Dad!" she exclaimed.

Her father laughed, as did Sam.

"Dinner's ready. Let's everyone take a seat at the table," Lorretta said as she carried a large pot from the kitchen.

Sam immediately went to her aid. "Here," he said. "Let me carry that for you."

"Thank you very much," she said as she returned to the kitchen and picked up a bowl of garden salad.

"No problem," Sam said, seeming eager to help.

"I want to sit next to Sam," Cloe said.

"No, I do," Clarissa said.

"Quiet down, you two. Both of you on this side of the table right now," Dan said, motioning to two empty chairs on his left.

The twins did as they were told.

Sam waited for Evie's mother to sit down before he took a seat next to Evie.

"Let's join hands and say grace over this delicious-smelling dinner your mother has made for us," Dan said. With all heads bowed, he prayed. "Heavenly Father, we come to You with grateful hearts for all of Your tender mercies and kindnesses. We are blessed beyond compare and know that all good and perfect things come from You. Thank You for our dinner guest, and please bless this food for the nourishment of our bodies. Amen."

"Amen" echoed around the table.

Evie didn't want Sam to let go of her hand, but he squeezed it gently just before he loosened his grip.

"Now, let's eat," Lorretta said as she began ladling the fish stew into bowls. "There's salad and bread too. Please help yourselves."

After Evie took her first bite, she said, "Gosh, Mom! This is so good."

"I agree," Sam said. "This is way better than any bouillabaisse I've had at any of the local restaurants." He put a spoonful of the broth into his mouth. "There's something different about yours—something delicious."

"It's the fennel," Lorretta said. "I think fennel adds more depth of flavor."

"Well, it sure is tasty—that's for sure," Sam replied. Addressing the twins from across the table, he asked, "How about you, girls? Are you enjoying your dinner?"

They lit up as if delighted to be included in the adults' conversation. "It's really good," Clarissa said.

"Yeah. It gots depths of flavor," Cloe added, which caused everyone at the table to laugh, including Clarissa and Cloe.

Evie's father addressed Sam. "I see you do construction work. How long have you been doing that, son?"

"Since fresh out of college, so for two years now. I'm a partner with my father in our contracting company."

"Do you like that sort of work?" Evie's father asked as he dipped his bread into his bowl.

"Yes, I do. I enjoy building things with my hands. It gives me a sense of accomplishment when we finish a job."

Dan nodded and smiled. "I can imagine that would be rewarding. I've always admired a man who is good with his hands."

"Thank you, sir," Sam said.

Evie watched as Sam glanced across the table at the twins, who were staring at him. They giggled when he smiled at them.

"I've seen you girls playing in the ocean in the mornings. You look like good swimmers," he said.

"I swim best," Cloe said.

"No you don't," Clarissa argued.

Evie laughed. "You both swim equally well."

That seemed to satisfy them.

"If everyone is finished with their dinner, we can have dessert," Lorretta said.

"I'll clear the table, Mom," Evie replied as she stood and began gathering the dirty dishes.

"I'll help," Sam said. "It's the least I can do for this fantastic meal."

After clearing the table, Evie and Sam helped serve the dessert of coconut cake and chocolate ice cream.

"This looks good," Sam said, chuckling. "I bet I can guess who helped pick out this yummy-looking dessert."

The twins giggled and shouted, "We did!"

Sam laughed again. "I figured that. I know how much you girls love your chocolate ice cream." He looked to Evie's father. "If you all like Italian food, there's a nice little restaurant I know that makes the best cioppino you've ever tasted."

Evie's mother's face lit up. "I would absolutely love to try that dish. Maybe we can all go there before we leave."

Evie looked to her dad.

"That sounds like a plan to me too," he said. "You just let us know when you're free to show us the way, Sam."

Sam seemed pleased. "How about tomorrow evening?"

"Tomorrow evening it is," Dan replied.

Evie couldn't believe what she was hearing. She was actually going to get to go out on a date with Sam. It would be with her entire family, but Evie didn't mind as long as she got to spend more time with Sam.

Unexpectedly, he took her hand underneath the table and gave it a gentle squeeze.

5

A FAMILY DATE

Wishing once again that she had more dresses to choose from, Evie put on her yellow button-up dress with capped sleeves for her date with Sam and her family. She fluffed up her hair, which she had chosen to curl for a change. She wanted to look nice for Sam.

He told her family he was taking them to one of the lesser-known restaurants that the locals preferred to keep for themselves.

Evie couldn't help but be excited. She had grown close to Sam over the past few days, and what had started as a juvenile infatuation felt as if it were growing into something more.

Much to her surprise, her father had given her permission to ride with Sam in his pickup truck as the rest of the family followed behind.

"This is a nice truck," Evie said as she admired the immaculate interior of his black vehicle.

"Thank you," Sam said. "I've only had it for a couple of months. It's my work truck, but I like to keep it looking nice. I'm sort of a clean freak—for a man."

"I'm kinda like that too. I like things tidy and organized. I'm even a neat painter," Evie said.

"I would love to see some of your paintings. You'll have to text me some pictures when you get back home," he said.

Evie smiled and said she would, but she was sad at the mention of going back home. She didn't want to leave the ocean just yet—or Sam.

After about a thirty-minute drive, they arrived at the restaurant. It was a small establishment, and the lot was crowded with patrons. After finding a parking space, Sam turned off the engine. "Let me get your door for you," he said as he stepped out of the truck.

He came around to the passenger side, opened the door, and held out his hand to her. Placing her hand in his, Evie stepped out of the truck and straightened her dress.

"You look very nice tonight," he said. "You look pretty in yellow with your blonde hair."

"Thank you very much," she said. "You look nice too."

He was wearing a blue pullover shirt and jeans. He opened his mouth to reply but was interrupted by her family.

"This looks like an authentic Italian restaurant," Evie's mother said.

"Oh, it is," Sam said. "They have exceptional food."

With Sam leading the way, they walked into the establishment.

"We have reservations at six for Wright," Sam told the attractive hostess who greeted them.

"Right this way," the woman said as she led them to a large, round table next to a window. "Is this all right?" she asked politely. She spoke with a thick Italian accent. Evie enjoyed listening to her speak.

Sam looked to Dan, who said, "This is fine. Thank you very much."

"You're welcome," she said. She handed each of them a menu. "Your waiter's name is Antonio. He'll be right with you." She turned and walked away.

Everyone looked at the menu.

"I don't know why I'm looking at this," Evie's mother said as she laid her menu aside. "I want to try that wonderful cioppino Sam recommended."

"Me too," Evie said, as did her father.

"What do you girls usually get to eat at Italian restaurants?" Sam asked the twins.

"Spaghetti!" they shouted in response.

Evie laughed at her sisters. "That's right," she said. "They love spaghetti."

After Antonio took their orders, he lit the candle in the center of the table. The white taper stood in an empty Chianti bottle and had wax dripping down. It was the perfect table setting for the intimate Italian eatery. As much as Evie loved her family, she wished she and Sam were there alone.

While they waited for their food to arrive, Dan passed around the bread basket and asked Sam about his family.

"It's just my dad and me," Sam said. "I lost my mom to breast cancer two years ago, and I don't have any brothers or sisters, so my dad is all I have here. We have some extended relatives back in Lexington, Kentucky, but I don't get to see them very much."

Hearing Sam say that caused Evie profound sadness. She wished he had a family like hers.

"I'm sorry to hear that about your mother," Lorretta said. Her empathy was apparent.

Sam nodded. "Thank you. I miss her so much. She was the best mother a son could ever hope for. She loved me fiercely." He shook his head and chuckled softly. "When I was a quarterback in high school, I swear I think she cried every time I got sacked. She never wanted to see me hurt in any way."

Lorretta offered a knowing smile. "That's what us mothers do. It's our job."

Antonio walked up to the table with part of their dinner orders on a large tray. Another waiter followed him with a second tray containing the remainder of their orders. After setting a plate before each of them, he asked, "Is there anything else I can get you? Would you like refills on your drinks?"

Evie's father answered, "Yes, please, and may we have some more bread?"

"Of course, sir," Antonio answered. "I'll be right back."

After her dad said the blessing over their meal, Evie watched Sam as he watched her mother take her first bite of cioppino.

Lorretta looked at Sam and nodded. "This is fantastic!" she exclaimed.

Sam appeared pleased. "I knew it wouldn't disappoint. They make the best I've ever had."

"I'm going to attempt to copy this recipe," Lorretta said.

"Well, I hope you can manage to do it, because this is outstanding," Dan replied. "How is your spaghetti, girls?"

Cloe nodded as she slurped a long strand of spaghetti into her mouth.

"It's good, Daddy," Clarissa answered.

"I'm glad, sweethearts," Dan said.

He had a look in his eyes that warmed Evie's heart. It was a father's unconditional love. That was the reason she was having such a difficult time with disappointing her father if she decided not to become a doctor like he wanted. She was afraid her daddy would never look at her that way again. She couldn't bear the thought of that.

"So I hear you like fishing, Sam," Evie's father said.

Sam wiped his mouth with his napkin. "Yes, sir. I love to fish. I'm not very good at it, but I enjoy doing it. It clears my mind like nothing else can, except for maybe a walk on the beach."

"It must be nice to be able to go to the ocean anytime you want," Evie said. "I love the beach."

At the mention of the ocean, the twins perked up. "Are you taking us out in the canoe tomorrow, Evie?" Clarissa asked.

Evie smiled at them. "Of course I am."

They giggled in response.

Antonio returned to their table. "May I get you anything else? Dessert perhaps?"

"Chocolate ice cream!" Cloe exclaimed.

"I'm sorry, miss, but we don't have chocolate ice cream," Antonio said.

Dan smiled at the two little girls. "We'll get you some ice cream on the way home." Looking around the table, he asked, "Would anybody else like dessert?" After ascertaining that everyone was too full for a sweet ending to the meal, Dan asked for the check.

"If you don't mind, sir, I'd like to pay the bill," Sam said.

"That won't be necessary, son. You brought us to this delicious restaurant; the least I can do is pay for it."

Sam seemed indecisive.

"Really. I insist," Dan said as he laid his credit card down on the table.

"Okay then, but at least let me leave the tip," Sam said.

"It's a deal."

Sam opened his wallet, took out a generous amount of bills, and placed them on the table for Antonio.

After they walked out of the restaurant, Evie's father gave her permission to ride to the ice cream shop with Sam.

Once they were both in the truck and buckled in, Sam released an audible deep breath.

Evie giggled. "What was that for?"

Sam laughed too. "I don't know. I guess I'm just relieved your dad didn't give me that dirty look he gave me that first day on the beach. I was worried he might try to body-slam me for liking his eldest daughter."

"So you like me, do you?" she asked teasingly.

Sam shook his head, appearing embarrassed. "Yes, Evie, I like you." He reached over and took her by the hand.

"That's good because I like you too."

"Oh, you do, do you?" He grinned.

"Yes. I've liked you since the first day I saw you," she replied softly.

"That's sweet, Evie, and I felt the same way about you too."

"You did?" she asked.

"Yes, I did. Couldn't you tell?"

"I hoped you did, but I wasn't sure."

They were quiet for a few moments. "I wish we didn't live so far apart," Evie said, saddened by the prospect of having to say goodbye to him in just a little more than a week.

"Me too," he replied. He glanced over at her and smiled. "But we'll stay in contact with each other. We won't lose touch."

"Do you promise?"

"I promise," he said as he brought her hand to his lips and kissed her fingers.

6

OF AGE

The following week, the Edwards family adhered to a familiar schedule of enjoying the ocean and the beach in the morning, sightseeing and shopping in the afternoon, and visiting with Sam in the evening. Evie was thrilled that her family had accepted Sam, especially her dad. Her parents permitted Evie and Sam to sit out on the deck in the evenings to talk and get to know each other. On occasion, they were allowed to go for ice cream as long as they took the twins along as chaperones.

On the evening before their last day at the beach, Evie summoned up enough courage to speak with her father. She had something important she wanted to ask him. Finding him sitting on the sofa, absorbed in the evening news, Evie decided to help her mother in the kitchen until the newscast was over.

When she heard her father click off the television, Evie tentatively walked into the living room. "Do you have a minute, Dad? I have something I want to talk with you about."

"Sure, Evie. What is it?"

She sat down beside her father on the sofa. "Well, I was wondering. Since you've gotten to know Sam and know he is a good and decent man, I was wondering ..." She paused.

Her dad laughed. "What is it, Evie? Spit it out."

"Would it be all right if after dinner, Sam and I take a walk down the beach together? We'll only take a short walk. Please, Daddy?" Evie pleaded.

Her father's mouth curled up slightly at the ends. "I'm tempted to tease you and get you all riled up, but I don't see a need for that. If it's all right with your mother, I see no reason why you and Sam can't take a short walk on the beach together—a short one."

Evie was so thrilled she couldn't seem to sit still. She jumped up off the sofa and bounced up and down. "Thank you, Daddy!" she exclaimed, immediately wondering what she was going to wear.

Her dad grew serious. "Now, I expect Sam to behave like a gentleman, and I'll be telling him that before you all go for your walk."

"Oh! He will, Daddy. He's always respectful." Evie couldn't wait to run to her mom, who was watching from the kitchen.

"He said yes, Mom. He said I could go if it was okay with you."

"Well, it's fine with me, sweetie. Just as long as you get back by your usual curfew, I'm fine with you taking a walk on the beach with Sam."

Evie squealed happily. "Thanks, Mom! After I go get dressed, I'll help you with dinner."

"I would appreciate that. You know how much I love cooking with you."

On her way to her room to get ready for her date with Sam, Evie passed her sisters, who were playing on the floor with their dolls. "Are you girls ready for one more day in the ocean tomorrow?" she asked.

Their faces lit up with youthful enthusiasm. "Yes!" they exclaimed.

"Will you take us way out in the water in our canoe?" Clarissa asked.

Evie bent down and stroked her sister's hair. "Of course I will. I can't wait."

After putting on the only dress she had left that Sam had not seen, Evie emerged from her room wearing a pink sundress. Her hair was down and straight. She wore pink lipstick and a pair of dangly white earrings.

"Well, don't you look nice," her father said as she walked past him on her way to the kitchen. "You look more like your mother every day. You're beautiful."

Her father's sweet compliment made Evie feel special. "Thank you, Daddy," she said as she bent down and kissed him on the cheek. "I'm going to go help Mom with dinner."

"Come to think of it, I should come help too," he said as he rose from the sofa. "I know your mom loves to cook, but I'm sure she could use some assistance."

Her mother looked surprised when she saw both of them walk into the kitchen.

"We're here to help," Dan said. "What do you want us to do?"

"Well, one of you can man the fryer for the fish, and one of you can peel and cut up the potatoes for the french fries."

"I'll take the potatoes," Evie said.

"Well then, I guess I'll take the fryer," her father said, laughing.

"Good. Then I'll work on the coleslaw and tartar sauce," her mother said. "This is fun, having both of you in the kitchen with me."

"I should do it more often so I can learn how to cook as well as you, Mom."

"Yes, you should," her father said. "The way to a man's heart is through his stomach, you know." He turned and winked at her. "That's how your mama managed to land a handsome hunk like me."

They all laughed at her father's silly comment.

The Edwards family and Sam were all seated around the table, enjoying their last dinner together. They were having fish and chips.

"This is delicious, Mrs. Edwards," Sam said. "I've never had coleslaw or tartar sauce as good as this. If you don't mind me asking, how did you make it so tasty?"

Lorretta thanked him for his compliment. "The secret to good coleslaw is to add a scant amount of sugar, and I like my cabbage grated instead of coarsely cut with a knife. Now, as for the tartar sauce, just a tiny grating of shallot makes all the difference in the world."

Sam took another bite. "It sure is good, and the fish and fries are great too." His facial expression appeared slightly introspective. "I sure am glad I got to meet all of you, and I want to thank you for your kind hospitality. I'm going to miss you."

Evie started to reply, but before she could say anything, her father spoke up.

"We've enjoyed meeting you too, Sam—especially Evie." Her father grinned mischievously. "I hear you want to take our daughter for a walk on the beach this evening."

Sam put down his fork. "Yes, sir, I would, if it's all right with you and Mrs. Edwards."

Dan nodded. "Her mother and I think that would be okay if you promise to treat our daughter with the respect she deserves."

Sam nodded. "Of course, sir. I wouldn't think of treating her any other way."

"All right then," Dan said. "Let's finish our dinner so we can see what's for dessert."

Evie watched as her father winked at her smiling mother. His love for his wife was obvious in many ways. Evie hoped to be loved as much by a man someday.

"Evie, can we go for a walk on the beach with you and Sam?" Clarissa asked while shoving a ketchup-laden french fry into her mouth.

"Yeah, can we?" Cloe asked.

Evie felt guilty for having to tell Clarissa and Cloe they couldn't come along. "I'm sorry, girls, but not this time. It'll be late and past your bedtime, but we'll get up early in the morning to go play in the ocean, okay?"

"Okay," the twins murmured, looking disappointed.

After enjoying the dinner, Evie and Sam helped clear the table while Lorretta and Dan served dessert: southern-style banana pudding.

Sam took his first bite and shook his head. "Just when I thought you couldn't make anything tastier, you go and improve on perfection, Mrs. Edwards."

Lorretta grinned, obviously soaking up the praise for her cooking abilities. "Thank you, Sam. This is a family favorite. I'd be glad to write down the recipe for you if you'd like."

"I would love that, Mrs. Edwards. I doubt mine will taste anything like yours, but I would like to make some for my dad. He would love this."

"I'll be sure to get the recipe to you before we leave tomorrow."

Hearing her mother say those words instantly made Evie's heart sink. She didn't want to leave tomorrow. She didn't want to leave Sam.

Evie and Sam insisted on washing the dishes while the rest of the family retired to the living room. As soon as they finished putting away the last of the clean dishes, they walked in to find everyone watching television.

"If it's okay, we're going for our walk now," Evie said.

"Sure," her father replied. "Just be back by ten o'clock." He looked at her and smiled.

"I will, Daddy. Thank you."

The sun was getting low on the horizon when Evie and Sam walked out the back door of the condo.

Evie inhaled a deep breath of ocean air. "Oh my gosh! I'm going to miss this place so much."

Sam reached out and gently grasped her hand. "I'm going to miss *you* so much."

On the sudden verge of tears, she said, "I'm going to miss you too, Sam. I'm really glad I met you."

"I'm happy to have met you too, darlin'."

Evie grinned when he called her darlin'. It made her feel special and as if Sam saw her as a woman instead of a child.

They walked slowly down the boardwalk in the direction of the spectacular horizon, planning to walk at the water's edge on the way back.

"Don't you just love this time of day?" Sam asked.

"Yes, I do. The beauty of impending twilight takes my breath away," Evie replied. "The colors the sun produces after it has disappeared are nothing short of miraculous. I'm always amazed at the different hues of the setting sun—how the sky goes from a deep blue to a teal and then yellow. It defies description and refuses to be captured."

"Spoken like a true artist," Sam said as he raised her hand to his lips and kissed it.

Evie smiled, both at his comment and at the sensation of his warm lips. She wondered if he would kiss her good night. She hoped so. Just the thought of his lips softly making contact with hers made her heart race.

Even though they had been walking slowly, they reached the pier in what seemed like only minutes.

"Let's go into the souvenir shop. I want to buy you something to remember me by," Sam said.

His comment made Evie smile. There was no way on earth she was going to forget him. She didn't need a trinket to remind her that she had fallen in love with him.

"Come on," Sam insisted as he tugged on her hand. "What would you like—a T-shirt or a conch shell?" He laughed. "I'll buy you anything you want."

Evie looked around the tiny shop. Her eyes landed on a pair of earrings. She walked over and picked them up. They were lovely: small seashells dangling from pearl studs. She liked them—until she looked at the price on the back. They were much too expensive.

"You like those, don't you? I can tell," Sam said.

Evie shook her head. "No, they're way too costly. I think I would rather have a T-shirt." She tried to pull Sam toward the shirts on the other side of the shop, but he wouldn't budge.

"Nope," he said, grinning. "It's these earrings. They're pretty, and they'll look even better on you. Now, come over here." He gently pulled her to his side. "We'll take these," he told the cashier as he took out his wallet.

Evie continued to protest, but Sam would not take no for an answer.

As they walked out of the shop, Sam handed her the small bag and asked, "Can you put these on for me so I can see you wearing them? I'd like to take your picture too."

Once again, Evie had to fight back tears. Looking into Sam's amazing hazel eyes, she put on the earrings, knowing they would forever hold a special place in her heart.

"How do they look?" she asked.

He looked at her for what seemed like several minutes. "They look awesome," he said. "*You* look awesome. You're the most beautiful girl I've ever seen."

Evie could feel her cheeks turning pink. "Thank you, Sam."

"You're most welcome, Evie."

They walked hand in hand to the end of the pier. Looking down into the deep blue sea, Evie said, "Can you imagine what humongous creatures live in such an enormous place?"

"No, I can't," he replied. "It's hard to believe you can be out in the middle of the ocean and not see land anywhere. It's kind of scary, isn't it?" He laughed as he grabbed her around her waist, pretending he was going to push her into the water.

She screamed and then giggled. "My dad will kill you if you toss me off this pier," she said.

"Don't I know it," he said, smiling.

He was still holding her by the waist, and she didn't mind at all. It felt nice to be close to him. They stared into each other's eyes. Evie wanted to speak from her heart—to tell him she loved him—but she couldn't seem to get the words out. She was fearful of sounding like an infatuated, silly girl. She waited for him to say it first. She wanted to hear him tell her he loved her, but he didn't. It seemed as if he wanted to, but he didn't say the words she longed to hear.

"I guess we should start back," he said, sounding as reluctant as Evie felt.

"I guess so," she replied.

"First, let me get a picture of you beneath the light," he said. "I want to remember you just as you are right now."

Evie smiled for his picture, even though her heart wasn't in it. After pulling her phone out of her pocket, she took a picture of him as well. After they each took a selfie of the two of them together, they began their slow walk back toward the condo.

They took off their sandals and strolled slowly in the surf. The foamy water tickled Evie's feet.

Holding Sam's hand, she said, "This is so wonderful—so magical."

"It is," Sam replied. "It's a lot less crowded down here too."

They were among only a few other people walking along the water's edge. It was dark except for the lights shining from the boardwalk and the full moon gleaming brightly in the sky. Its glowing reflection danced on the rippled water of the ocean. It was an incredible sight. Evie couldn't believe she was there—with Sam. "This is the most romantic moment of my life," she whispered.

Sam gazed deep into her eyes. "It is for me too, Evie." Moving closer to her, he wrapped his arms around her waist. "Would it be all right if I kissed you?" he asked softly.

"I was hoping you would," Evie answered.

As he moved his face closer to hers, she stood on her tiptoes and wrapped her arms around his neck. He smiled at her just before he gently placed his moist, soft lips against hers.

Feeling as if she were melting into him, she let herself enjoy the sensation of his passionate embrace. She had been kissed before but never like this. She had never experienced anything like what she felt at that moment. Desire like she had never felt before burned inside her. She wanted him desperately. Had it not been for the promise she had made to herself to stay chaste for marriage, she felt certain she would have given herself to him.

When he ended their kiss, she felt her heart sink. She wanted to beg him not to let her go, but she knew she couldn't.

Still holding her in his arms, he gazed into her eyes. "That was amazing," he whispered. "I …" He paused.

"What is it, Sam?"

He shook his head and smiled. "Nothing. That was just a fantastic kiss."

"It was for me too," Evie said, still wondering what else he had wanted to say.

Hand in hand, they continued their walk in the surf, and Evie wished that moment in time would last forever.

7

GOODBYE

I t was the girls' last day to play in the ocean. They couldn't have
asked for a more perfect day. The sun was beaming, and the
temperature was a balmy eighty degrees.

As they stepped onto the beach, Evie waved at Sam, who
was putting the finishing touches on his construction job. The
performance stage he had built looked fantastic and blended
seamlessly into the existing boardwalk and its surroundings. He
had done an impressive job. He smiled and waved back to Evie. He
had been invited over for a late lunch before the Edwards family
started for home. Evie couldn't wait to see him again.

As she had done the previous mornings of their vacation, Evie
took her baby sisters out in their inflatable canoe. Evie adored
hearing the sound of her sweet sisters' laughter. They were usually
all giggles and shrieks in the water, but the added excitement of
it being their last day, paired with a particularly agreeable ocean,
made that day especially enjoyable.

Evie lingered in the unusually warm water as her sisters ran
back to their beach chairs for a quick drink.

She was looking forward to one last swim in the ocean after she finished playing with her sisters. Her eyes shifted in Sam's direction. She was also looking forward to perhaps some more time with Sam.

When she saw her sisters running back to the water's edge, Evie began trudging through the knee-deep water to retrieve her sister-filled canoe and drag it back out into the ocean in anticipation of another wave to carry them back in.

They laughed over and over as the canoe successfully mounted an approaching wave and carried them back to the shore.

It was Cloe's turn to ride up front, so the two had switched places. They were so cute that Evie couldn't help but smile at them.

"Are you guys ready?" Evie asked enthusiastically.

"Yes!" they shouted.

"All right then, here we go." Taking hold of the canoe, Evie pulled them back out into the waves.

Once they were out past the break, Evie treaded water while she watched and waited for another wave to appear and carry her sisters back to shore.

Momentarily distracted by her mother standing on the beach and waving them in, Evie lost her grip on the corner of the canoe. A huge wave came pounding down upon them, capsizing the canoe. Evie didn't panic, because she knew her little sisters could swim like fishes.

She saw Cloe swimming to shore with Clarissa right on her heels. Evie was right behind them. All three were giggling and having a wonderful time.

Evie couldn't have imagined what happened next. Everything occurred in an instant. From the corner of her eye, Evie saw something sleek and shiny break the surface of the water and then disappear. During the moments that followed, Evie's eyes darted around her. Suddenly, she saw a large splash of water where

Clarissa had been swimming. The little girl let out a primal, bloodcurdling sound unlike anything Evie had ever heard. She frantically swam the short distance only to find the water around her baby sister blooming red. Panic-stricken, she gathered her sister in her arms and began carrying her to shore.

After that, every sound Evie heard was muffled—the pounding surf, her mother's screams. The only sound she could hear clearly was the sound of her own heart thumping in her ears.

By the time she reached the water's edge with Clarissa, her parents had run down from their spot on the beach. She laid her injured sister down on the sand at the feet of her frantic-looking mother and father.

Clarissa's left side, including her arm and shoulder, were missing, and blood was pulsating with each beat of her heart out of the tremendous wound in her tiny body. For a few moments, she was conscious and moaning, but then her beautiful brown eyes rolled back into her head, and she fell quiet.

As Evie held on to a hysterical Cloe, she could feel Sam's arms around her from behind. Evie watched in horror as her mother and father worked feverishly to stop the bleeding and save their baby girl's life. Their efforts were to no avail. Clarissa died in their arms on the beach that day—and it was all Evie's fault.

8

A LIFE OF AMENDS

Thirteen Years Later

Having completed her bachelor's degree and four years of medical school at the Marshall University School of Medicine in Huntington, West Virginia, from which she had graduated at the top of her class, thirty-one-year-old Dr. Evie Edwards was in her third year of surgical residency. She was two years shy of becoming a partner in her father's practice; however, there was still plenty of learning left to do before she became a practicing surgeon.

It had been a long and difficult road. The years and years of studying and residency were challenging at best. The nearly eighty-hour workweeks were exhausting, leaving Evie feeling depleted most of the time.

Living in her own apartment within walking distance of her residency at Cabell Huntington Hospital made life a little bit easier; plus, her neighborhood was nice. She felt safe there—safe enough to go out for a jog or a walk in Ritter Park even in the predawn darkness.

It was a pleasant, early summer Sunday morning and one of Evie's few days away from the hospital. She averaged four to five days off a month, so she tried to make the most of each one. The rest of her days were consumed with her residency and studying for her yearly ABSITE exams. Time for eating and sleeping was limited.

It was barely daylight outside when Evie got out of bed and got ready for a jog around the park. There was a mile-long gravel jogging pathway around the entire vast and picturesque park. Evie loved living close to one of Huntington's most beautiful landmarks. She appreciated being able to enjoy it whenever she had the opportunity.

Evie's busy life didn't always leave time for self-reflection, but that day, as she was pulling her lengthy blonde hair back into a ponytail, she looked at her face in the mirror. What she saw caused her to wince. Her blue eyes were bloodshot, and her face had taken on a dull pallor.

Sighing, she put on her black running shorts and a gray T-shirt—a perfect choice, Evie thought, since the dismal colors suited her mood. Her decision to follow her parents' wishes for her life rather than her own was easier to swallow on some days, but this wasn't one of those days.

After having a cup of strong coffee, Evie grabbed her keys and headed for the door. Once outside, she breathed in the fresh summer air. It had rained the night before, so the cool air smelled as if it had been freshly laundered.

She started out with a walk, which she did in silence. She preferred it that way. She didn't run to music. It interfered with her thoughts.

That day was Cloe's eighteenth birthday. She had just graduated from high school, making it through by the skin of her teeth. Her grades were subpar, to say the least, so college wasn't likely in her future, not that she wanted it to be. Cloe reminded Evie of a 1960s wild child. Her hair color changed almost on a weekly basis, with purple being her favorite of late. Multiple oversized piercings marred her otherwise feminine facial features.

Evie felt sorry for her mom and dad. She knew raising Cloe must have been a challenge at best. Evie couldn't imagine the emotional pain they had endured. She had witnessed some of it firsthand, especially before and during her college years while she was still living at home. She'd tried her best to support Cloe and maintain a relationship with her during those years, but Cloe had refused to allow it. Evie couldn't fathom how Cloe must have felt. Losing her twin at such a young age must have been like losing half of herself. She was withdrawn and unreachable.

Evie was due at her parents' home at seven o'clock for a birthday dinner planned for just the four of them. A pool party for Cloe with some of her dubious friends would follow. Evie wasn't looking forward to dinner. Frankly, she didn't like going to her childhood home. She couldn't understand why her parents hadn't moved away after Clarissa's death. She couldn't fathom how they could still live there, surrounded by memories of their dead little girl. Evie had had a difficult time living there during her college years. Now she could barely stand to walk through the front door. The house was haunted with Clarissa's childish voice and youthful giggles. It made Evie want to cry every time she went there, which, thankfully, because of her residency hours, wasn't often.

Evie thought long and hard about what to get Cloe for her coming-of-age birthday. Finally, she settled on a pair of pearl stud earrings with a delicate matching necklace. Pearl was Cloe's birthstone, and although the jewelry was more than Evie could afford, she splurged and bought it for her sister anyway.

After a self-punishing six-mile jog around the park, Evie returned home breathless. She came into her apartment and locked the door behind her. After chugging a bottle of water, she headed for the bathroom, shedding her clothes as she walked.

As she stood in the shower with the warm water beating down on her skin, she thought about her life—a life she didn't want. She knew in her heart that she couldn't go on this way. She had made the decision to go into medicine out of guilt and was staying in it out of love and respect for her parents. But what about love and respect for herself? She had lost that long ago and wasn't sure if she could ever find it again. She wanted to be happy in the life her parents had chosen for her. She just didn't know how.

After following the long, circular driveway, Evie parked outside her parents' lovely home. Immediately, she was vexed by a combination of feelings. The place felt like home on the outside. It was a stunning two-story redbrick colonial-style structure with four massive white columns in the front. The outside was warm and welcoming, just as it always had been. It was home. But on the inside, it was different; it was unsettling. It reeked of memories of Clarissa. For the life of her, Evie couldn't seem to remember her beloved sister as the carefree, adorable child she had been. When Evie thought about her, she could see only her maimed and bloody body lying dead on the beach in Virginia.

Tears rolled out of Evie's eyes and down her cheeks. The guilt was almost more than she could bear. It was all her fault Clarissa had died that day, and she knew it. If her parents ever found out, they would hate her for the rest of her life.

Evie sighed deeply and summoned her courage to go inside. She picked up Cloe's wrapped birthday gift and opened her car door. Just as she was getting out of her car, she saw her mother open the front door.

"Hi, sweetie," her mother said. "I was beginning to wonder if you were going to come inside."

Evie forced a smile. "I'm sorry, Mom. I was on the phone with a friend," she lied.

Her mother greeted her with open arms and hugged her tightly. "I'm so glad you were free today and could come over."

"Me too." Evie lied again. It wasn't a complete lie but close to it.

"Well, let's get inside. Dinner's almost ready."

Her father, whose hair had seemed to turn completely gray overnight, met them in the hallway, at the foot of the stunning curved staircase that led to the upstairs bedrooms. Evie had always loved that staircase. It gave the home personality and an air of elegance.

"Hi, honey," her father said. "How are they treating you at the hospital?"

Evie forced another smile. "It's okay. It's very hectic and demanding, but I'm doing all right."

"Good," her father said. "In just a few more years, you and I can be partners. I'm so looking forward to that."

Evie could see the joy in the eyes of her father, which eased her apprehension a bit. It made her feel good inside to make her parents happy. Too bad it came at the cost of her own happiness.

Just as they were heading to the kitchen to finish preparing dinner, Cloe noisily descended the staircase. "Hey, Evie," she said, sounding unusually cheerful. "I'm eighteen today," she announced, as if Evie didn't already know. Raising her arms in the air and laughing, she shouted, "I'm free at last!"

Evie looked at her sister. Her eyes went immediately to her vibrant purple hair and a large septum nose piercing. She also had a large hoop through each eyebrow and one through both her upper and lower lip. She was a spectacle dressed in an oversized black T-shirt that had the ribbed band cut from the neckline so that the ragged edge plunged deep into a logo of a local band Evie found questionable. The shirt was paired with jean shorts cut so high above her thighs that they revealed the entire white pockets of her pants.

"You're not entertaining your guests at your birthday party wearing that, are you?" her father asked with a disapproving expression on his face.

"I'm eighteen now. I can do and wear whatever I want," Cloe answered belligerently.

"You don't have to be so unpleasant about it," her mother said.

Cloe sauntered past them and headed toward the kitchen. "What's for dinner anyway? I'm starved."

The rest of the family followed after Cloe.

"Since it's been a warm day, I thought a nice, cool Caesar salad with grilled chicken would be good, along with your favorite twice-baked cheddar potatoes," Lorretta said, addressing Cloe. "And, of course, cake and chocolate ice cream for dessert."

"That's okay, I guess," Cloe said with a shrug.

Evie smiled at her mother, who looked a bit hurt by Cloe's lack of enthusiasm and appreciation for her dinner menu. "It sounds delicious, Mom," Evie said.

Her father chimed in. "It sure does."

"Well then, let's eat," her mother said. "I could use a little help getting it to the table."

Evie picked up the large crystal bowl of salad. The aroma of the garlic croutons, grated parmesan, and grilled chicken strips on top greeted Evie's nose. "This smells great, Mom."

"Thank you, sweetie," her mother said as she placed a platter of twice-baked potatoes on the elegant white-linen-covered table. "I hope you all enjoy."

"We always do, Lorretta," Dan replied, smiling.

Once they were all seated at the table, her father requested that they all join hands and say grace over their meal. Cloe rolled her eyes as she accepted Evie's outstretched hand. Her father began his prayer.

"Dear heavenly Father, we thank You for the abundant food before us and for the precious hands that prepared it. Please bless it for the nourishment of our bodies, and wrap us in Your loving arms of protection. Amen."

All around the table said, "Amen," except for Cloe.

After everyone had served him or herself, Evie took a bite of her chicken Caesar salad. The first thing she tasted was the hint of garlic in the dressing. "This is so good, Mom. I really miss your food. You're such a phenomenal cook."

"Yes, Lorretta, this is absolutely delicious," Dan said.

Evie expected her sister to offer a compliment, but she didn't. Cloe just sat there frowning while she ate her dinner.

Out of nowhere, Cloe's frown turned upside down. "Guess where I'm going, Evie," she said.

"This is not the time, Cloe," her father said angrily.

"I think it's the perfect time," Cloe said defiantly. "I'm leaving for Paris tomorrow," she announced, grinning at Evie.

Evie could feel her mouth drop open. She was momentarily in shock. She didn't understand. What business did Cloe have in Paris, unless it was to rub it under Evie's nose? Cloe knew that Paris was Evie's dream, and now here she was flaunting it, and it was painfully obvious she was enjoying it.

"What—why are you going to Paris?" Evie asked. Her feelings were hurt, and she was on the verge of tears. Why would her only sister want to hurt her like this? She didn't understand.

"Just for the hell of it." Cloe shrugged. "I'm going with a group of my friends just to hang out in the art museums and see what it's like on the other side of the world."

Evie was speechless. She looked from her mother to her father. Neither of them would look her in the eye. Thinking quickly and not willing to let Cloe know she had gotten to her, Evie replied, "Well, I hope you have a safe trip and a wonderful time. How long will you be gone?" she asked nonchalantly as she took another bite of salad.

Cloe seemed disappointed at Evie's unemotional reaction to her surprising news. "It's just a one-week trip," she answered, obviously deflated.

Evie took another bite of her dinner. "Mom, this potato is divine."

Her mother smiled softly. "Thank you, Evie."

Glancing over at Cloe, Evie felt her heart soften slightly. Instead of the harsh young woman before her, Evie remembered the kind and gentle child Cloe used to be. Her heart went out to her sister. She wished there was something she could do to help her. So much of her short life had been shadowed by pain; it was difficult for Evie to bear.

Evie picked up the pink-wrapped gift she had brought for her sister and handed it to Cloe. "I know we're supposed to wait for the cake and ice cream, but I can't wait that long. Would you please open my gift now?"

Cloe laid down her fork. "I guess," she said as she accepted the present.

She tore off the wrapping, which revealed a small white box. Removing the lid, she looked at the refined pearl stud earrings and matching necklace. At first, Evie saw the slightest glimpse of her darling little sister. Cloe's chin quivered slightly before her face turned stony again. "It's pretty," she said as she quickly laid it down on the table. "It's not my style, but thank you."

"Cloe Ann Edwards," her mother said crossly. "Can't you at least show a little bit of manners when someone gives you a gift? I don't know what's happened to you."

Tears were pooling in her mother's eyes. Evie didn't know if they were angry tears or tears of disappointment. She assumed they were a combination of both.

"Sorry," Cloe said disingenuously.

"It's all right," Evie said. "I put the gift receipt in the box. You can exchange them if you like."

Cloe looked at Evie and shrugged again.

"If everyone is finished, I guess we should have our cake and ice cream now," Lorretta said as she wiped away her tears and began clearing the table.

"I'll help you with that, honey," Dan said as he stood and followed her into the kitchen with his hands full of dirty plates.

Evie didn't know what to say to Cloe, so she remained quiet until her parents returned with a glowing birthday cake. They were singing "Happy Birthday."

The smile on Cloe's face appeared duplicitous, as if she just wanted this thing to be over with as soon as possible.

After they ate their cake and ice cream, Cloe opened her large gift from her parents: a new piece of designer luggage for her trip to Paris and a greeting card with cash inside.

"Thank you," Cloe told them as she looked down at her watch. "It's almost time for my friends to get here, so I'm going up to my room to get ready."

Evie's parents' disappointment was written all over their faces, but they remained quiet. Once again, Evie's heart went out to them. She watched as Cloe got up and went upstairs, leaving her gift from Evie lying on the table.

9

A DAY IN THE LIFE

It was early Monday morning, and Evie was running a bit late for rounds. After getting dressed in green scrubs and a lab coat, she pulled her hair back into a ponytail and quickly scarfed down a piece of toast and a strong cup of coffee. After grabbing her backpack off the sofa, she headed out the door.

During her brisk walk to the hospital only two blocks away, Evie tried to convince herself that her life wasn't so bad. In fact, many people would have loved to be in her position. She knew that and was determined to try to start embracing her life rather than resenting it. She owed it to herself, and she owed it to Clarissa.

It was a foggy morning, so she carefully checked traffic both ways before crossing her only large thoroughfare, Hal Greer Boulevard. The hospital was directly across the street.

Slightly out of breath, Evie walked through the front doors, down the hallway, and into the elevator. After she pressed the button for the third floor, the doors closed, leaving Evie a few seconds to collect herself. She released a deep breath as the doors opened, and a new day began.

Her four companion residents were gathered around the nurses' station, waiting for Dr. Stone, a fifth-year surgical resident, to begin their rounds.

Shortly after five o'clock, Dr. Stone arrived. "Is everyone here?" he asked abruptly, as if he wasn't the one who was late.

"Yes, sir," answered the group of five.

"Then let's begin," he said as he looked down at the tablet in his hand.

Walking into their first patient's room, Dr. Stone apologized to an elderly woman who was lying in the bed. "We're sorry to wake you so early, Mrs. Howard. How are you feeling this morning?" he asked loudly.

"I may be old, young man, but I'm not deaf," she answered.

Evie couldn't help but smile. The old woman had spunk, and Evie admired that.

"Sorry," Dr. Stone said quietly.

"But to answer your question, I'm feeling pretty good this morning. My stomach is sore, but that's to be expected, I guess," Mrs. Howard replied.

"Yes, ma'am, it is," Dr. Stone said. Turning to address the group of residents, he asked, "Who would like to do the honor of refreshing our memories on this case?"

All five hands shot up in the air.

"Why don't you take this one, Dr. Edwards?" Dr. Stone asked.

Evie didn't need to look down at her tablet. She had already read the nurse's notes on Mrs. Howard's vitals and overnight complaints. She liked Mrs. Howard, so she was glad Dr. Stone had chosen her for this case.

"Our patient, Mrs. Ella Howard, is a ninety-year-old woman who underwent surgery yesterday morning for a bowel blockage. The blockage and necrotic tissue were dissected, and the wound was closed without incident. The patient's vitals were stable overnight, with one complaint of pain, at which time she was administered three milligrams of intravenous morphine."

"Very good, Doctor," Dr. Stone said. "Mrs. Howard, would you mind if we examined your incision?"

"I don't mind," she said as she pulled down her covers and lifted her gown to expose her stomach.

After removing the bandage and inspecting Mrs. Howard's abdomen, Dr. Stone said, "Dr. Edwards, please come up and examine the patient, and tell us your findings."

Evie smiled down at Mrs. Howard before looking at the vertical incision on her stomach. After putting on a pair of exam gloves, she gently palpated the area. Mrs. Howard grimaced.

"I'm sorry if I hurt you," Evie said.

Mrs. Howard smiled. "That's okay, sweetheart."

Pleased with what she saw and felt, Evie looked at Dr. Stone. "The tissue around the incision looks good. No signs of redness or infection are found."

"What would you recommend?"

"Due to the advanced age of our patient, I would suggest she stay in the hospital for another five to seven days for observation before releasing her."

"Very good, Dr. Edwards," Dr. Stone said. "I concur."

Evie made eye contact with Mrs. Howard.

"Thank you, Dr. Edwards," the elderly woman said as she reached out her wrinkled hand. Evie received it and held it gently. Smiling, Mrs. Howard squeezed Evie's hand before releasing it. Evie smiled back.

"We'll see you during rounds this evening, Mrs. Howard," Dr. Stone said loudly.

"I'll be here!" Mrs. Howard shouted back.

Evie stifled a chuckle.

Standing alongside her attending physician, Evie was scrubbing for surgery. She had profound respect for Dr. Dailey. He was attentive and kind to his residents but tough on them when he needed to be.

"Have you come to a decision about your specialty?" Dr. Dailey asked. "You really should have decided by now if you're going to."

Evie had been trying to answer that question for herself for a long time. "As you know, my father is a general surgeon and wants me to join him in his practice as soon as I graduate," Evie answered.

Dr. Dailey continued to scrub his hands and forearms. "You didn't answer my question. Whether or not you choose to specialize, you need to choose for yourself—not for your father."

"I know," Evie answered softly. "I'm just not sure I want to go for a fellowship for a specialty. I can't decide if I want to commit myself to another three years of education or just go ahead and join my father's group upon graduation."

"I know, but whether or not you decide to go for a fellowship, would you like my opinion on where you would thrive and be happiest?" Dr. Dailey asked with a sideways smile.

Evie turned to face him. "Yes, sir, I would very much like to have your opinion."

"Well, since you asked," he said, chuckling. "In my observation, I think one of two specialties would be ideal for you. It may sound odd, but I think you would make a wonderful pediatric surgeon, and at the same time, I think you would be just as fulfilled as a general surgeon working primarily with geriatric patients. I've observed you while administering to both of these age groups, and I can see it in your face and in your eyes. You have a gift, Evie.

You seem to connect to both the young and the old with the same amount of exuberance and empathy."

Evie thought for a moment about what Dr. Dailey had just said. He was right. She did seem to have an affinity for children and the elderly.

"Thank you for the compliment and for your opinion, Dr. Dailey. I appreciate that very much," Evie said as she finished scrubbing up.

Dr. Dailey nodded. "You're welcome. Now, let's go get that hot appendix out of our patient."

Gowned up and ready for surgery, Evie stood silently on one side of her patient while Dr. Dailey stood on the other. Evie looked down at the face of the twenty-one-year-old young woman on the table, who was probably about to undergo an emergency appendectomy. She was experiencing pain in her lower abdomen, was running a fever, and had an elevated white blood cell count, which were all the classic signs of appendicitis. A breathing tube had been inserted into her lungs, and she was under general anesthesia.

Just before commencing, Evie did what she always did before performing a surgery: she said a quick silent prayer for her patient.

The sound of Dr. Dailey's voice startled Evie a bit. "Please proceed, Dr. Edwards."

Evie focused her attention on her patient's sterilized stomach and made an umbilical keyhole puncture and inserted the port with a trocar. She then released carbon dioxide gas to inflate the patient's abdomen, after which she inserted the laparoscope through the port to examine the appendix. Looking at the image on the monitor, she could see that the appendix was red and swollen and needed to be removed.

"The appendix is hot, as we suspected," Evie told Dr. Dailey. "There's definite blockage from the appendix to the intestine. There is distention and swelling."

"Looks that way," he replied. "Let's get that out, shall we?" He looked at her expectantly.

Evie made two more small incisions in the upper right and lower left quadrants of her patient's abdomen to use for inserting instruments. She clamped the end of the appendix, severed the inflamed organ, and detached it. Using staples, she closed the inside wound. She then inserted the diseased appendix into a surgical bag and successfully removed it through the port.

Even though the entire procedure took only thirty-five minutes, Evie could feel the perspiration on her forehead. She breathed a deep sigh of relief as she removed the other instruments and closed the three insertion wounds with sutures and glue.

"Beautiful job, Doctor," Dr. Dailey said. "Congratulations."

Evie smiled behind her mask, but her eyes stung with the threat of tears. The satisfaction she felt at having just saved a life was extremely emotional and beyond description. "Thank you, Dr. Dailey," she said.

Throughout her busy day of performing surgeries and making her evening rounds, Evie couldn't seem to stop thinking about whether or not to choose a specialty. Dr. Dailey had hit the nail on the head—her choice was between doing a fellowship in pediatrics or going directly into general surgery with a specialty in geriatrics—but Evie couldn't seem to decide which she wanted to do.

It was seven o'clock in the evening, and she felt weary from her long shift. She was in no frame of mind to make the decision now, nor did she have to.

She had been on her feet for fourteen straight hours by the time her group of residents finished the day the same way they had started: by following Dr. Stone into the room of their final patient of the day, Mrs. Howard.

Dr. Stone looked to Evie. "Carry on, Dr. Edwards," he said.

"How are you doing this evening?" Evie asked her patient, making sure not to speak too loudly.

Mrs. Howard grimaced. "I'm not feeling too well, sweetheart."

Evie could see that her patient was frightened. To be honest, so was Evie. She wanted Mrs. Howard to make a full recovery and go home happy to be with her children and grandchildren.

"May we take a look at your tummy?" Evie asked softly.

Mrs. Howard nodded. "You can. I like you."

Evie smiled at the elderly woman's sweet comment. "I like you too, Mrs. Howard," she said as she pulled down the covers and lifted her patient's gown. After removing the bandage, Evie could see that there was some inflammation beginning to form in the incision. Looking to Dr. Stone, she said, "We're going to have to start her on some tetracycline."

He nodded his approval of her proposed treatment.

Mrs. Howard reached out for Evie's hand. "Is it serious?" she asked, appearing nervous.

"It could be, but more than likely, it's just a little infection. We'll start you on some IV antibiotics right away. That should clear it right up." Evie smiled. "Don't worry. We'll take good care of you."

"Thank you, sweetheart," Mrs. Howard said as she held tightly to Evie's fingers.

"You're very welcome," Evie said as she stroked her patient's weathered hand.

It was after eight o'clock in the evening when Evie and her group finished their rounds and the patient charting work that followed.

"Who wants to go to the cafeteria to get something to eat before they close?" Elizabeth asked. "I'm starving to death." Elizabeth Stewart was a tall, gorgeous redhead with emerald-green eyes. She was one of Evie's closest friends of the group, as was George.

"I'll go," George said. "My stomach's been growling since noon." George Baisdan was rather short and had dark brown hair and eyes. Evie liked him. He had a vulnerable side to him that Evie found endearing. He wasn't afraid to show his true feelings. She admired that.

"I'm ready," Evie said. Although she was worried about Mrs. Howard, she was hungry and thirsty. She hadn't had time to stop for lunch. "Let's go," she said to Elizabeth and George. Addressing the other two residents, Linda and Lonnie, she asked, "Are you sure you don't want to come eat with us?"

The two declined, saying they wanted to go home and go to bed.

That was Evie's next desire after eating. She wanted to go home and plop into bed to get some much-needed sleep.

After getting their food in the cafeteria, the three cohorts sat down in a four-person black vinyl booth. Elizabeth and George sat on the side opposite Evie. Evie looked at her friends' food trays and laughed. All of them had enough food on their plates to feed an army.

Evie started with a salad and planned on finishing with a slice of cherry pie, with a turkey sandwich in between. The first bite tasted heavenly. The cool, crisp lettuce coated in creamy ranch dressing was exactly what she had been craving since noon.

"How can you choose salad over pizza?" Elizabeth asked with her mouth full.

"Yeah," George said. "There's just something not right about you." He laughed as he took a huge bite of pizza.

"I just like salad," Evie said, laughing along with her friends. "Guess what?" she added. "I'm not certain, but I think I've decided on a specialty."

"Well, it's about time," George said. He had started medical school knowing he wanted to become a plastic surgeon.

"Yeah," Elizabeth said. "Are you coming into cardiovascular with me?"

Evie shook her head. "Nope. I don't think I'm going to fellowship at all. I think I'm going directly into general surgery with a specialty in geriatric patients."

George wrinkled his nose. "That's not a very sexy specialty."

Elizabeth punched him playfully on the arm. "I think it's a wonderful calling. I hope when I get old and gray, I'll have a special doctor like Evie to take care of me."

"Thank you," Evie said, grinning. "I still haven't decided for sure. I'm still drawn to pediatrics too." She shrugged. "I sure am indecisive, aren't I?"

She took another bite of salad, wondering what her father would say should she choose to apply for a pediatric fellowship.

10
REWARDS

Evie stowed her overnight bag in the bin and took her seat by the window. The airplane was almost to capacity when she sat down. She was happy with her seat. It was just in front of the wing, so she would have a bird's-eye view of the scenery around and below her. She would enjoy that very much.

She looked up to see a frantic-looking man hurriedly enter the plane. The flight attendant looked at the man's ticket and pointed to the empty seat next to Evie. Evie's mood immediately soured. She had hoped the seat would remain empty. She wasn't in the mood to make idle small talk with a stranger on a plane, when she could use that time to silently rehearse her presentation speech.

Watching the man as he stored his luggage in the overhead bin, she felt there was something vaguely familiar about him, or maybe he just reminded her of someone.

He sat down in his seat and buckled his safety belt. Releasing a sigh, he looked over at Evie and smiled politely. Evie smiled back. She noticed he was looking at her peculiarly.

"I apologize for staring. It's just that you look like someone I used to know," he said.

"I know what you mean," Evie said. His voice sounded familiar. "You remind me of ..." She paused. Looking into his hazel eyes, she suddenly remembered. "Sam?" she asked quietly. "Is your name Sam Wright?" Saying his name brought back a flood of emotions.

"Evie?" he asked disbelievingly with a huge grin on his face.

"Yes," she replied. "I'm Evie Edwards. I'm surprised you remember me."

"Remember you—how could I forget you?" he asked. His grin evolved into a serious expression.

They sat there in silence, staring at each other, for several moments. All the feelings Evie had had for Sam at the beach so long ago came rushing back with a vengeance.

"It's so good to see you, Evie," he said.

Evie could tell his words were genuine. She could see it in his familiar gaze. She had never forgotten his sincere hazel eyes.

"It's good to see you too, Sam," she said. "How are you? How have you been?"

Before he could answer, the flight attendant announced their takeoff and asked that all passengers have their safety belts buckled and their seats in the upright position. As the plane began to accelerate, so did Evie's heart. She felt like a silly teenager in love all over again. The truth was, Evie had never gotten over Sam. She had dated very little after their short summer romance. Everyone she went out with couldn't seem to measure up to Sam.

When they were in the air, making their ascent, Sam answered her questions. "I'm doing fine. Still working with my dad, but we're based out of Lexington, Kentucky, now."

"You are? What prompted your move to Kentucky?" Evie asked. "I thought you would never leave Virginia Beach."

He ignored her questions. "What are you doing now?" he asked as he turned in his seat toward her. "If memory serves me correctly, you were going to become an artist. Are you on your way to Paris?" he asked with a charming smile. "Please say yes."

Evie smiled and shook her head. "No, I'm on my way to a medical conference in Boston. I'm making a presentation there about an article I wrote that was published."

Sam's eyebrows went up in surprise. "Oh wow! I knew medicine was on the table for you, but I thought for sure you'd go in a different direction. Well, anyway, I hope that makes you happy."

Evie nodded softly as she thought of the life that never had been. "Yes, I became a doctor. I'm in my third year of surgical residency." Surprisingly, it didn't make her sad to say that. She found it odd, but it actually made her smile. "I guess sometimes dreams can change, Sam," she said. "So how are things with you?"

Sam's face remained somber. "I'm good," he answered unconvincingly. "I'm …" He paused. "I'm on my way to Rockport."

"That's nice. Is it for work?" Evie asked.

Sam seemed hesitant to answer. "No," he replied. "My fiancée is there. Her family lives in Rockport, and I'm flying up there to help her make the move to Lexington."

Evie couldn't help the twinge of jealously that clouded her brain as she digested his comment. She knew it was silly, but it hurt her to know he had found someone else. But why wouldn't he have? They hadn't spoken a word since the day Clarissa died. What had she expected him to do—carry a torch for her the way she had carried one for him?

Somehow, Evie was able to take control of her slightly irrational emotions. She offered him her left hand. "Congratulations," she said as sincerely as she could. "When is the big day?"

He took her hand and held on to it. "Not for a while yet. Martie wants a Christmas wedding."

"Martie," Evie repeated. "Well, Martie is one lucky lady. I hope she knows that."

Sam grinned. "I don't know about that. Now, how about you? Are you married or seeing anyone seriously?"

Evie laughed. "Apparently, you don't know anything about the life of a surgical resident. I barely have time to eat or sleep, much less date."

"I'm sorry to hear that," Sam said. "I really am. You were a remarkable young woman all those years ago, Evie, and I can't imagine anything has changed."

He gazed into her eyes in a way he shouldn't have. He was looking at her the same way he had during their brief two-week love affair many years earlier.

Evie wondered if he could see the same wistful look in her own eyes.

Sam was still holding her hand, and she had no desire to pull it away. They talked and laughed during the entire flight. Without mentioning Clarissa, they talked about their short time together thirteen years earlier and agreed that it didn't seem like it had been that long ago.

"You haven't changed a bit, Evie," Sam said softly. "You're just as beautiful as you ever were. If it's possible, I think you're even more so."

"Thank you, Sam. I needed to hear that. I figured that medical school and residency had aged me significantly."

"No, not at all," he said reassuringly.

Evie swallowed hard. She wanted to tell Sam she still had feelings for him, but how could she? She had no right. As the passionate emotions from thirteen years earlier continued to overwhelm her, she found it difficult to keep them in.

Sam was still holding her hand when the flight attendant announced that they would be making their descent and arriving at Boston International Airport in just a few minutes.

It was only then that Evie felt Sam let go of her hand. Their short interlude was over, and Evie was profoundly saddened by that.

As the landing gear lowered and the tires made impact with the runway, reality reared its ugly head. Evie had to let Sam go—again—knowing she would never see him again.

As the passengers began to exit the plane, Sam turned to look at Evie. He appeared as sad as Evie felt. "I can't tell you how good it was to see you again, Evie. I just ..." He trailed off.

"I was thrilled to see you again too, Sam," she said. "I truly am glad for you and Martie. I wish you nothing but happiness."

"Thank you, Evie," he said. "I appreciate that."

After one more smile, they stood and retrieved their bags from the overhead bin. They exited the plane and walked to the car rental office together. Once they had procured their rides, Sam walked her to her car, where they said one last goodbye.

"I don't know what to say," Sam said as he gazed at her. "I have a lot I would like to say to you—but I can't."

A tear rolled down Evie's face. "I understand" was all she could manage to say.

He leaned in and kissed her on the cheek, lingering there for a moment. It took all Evie had not to declare her feelings for him.

"Take good care of yourself, Evie."

"I will. You too," she whispered tearfully.

As he turned to walk away, Evie waved one last goodbye. Once in her car, she allowed herself to release the tears that had been on the surface since the moment Sam told her he was engaged.

Evie had told him she understood, but she didn't. She didn't understand why so many bad things had happened to her in her life. She didn't understand why she had lost her baby sister, Clarissa. She didn't understand why she'd had to let go of her childhood dream. Now she had to lose Sam all over again. She didn't understand any of it.

11

AN OVERDOSE
OF REALITY

Although her trip had been dampened by having to say goodbye to Sam, Evie was pleased with how her presentation had gone in Boston the previous week. Standing in front of an audience of her peers and superiors, she had felt nervous during her speech but hoped they hadn't noticed.

She couldn't seem to get Sam off her mind. It had been an incredible coincidence that they had found themselves on the same plane at the same time. Fate was funny that way.

As Evie, Dr. Stone, and the other residents made their morning rounds, Evie's phone kept vibrating in her pocket. The caller was persistent. As soon as one call went unanswered, the person called back. Evie rejected every call, but still, they kept coming. As she stood inside a patient's room, the calls continued. The vibrating sound was apparently annoying Dr. Stone.

"Why don't you step out and take that call?" he told Evie abruptly.

"Sorry, sir," Evie said as she stepped outside the doorway and took her phone out of her pocket. It was her father calling. Evie called him back.

"What's going on, Dad?" Evie asked crossly. "I'm making rounds. I'm not supposed to be—"

Her father cut her off. "It's Cloe. She's in the emergency room."

"What happened?" Evie asked as her heart began to pound.

"She overdosed," her dad said, sounding as if he were about to break down.

"I'll be right there," Evie said.

Just as she finished her call, Dr. Stone and the other four residents walked out of the patient's room. He looked at Evie with a scowl on his face.

"My sister's in the ER," Evie said as her eyes pooled with tears.

"Go," Dr. Stone said without hesitation.

"Thank you, sir."

Evie turned and hurried toward the elevators.

Before entering Cloe's room, Evie discussed her condition with the attending ER physician, Dr. Moses. He told her that Cloe had overdosed on heroin and that the paramedics had had to administer three doses of naloxone to pull her out of it. "They said they almost lost her on the way to the hospital," Dr. Moses said. "She's one lucky young lady."

Evie could think of a lot more words to describe her sister other than *lucky*—*entitled, careless, inconsiderate,* and even *stupid.* Although relieved Cloe was still alive, Evie was furious with her.

When she entered Cloe's hospital room, Cloe was lying flat on her back on the bed. Evie looked at her parents, who were standing together off to the left side. Her father had his arms lovingly wrapped around her distraught-looking mother.

Evie walked up to the right side of Cloe's bed. She looked thinner and more haggard than she had just a few weeks earlier when Evie last saw her. Cloe looked up at her defiantly.

"Spare me the speech, sis," Cloe said, rolling her eyes.

Evie couldn't believe what she was seeing and hearing. Didn't Cloe have the slightest idea how close she had come to death? Did she not realize the dangerous game she was playing with her life?

"Heroin, Cloe? Are you serious?" Evie asked sternly. "Have you lost your mind? You could have died."

Cloe smiled smugly. "Well, I didn't die, did I?"

"Not from lack of trying, huh, Cloe?" Evie asked with a disgusted sigh.

Evie had much more to say but was interrupted when Dr. Moses came into the room. He addressed Cloe, but most of his attention was paid to Evie. "She's been given naloxone and IV fluids. It seems that the heroin has been significantly flushed from her system. Her vitals are back to normal, as is her oxygen level." He looked to Cloe. "I think we can release you to your parents. I would strongly suggest you seek professional help through a drug rehabilitation program. I can suggest—"

Cloe cut him off. Raising up in bed, she said insolently, "I don't have a drug problem. I was just trying something. I did something stupid. That's all."

"All right then, I'll sign your release papers," Dr. Moses said as he glanced over at Evie with a look of frustration.

Evie knew there was nothing else Dr. Moses could do. He couldn't force Cloe into rehab. Evie knew the drill. Until Cloe was ready to stop the runaway train that was her life, there was nothing anybody else could do to save her.

12

AN OFFERING OF HOPE

I t had been two weeks since Cloe's overdose and subsequent visit to the emergency room. She was still living at home with their parents and still unwilling to acknowledge that she needed help with her drug problem.

Evie visited as much as her busy hospital schedule would allow. Even though she was absent in body, she was there in spirit. Cloe was never far from her mind. Evie had lost Clarissa; she couldn't bear the thought of losing Cloe too.

With her head down and her focus on her sister, Evie walked hurriedly through the automatic doors of the hospital. After almost bumping into someone, Evie came to an abrupt stop. Looking up, she saw that it was Dr. Moses. "I'm sorry, Dr. Moses. I wasn't paying attention to where I was going."

He smiled at her. "No problem," he said. "How are you doing this morning, Dr. Edwards?"

Impressed that he remembered her name, Evie returned his smile. "I'm fine, sir. How are you?"

"Just fine, thank you." He looked thoughtfully at her, as if wanting to ask her something.

He was an eye-catchingly attractive man with a short mustache and goatee. He had light brown skin, dark brown eyes, and a charismatic smile. Other than his smile, his most striking feature was his shiny black hair, which was slightly wavy.

"You seem to be in quite a hurry this morning. I don't suppose you'd have time for a cup of coffee, would you?" he asked with a hopeful expression on his face.

Pleasantly surprised by his offer, Evie checked her watch. She had about twenty-five minutes to spare. "As long as you don't mind a quick cup, I would like that."

"Don't mind at all," he said as the two headed toward the hospital coffee shop.

As they reached the ordering station, Dr. Moses asked Evie what she would like.

Pleased by his gentlemanly gesture in paying for her drink, she asked for a large black coffee.

"I was wrong about you," he said, smiling. "I figured you would want one of those froufrou specialty coffees."

Evie laughed. "Froufrou drinks would never have gotten me through medical school. Besides, I'm a simple girl with simple needs," she said as he placed their orders and paid for their drinks.

After receiving their cups of coffee, Dr. Moses led the way to a vacant small, round table. Evie was impressed when he pulled her chair out for her and waited for her to sit first.

"So since we're running short on time, I would first like to ask you—how's your sister?"

Evie's smile quickly faded at the mention of her troubled sister. "She's still denying that she has a problem. I don't know what to do to help her."

"I've been thinking about that," he said, which surprised Evie. "Since she's not open to any type of rehabilitation, what about a tried-and-true family-based intervention? Have you thought of that?"

Evie hesitated. "I hadn't really thought about that. Cloe is so volatile; I'm not sure we could get her to sit still for that, but at least we could give it a try." She smiled at him. "Thank you for your concern for my sister and for your suggestion. I'm going to discuss it with my parents tonight."

Grinning back at her, he said, "You're most welcome, Dr. Edwards."

"Please call me Evie," she said.

"Only if you'll call me Eric."

"Okay, Eric." It felt odd to call an attending by his first name, but she liked it. She also liked being the envy of almost every woman in the coffee shop. She couldn't help but notice the jealous glances she was getting. Eric was probably used to getting that kind of attention from the ladies, but the experience was new to Evie.

As they chatted over the next few minutes, Eric seemed to only have eyes for her.

Glancing at her watch, she saw that it was time for her to go. "I gotta run," she said as she rose to her feet.

He did the same. "I hope you have a good day, Evie," he said.

"You too, Eric," she said.

"Would you be open to having dinner with me sometime?" he asked.

Although slightly taken aback by his offer, Evie was thrilled. "I would love to, but you know what my schedule is like."

He laughed.

Evie enjoyed the sound of his laughter. It was deep and alluring.

"Yes, I remember those residency days. Here," he said as he offered her his business card. "My personal cell number is written on the back. Just let me know when you're free. I'll do my best to accommodate your schedule."

Evie smiled and took the card from his hand.

After they said their goodbyes, Evie headed for the elevators. If she didn't hurry, she would be late for morning rounds. As the elevator rose, Evie's mind wandered back to her coffee break with Dr. Moses. He was a successful and good-looking attending, yet he seemed to want to spend his time with her. Evie had to admit she was flattered and perhaps a little terrified. After all, her experience and track record with men left a lot to be desired.

After making their evening rounds, Elizabeth, George, and Evie went to the cafeteria for dinner. Evie didn't tell them about having coffee with Dr. Moses and his subsequent invitation to dinner. For some reason, she felt as if keeping the news to herself made it more special. She couldn't help but smile when she thought about Eric. She found his consideration of her sister's health endearing.

"What's that smile all about?" Elizabeth asked. "That looks like a man-made smile to me." She laughed.

Evie giggled at her astute friend. "I'm just glad to be done for the day. I'm so tired I might just go to sleep right here in this booth," she said as she took a bite of her hot dog. She felt guilty for eating it. She tried to eat healthy foods, but the hospital made the best hot dog sauce she'd ever had, including her mother's—and that was saying something.

"I'm glad you're going into cardiovascular, Elizabeth," George said as he took another bite of his hot dog. "I'm going to need your services before long if I keep eating as unhealthily as I have been lately."

The three friends chuckled.

"I'm so glad Mrs. Howard is doing better," Evie said. "She should get to go home soon if she keeps improving."

Elizabeth and George looked at each other.

"What is it?" Evie asked as she took another bite of her mouthwatering hot dog.

"It's just—I don't know. You seem to get awfully attached to your patients," Elizabeth said.

Evie took her friend's statement to heart. She had to admit it stung a little. "I can't help it," she said. "I care about people. That's just the way God made me."

Elizabeth appeared regretful. "I'm sorry, Evie. Don't listen to me. Sometimes I don't think I care enough. Who am I to judge you for caring too much?"

Evie grinned at her friend. "Don't worry about it," she said.

She looked over at George, who had just finished his second hot dog. Exhaustion showed on his face. He looked as if he were about to drop at any minute.

"Are you sure you're okay to drive home, George?" Evie asked.

"Yeah, I'll be all right. It's a short drive. Wanna ride home?" he asked.

"No, thanks," Evie replied. "I'm looking forward to the warm, fresh air and a short walk home."

"Okay. Be careful," George said as the three friends stood and gathered their backpacks.

They walked out of the cafeteria together and out the hospital's double sliding doors. After saying their goodbyes in the parking lot, they headed their own separate ways.

After Evie got home, took off her scrubs, and got into her nightshirt, she stretched out on the sofa with her cell phone in hand. She yawned as she dialed her mother's number.

"Hi, sweetie. How are you?"

"I'm okay, Mom. Just tired," Evie answered. "As soon as we get finished talking, I'm going straight to bed. I know it's early, but I'm bushed."

"Aw, sweetie, I feel so bad for you. Residency is one of the most difficult things one can put themselves through."

"It sure is hard. But I only have two more years if I don't specialize. I'll make it somehow," Evie said with a sarcastic chuckle.

"I know you will, sweetie. Do you know if you'll be free on Sunday? Would you like to come over for dinner?"

Evie took a deep breath. She wasn't sure how her mother was going to react to her suggestion of a family intervention for Cloe, but she had to ask. "Mom, I'm available on Sunday, but instead of dinner, I have an idea. Actually, it was Dr. Moses's idea."

"What is it, Evie?" her mother asked. Her apprehension was apparent in the tone of her voice.

Evie asked her mother's opinion on the intervention for Cloe.

"Well, I'll have to talk it over with your father, of course, but I can't see where we have anything to lose if we give it a try," she said quietly, obviously fighting back tears.

Hearing the deep sorrow in her dear mother's voice broke Evie's heart. It hurt her to hear her mother's pain.

13

SOUL CLEANSING

Evie arrived at her parents' home at two o'clock on the following Sunday afternoon. Her stomach was slightly upset. The intervention wasn't going to be easy. Cloe would see to that. Evie was sure of it.

When she walked through the front door, her mother was standing in the living room, and Cloe was descending the staircase. Cloe's hair was blue this time, and she looked sickly, sullen, and tired. She made no attempt to smile or make Evie feel welcome.

"What are you doing here?" she asked Evie in a loathsome tone.

"Cloe Ann," her mother said. "That's no way to greet your sister."

Cloe stopped and rolled her eyes like a juvenile. Evie could already see that the intervention was going to be challenging at best.

"Would you mind coming into the living room and talking with us, Cloe?" Evie asked quietly. "After days of nonstop hospital talk, I'd really like some family time on my day off."

Cloe shrugged. "I guess," she said as she turned and headed toward the living room. "It's not like I have anything else to do."

Her father was already seated, and Evie noticed that her mother had snack foods and drinks on the circular coffee table in the center of the sitting area. That was her mother—always accommodating.

Evie took a seat on the sofa, and Cloe plopped down on the opposite end. It seemed Cloe wanted to be as far away from Evie as she could get.

Evie took a moment and looked at her little sister. For such a young woman, there seemed to be tremendous pain hidden beneath the lines of her face. It tugged at Evie's heartstrings to see her baby sister hurting. She wanted so much to help her, but she didn't know how. She wanted to wrap Cloe in her arms and make the pain evaporate, as she had done so often when Cloe was little, but she knew this hurt wasn't going to fade with just a hug. She wasn't sure how to make it disappear. She needed guidance. Silently, she said a quick prayer for God's help in what she was about to do. As if quietly approaching a wounded animal, Evie scooted closer to her sister on the sofa. Cloe looked at her as though she were going to bolt.

"Please, Cloe, talk to me. All I want to do is talk."

"About what?" Cloe sneered. "About what a screwup I am?"

Evie reached over and took Cloe's hand. At first, she thought Cloe was going to snatch it away. She started to—Evie could feel it—but she didn't, and Evie was glad. She smiled at her beautiful sister with blue hair and piercings. She felt a tear trickle down her face. Oh, how she loved Cloe. If only Cloe had known how much she was loved.

"No," Evie replied. "I don't think you're any more screwed up than the rest of us. You're just ..." Evie thought for a moment. "I think you're just heartbroken, and you don't know how to deal with it. Do you want to talk about the reason?" She knew the reason. It was Clarissa. "Trust me, Cloe, talking about it will help. I promise you it will."

Cloe pulled her hand away. "Why now?" she asked hatefully. "Why are you so concerned now?"

Evie's tears continued as she gently took her sister's hand again. "Because I feel like I'm losing you, Cloe, and I don't want to lose another sister. I couldn't bear it."

Cloe whipped her head around and glared at Evie. "I haven't heard you mention her name once since that day on the beach," she spat. "Why is that, Evie? If you loved her so much, why is it you never mention her name?"

Cloe looked at Evie with such disdain that Evie could barely maintain eye contact.

"I don't ..." Evie paused. Tired of trying to hold off a flood of tears, she let them flow freely down her face. Clearing her throat, she said, "I haven't talked to you—any of you ..." She hesitated again and looked around the room at her mother and father. Her eyes came back to rest on Cloe's bowed head. "I can't say her name to any of you because her death was my fault. I'm the reason she died that day."

The room fell silent. Without letting go of Cloe's hand, Evie retrieved a napkin from the coffee table and wiped her face.

Cloe slowly turned her head to face Evie. She was crying too. "No. It wasn't your fault. It was mine."

Evie gave her sister time to elaborate, but Cloe didn't say another word. She just sat there crying. Evie silently prayed once again for God's guidance before she spoke. "You were only five years old, honey. Nothing was your fault."

"Yes, it was!" Cloe exclaimed loudly. "Clarissa ..." She paused. It appeared as if saying her sister's name out loud caused her great sorrow. "She asked me if she could ride up front in the canoe that morning, but I wouldn't let her. I wouldn't let her take my turn. If I had, she would still be alive."

Cloe looked at her so hopelessly and helplessly that it caused Evie's heart to ache. Sobbing uncontrollably, Cloe forced her words out in broken spurts: "I didn't want to tell you all. I knew if I did, you would hate me."

Evie gathered her broken little sister in her arms and held her while she cried. She glanced at her silent parents, who were also crying and looking as if they didn't know what to do. Her mother appeared as if she were about to get up out of her seat, but Evie shook her head. She was afraid of overwhelming Cloe and causing her to retreat back inside herself again.

Feeling the weight of the world on her shoulders, Evie chose her words carefully and spoke softly. "Cloe, honey, you were just a baby. You didn't know what was going to happen—none of us did but especially not you. Do you think you can accept that as truth?"

Evie could hear Cloe's sobs subsiding. "I don't know," she whispered. "I want to—I just don't know how."

"We'll help you," Evie said as she stroked her sister's blue hair.

Cloe pulled back and looked intently at Evie. She appeared first relieved but then troubled. As if able to read the buried pain in Evie's eyes, Cloe reached out and touched Evie's face and asked softly, "What did you mean when you said Clarissa's death was your fault? You didn't do anything wrong."

Evie didn't know what to say. Her first inclination was to keep her secret buried, where it belonged, where it couldn't hurt anyone but her, but staring into Cloe's understanding eyes for the first time in years gave her the strength to tell the truth. "I knew there were sharks in that water where we were. A sandbar shark brushed up against me in the water a few days before it took our sister, and I didn't tell you all, so it was my fault," Evie said as she bowed her head in shame. "And I accidentally let go of the canoe right before you all spilled out into the ocean. If she had still been in the canoe, she wouldn't have—" Evie couldn't hold back the sobs any longer. They racked her body as Cloe held her tightly.

"Don't cry, Evie," Cloe said softly. "It wasn't your fault either."

"No, it wasn't," their father said as he and their mother came over and knelt down beside Evie and Cloe. "What happened that day was a horrible freak accident, but it was an accident nonetheless." Looking at Cloe, he continued. "You had no control whatsoever over what happened." Turning his gaze toward Evie, he added, "And I saw the shark that took our baby that day. It was definitely gray—sandbar sharks are brown."

"But I let go of the canoe," Evie said, barely able to make eye contact with her parents.

"I saw the size of that shark, Evie," her father said somberly. "A little rubber canoe wouldn't have stopped him." He paused and shook his head. "Don't think for one minute that your mother and I haven't blamed ourselves for what happened to our baby. What if we had chosen a different condominium to stay in or a different date to take you all to the beach?"

Evie looked at her father and mother. They had tears in their eyes. The entire family had suffered an almost insurmountable loss—a loss so devastating that it had taken thirteen years for them to be able to even speak about it. Thirteen years of self-hatred and blame. Thirteen years of shame and guilt. Evie thought that was enough. It was time to reconcile and begin to heal.

"Maybe none of us are to blame for what happened to Clarissa." It was the first time Evie had uttered her sister's name aloud. It caused her a combination of pain and relief—mostly relief.

"Of course we weren't," her mother said tearfully. "My sweet babies." She cried as she stood and opened her arms. Evie and Cloe stood and walked into their mother's warm embrace. "I love you girls so much. I can't describe how full of love my heart is for you. And I love Clarissa too, and I always will," she whispered.

Evie watched as her father stood and joined in for a loving family hug. It felt wonderful and long overdue as far as Evie was concerned. She sighed deeply in the knowledge that she was forgiven and loved.

14

PROGRESS

I t had been three weeks since Cloe's successful intervention. Cloe was in an in-patient rehabilitation facility and was doing well. Evie was so happy that she could barely contain her smile. Not only was Cloe healing, but so was the entire family. Evie could now take a breath without the guilt of Clarissa's death squeezing the air out of her. Without the guilt, she could love Clarissa and remember her with fondness and gratitude.

As Evie was leaving the hospital after a rewarding and successful day, she happened upon Dr. Moses in the lobby. With his bag in hand, he appeared to be on his way out for the day as well.

"Well, hello there, Evie," he said, smiling handsomely.

"Hi, Eric," Evie said. It still felt weird to call him by his first name, but he grinned even bigger when she did.

"Looks like we're leaving at the same time today," he said. "If you're not too tired, would you like to join me for a quick dinner? I don't know about you, but I'm starving."

Looking into his inviting dark brown eyes, Evie couldn't resist. "I think I would love that. I'm certainly not dressed for dinner," she said, looking down at her pink scrubs and white lab coat.

"I think you look beautiful," he said with another endearing smile.

Evie reciprocated with one of her own. "Thank you," she said, wishing she felt beautiful.

"We can take my car, and then I'll drop you back off to pick up yours," Eric told her.

"Oh, I don't drive to work. I walk. I live just two blocks away."

"Okay then, I'll just drop you off at your home after we eat."

Evie nodded happily. "Sounds like a plan to me," she said.

As the automatic hospital doors opened, they walked through and out into the parking lot. When Eric pressed the key fob in his hand, the lights on an impressive black luxury car blinked.

"I like your car," Evie said, wondering if she would ever be able to afford such an extravagance on her own.

"Thank you," he said. "I just got it a few weeks ago. It was a birthday present to myself." He laughed.

"Well, happy birthday," Evie said as he opened the passenger door for her.

"Thank you. I just turned thirty-six, so I decided I deserved to buy myself a nice new ride," he said as she climbed into the plush leather seat. He closed the door gently behind her.

After tossing his bag into the backseat, he got into the driver's side. "Now, where would you like to eat, Dr. Evie?" he asked with a grin.

"Hmm, I don't know. What are you hungry for? After all, it is your birthday, and it'll be my celebration treat, even though it's late."

"I wouldn't think of letting you buy my dinner. My mom raised me better than that." He grinned again. "After all, this is our first date."

The thought of their first date made Evie smile too. "Well, at least you get to choose where we go to eat—for your birthday."

"Well, before I so luckily bumped into you, I was thinking about Mexican. What do you think? Do you like Mexican food?"

"It's one my favorites," she replied.

"Good then. We're bound for Mexico," he said as he started the car.

Evie liked the smooth sound of the engine. It purred softly, as if giving a glimpse of its awesome power. She sank into the soft gray leather seat and smiled. "You have great taste in cars," she said.

"I have to admit, my dad is the car enthusiast in the family. He sort of guided me to this one," he told her.

"Well, he definitely guided you in the right direction."

"I'm lucky to have him and my mom. They live up in Charleston. I'm glad they're relatively close and are both in good health."

"Mine too," Evie said. "What do your parents do for a living?"

"Dad is a banker and car enthusiast extraordinaire," he said with a sideways smile. "And Mom is a teacher."

"That's nice," Evie said. "I've always admired teachers."

"I know your father is a surgeon, but what does your mom do?" Eric asked politely.

"She's a doctor too. She's a dermatologist."

Moments later, Eric pulled into the parking lot of a colorful Mexican restaurant. "Is this okay? Have you eaten here before?" he asked.

"Yes, I have, but it's been a long time."

"Well, it's only gotten better with age—just like me." He laughed heartily.

Evie laughed too. She liked him. She found it odd, but she felt comfortable and safe with him, even though they barely knew each other.

"Let me get your door, and we'll get inside and eat. I, for one, am famished."

She waited while he opened the door for her. Offering his hand, he helped her out of the car. He guided her toward the restaurant with his hand barely touching the small of her back. She enjoyed the sensation of his gentlemanly touch.

Once they were seated and had ordered their meals of green chili enchiladas with rice, they began to munch on the chips and salsa already on the table.

"This is good," Evie said as she crunched on a homemade chip.

"It only gets better from here," Eric said with another one of his contagious smiles. After dipping a chip into the salsa and eating it, he looked at her seriously. "If you don't mind me asking—and feel free to tell me if you don't want to talk about it—but I was wondering about your sister. How's she doing?"

"I don't mind you asking at all," she answered. "As a matter of fact, I was going to bring up the subject. I need to thank you, Eric."

He tilted his head and looked quizzically at her, so she continued.

"We did as you suggested. The family had an intervention for Cloe, but it turned out to be one for all of us. It was a great success." She watched as a compassionate and pleased expression graced his handsome face. "Cloe is in a rehabilitation center right now, and she's doing splendidly." Evie felt a tear roll down her cheek. It had no sooner fallen than his gentle finger wiped it away. "And it's all thanks to you, Eric."

He opened his mouth to speak, but the waiter interrupted. He placed their plates of food before them. "The plates are hot, so be careful," he said. "May I get you two anything else?"

Eric looked at Evie and grinned. "No, thank you," he said. "I think we have everything we need right here."

15

ONLY GETTING BETTER

Eric had been right. Five months into their relationship, things were only getting better. They saw each other whenever their busy schedules allowed but had fallen into the habit of speaking every night on the phone before bed.

Since Eric, things had changed for Evie for the better. Her entire outlook had changed. She was halfway through her third year of surgical residency and was thriving and learning to the best of her ability. She didn't want to be just a good surgeon; she wanted to be a phenomenal surgeon.

It was Thanksgiving Day, and she had the day off, as did Eric. He was accompanying her to her family's home for dinner, and then they were going to drive up to his parents' home for dessert.

After having slept in for a change, Evie awakened that morning with an appropriate feeling of thanksgiving. Happily, she hopped out of bed and headed to the kitchen to make herself a cup of coffee before getting her shower.

While waiting for her coffee to brew, she turned on some music and looked out the window. It was unseasonably cold and spitting snow, so she decided to wear her favorite warm turquoise sweater and a pair of jeans.

After taking a few sips of coffee, with her favorite oldies music playing in the background, she headed off to the shower.

The water felt exhilarating, and it felt good to have the day away from the hospital. Sometimes she wasn't sure if she was going to be able to physically survive another year and a half of residency. She looked forward to a day when an eighty-hour workweek wasn't the norm.

As she shampooed her lengthy blonde hair, she noticed how long it had gotten. It was almost halfway down her back. She didn't have time to get a haircut, but she didn't mind. She liked her hair long. She was blessed with thick, healthy hair like her mother's.

After showering and getting dressed, she blow-dried her hair. Since it was a special occasion, she decided to style it with the curling iron, making soft spiral curls. She then applied some mascara to her full lashes and some pink lipstick to her lips.

Feeling a degree of confidence in how she looked, she waited impatiently for Eric to arrive. She couldn't wait to see him and spend the entire day with him. She anxiously looked at the clock. He was fifteen minutes late.

Hearing his car pull into her driveway, she walked to the door to let him in. He had barely gotten out of his car, when she shouted, "You're late, Eric!"

He laughed. "I know, Mom," he replied jokingly.

"That's not funny, Eric," Evie said with her hands placed playfully on her hips.

He was still grinning when he came inside and closed the door behind him. "I'm sorry, baby doll. I'll try to be on time next time," he said as he took off his coat. Pulling her to him, he whispered into her ear, "You smell delicious and you look beautiful."

His smooth, seductive voice against her skin caused millions of goose bumps to form on her body.

She moaned in his embrace. With her arms around his neck, she laid her head against his chest and shoulder. As she did, one of her favorite old songs, "How Deep Is Your Love" by the Bee Gees, started playing.

"Oh man! I love this old song," Eric said excitedly. "May I have this dance, my lady?"

"I was hoping you'd ask," Evie answered with her head still resting against his shoulder.

As they began to sway to the music, Eric said, "I admit this might be a deal breaker for you, but I love disco music." He chuckled.

"Shut up, Eric." Evie giggled. "You're spoiling the mood."

"Oh! I got ya," he said as he pulled her in closer.

As the romantic melody played, they held each other and danced in the foyer of her apartment. It was their first dance, and for Evie, it was dreamlike. Eric hummed softly into her ear as they swayed to the beautiful music. He was a good dancer, and in his arms, she felt safe, warm, accepted, and—dare she say—loved.

She moaned contently in his arms, hoping in vain that the song would never end. Sadly, the song was over much too quickly. Evie wished the feeling she was experiencing could go on forever.

Eric seemed hesitant to let her go, which pleased her to no end.

"Evie," he said softly and seriously, "there's something I've been wanting to tell you."

Evie's mind ran rampant. He sounded so somber, as if something were wrong. *Please don't let it be bad*, she prayed silently as she pulled back to look into his face. He was handsome even without his trademark smile. "What is it, Eric?" she asked. "You're frightening me."

Still holding her firmly in his arms, he smiled softly. "I want to tell you …" He paused again, causing her heart to pound. "I'm in love with you, Evie. I love you." As he said those three words, his alluring dark eyes pooled with tears.

Evie couldn't readily respond. It seemed as though his unexpected declaration had robbed her of words. Finally, she smiled as she gazed into his eyes. "I'm in love with you too, Eric. I think I have been for a long time," she said with tears streaming down her face.

"You are?" he asked, sounding relieved. "You scared me there for a minute."

"Yes, I am," she replied softly. "I love you, Eric Moses."

He grinned and looked deep into her eyes. She knew she could never tire of staring into his sensual dark eyes.

It appeared he was going to kiss her, but he was taking too long to suit Evie. She stood up on her tiptoes and gently placed her lips against his. It was their first kiss as lovers, and it felt different from before. It felt more meaningful and more stimulating. Apparently, Eric felt the same, as his hands began to explore her body in a way he hadn't done before. Evie liked the way his touch made her feel. His gentle hands searched and stroked her back, coming ever so close to her breasts. His touch fueled her in a way she never had experienced before. It made her want him. She wanted him to carry her off to her bed and make sweet, passionate love to her. She let her mind wander for a moment to what that would feel like. It was blissful, and she wanted to badly, but she couldn't. Swallowing hard, she pulled back.

"What's the matter?" Eric asked. His voice sounded raspy.

She looked into his dark eyes again. With her palms resting against his warm chest, she said, "I can't, Eric. I haven't—" She broke their gaze. Looking down, she said, "I'm embarrassed to tell you this. It might sound silly for a woman my age."

"What is it, Evie? You never have to be embarrassed with me. Tell me."

Still not meeting his eyes, she said, "I've been saving myself for marriage."

Eric was silent for a moment. With his fingers beneath her chin, he gently lifted her head. Their eyes met once again. He smiled tenderly at her. "You are a very special woman, Evie Edwards," he whispered. "I've never met a woman like you before."

Evie returned his smile. "So you're okay with not making love?" she asked.

He chuckled sexily. "Well, I wouldn't go that far. I'm not okay—but I'm okay," he said with a wink.

"You're the sexiest man I've ever met," she said as she quickly kissed him on the lips again. "Resisting you isn't going to be easy."

"Well, thank you for the compliment, you sexy little thing you." He pulled her close and hugged her tightly. "I wish they'd play another Bee Gees song."

Evie giggled at her witty lover.

After enjoying the luxury of spending a leisurely morning of talking and laughing on Evie's sofa, Evie and Eric arrived at Evie's parents' home at three o'clock in the afternoon. Dinner was supposed to be ready at four, but they wanted to get there early in case her mother needed help with any last-minute preparations.

They pulled into the driveway and walked hand in hand up to the front door. Just before going in, Eric surprised Evie with a kiss. Their lips had no sooner met than Cloe opened the door.

"You two need to get a room," she said, laughing.

Evie and Eric laughed too. "Hey, sis! How are you?" Evie exclaimed, although just looking at Cloe's face answered her question for her.

Cloe was glowing and gorgeous. Her dull purple hair was gone, replaced by her natural brown color with shimmering blonde highlights. She was wearing it long and straight, and it suited her perfectly. All of her piercings were gone, except for a tiny stud in her left nostril. It wasn't Evie's taste, but she had to admit it matched Cloe's spirited personality. She had gained some much-needed weight as well. Gone was the gaunt, frowning face of the broken sister Evie had known for so long, replaced with the sweet smile and mended heart of a sibling Evie loved dearly.

Evie stepped inside the door and grabbed Cloe in a heartfelt hug. "I love you, Cloe," she said. "You look beautiful."

Cloe giggled. "I love you too, sis." She hugged Evie back. "Come on in, Eric," Cloe said while still locked in Evie's hug.

Evie laughed as she released Cloe. "I'm sorry, Eric."

"What's all the commotion in here?" her father asked as he entered the foyer. He wore a warm, welcoming grin. "There's my soon-to-be partner," he said to Evie. "And there's my favorite ER doc," he said as he reached out and vigorously shook Eric's hand. "Come on into the living room, and have a seat."

As they sat down, Evie was about to ask if her mother needed any help in the kitchen, when Lorretta walked through the doorway. Standing by Dan's chair, her mom seemed radiantly happy, which warmed Evie's heart.

"I've been cooking and baking all day," she said, looking a bit frazzled. "But I hope it all tastes good."

"You know it will, honey," Dan said. "Your food always tastes delicious. Now, come sit down on my lap." He quickly grabbed his wife and pulled her down on top of him.

They all laughed as Lorretta squirmed to get free from her husband's playful grasp.

Evie looked over at Cloe, who was smiling. There were no words to describe the thankfulness Evie felt for having her sister back.

"You look so pretty today, Cloe," Evie said. "I love your dress. Is it new?"

Cloe was wearing an attractive black A-line dress with a pair of open-toed black shoes with short heels.

"Thank you," Cloe answered. "Yes, it's new. I made it myself." Cloe had a glow about her, as if she were keeping some wonderful secret.

"You made it?" Evie asked, surprised. "What's going on, Cloe? I know you, my sister; there's something you're not telling me."

Cloe's smile brightened. "I just enrolled in an online fashion design class. I want to become a clothing designer," she said, looking hopeful, as if wanting Evie's approval.

Evie's mouth dropped open. "Oh my gosh, sis! I think you'd make a wonderful designer."

"You do?" Cloe asked, looking happily surprised.

"Yes, I do. You have such a gifted eye for fashion. I can just see you becoming a great success."

Cloe laughed. "Maybe I can design your wedding gown."

Evie blushed as Eric reached over and grasped her hand.

"You never know," he said, laughing.

Just then, Evie's cell in her pocket rang.

"Oh no!" her mother said. "I hope you don't have to leave."

Evie looked at the screen. Her heart flipped in her chest when she saw the caller's name. It was Sam calling. She frowned at the phone for a second. Quickly trying to make sense of the complex feelings she was having of simultaneously wanting to ignore the call and wanting to speak with him, she found herself pressing the answer button. "Excuse me for a second," she said as she walked into the foyer to take the call. "Hello," she said hesitantly.

"Hi, Evie. It's Sam," he said solemnly. "I wasn't sure if you still had the same phone number."

"Yes, it's me, Sam. How are you?"

"To be honest, I've been better."

"What's the matter?" Evie asked, feeling confused.

Sam paused for a moment. "You're what's the matter, Evie."

Her heart began to pound in her chest. "I don't know what you mean."

"Well, I'm about to get married in less than a month, and all I can think about is you. I love you, Evie. I always have," he stated quietly.

Shocked and overwhelmed, Evie didn't know what to say. Part of her was happy to hear that Sam still loved her, but then there was Eric. She loved Eric.

"I need your help, Evie. Tell me what to do. Give me a reason to call off this wedding. Can you do that?" he asked, sounding desperate.

Pushing aside her sudden resentment at him for putting her in this predicament, Evie thought for a moment. Part of her wanted to tell him that she still loved him too. Deep down, she did have a special place in her heart for him. While thinking about what to say, she glanced into the living room. Eric looked back at her, smiled softly, and winked. That was all the answer she needed. Eric was in her heart now. She loved him dearly. Sam was a love from the past—a past love that seemed destined to stay there.

"I'm sorry, Sam, but I can't say what you want me to say," Evie whispered, on the verge of tears. "There was a time when I was certain I loved you, but I'm not that person anymore, and so much has changed. Really, you don't even know me, and I don't know you. I'm so sorry."

"I am too, Evie. I'm sorry," he said before he ended the call.

Evie took a deep breath, put her phone back in her pocket, and returned to her place beside Eric, where she belonged.

"Everything okay, baby?" he whispered.

Evie smiled. "Couldn't be better, handsome," she answered honestly as she looped her arm through his.

16

HOLIDAY SEASON

It was Christmas. Although her family hadn't celebrated the holiday much since Clarissa's death, it was still Evie's favorite time of the year. It was sacred to her. Even with her hectic schedule as a resident, she had never missed a midnight Christmas Eve candlelight service at the church she had grown up in, which her parents and Cloe still attended. It did her heart good to worship and celebrate the birth of her Lord and Savior, Jesus Christ.

With Cloe's remarkable recovery and the restoration of her family, Evie was hoping for an old-fashioned Christmas at home.

She was scheduled for clinicals on Christmas Eve until around seven o'clock in the evening but had Christmas Day free, as did Eric. She was thrilled when he accepted her invitation to the church service and then to Christmas Eve and Christmas morning with her family. Afterward, their plan was to drive up to spend Christmas afternoon with Eric's family in Charleston.

Christmas Eve morning came with the first measurable snow of the season. Evie delighted in brushing the billowy white flakes off her car while it warmed up. It was too cold to walk to the hospital anymore.

As she sat in her car, blowing her warm breath on her hands, her cell rang. It was Eric.

"Hi, baby doll," he said. "Merry Christmas Eve, Evie." He chuckled.

Grinning, she answered, "Hi, handsome. Merry Christmas Eve to you too."

"You at work yet?" he asked.

"Not yet. I'm just sitting here until my car warms up. How about you?"

"Just pulled into the lot."

Evie couldn't stifle a giggle. She was overly excited to spend her first Christmas with the man she loved.

"Why are you giggling, you silly girl?" he asked.

"I'm just happy," she replied seriously. "I've never been this happy before."

She could hear him sigh. "Me either, Evie. You make me happier than I ever thought possible."

"I hope this feeling never ends," she said.

"If I have anything to say about it, it won't."

Evie savored his perfect response.

"Now, get your sexy self to work before you're late, and be careful driving. The roads are a bit slick."

"I will," she said. "I can't wait to see you tonight." It would be the first night they'd spent under the same roof. Evie was excited to know that the love of her life would be in the room right next to her all night long.

"I can't wait to see you either, baby doll." He paused before whispering, "I love you, Evie."

Every time he said those words to her, they brought with them the threat of happy tears. This time was no different. "I love you too, Eric," she replied.

After finishing evening rounds with the group and Dr. Stone, Evie, Elizabeth, and George gathered in the cafeteria to exchange Christmas gifts over coffee. They had promised each other nothing extravagant. Evie received a blue hand-knitted neck scarf from Elizabeth and a pair of gloves from George.

Evie loved her friends and fellow residents. They had known each other their entire residency. Evie could see their friendship lasting for years and years to come. She hoped they felt the same way about her.

After finishing their coffee and walking out to the parking lot together, the three wished each other one final "Merry Christmas" before heading to their cars.

Evie squealed when she heard Eric's car pull into her driveway. She was excited, to say the least. They had a couple of hours of alone time to spend together before they left to meet her parents and Cloe at church.

She opened the door to let Eric in. As soon as he crossed the threshold, she grabbed him around the neck and gave him a deep, meaningful kiss.

"Whoa! I dig this greeting," Eric said with a laugh. "What's going on?"

"It's Christmas," Evie said with her arms spread wide.

"Yes, baby, it's Christmas. Speaking of which, I forgot your gifts in the car. I'll be right back."

They had decided to exchange their gifts privately before heading over to church and then to her parents' house.

Eric came back with several festively wrapped packages. Evie hoped that one of them contained an engagement ring. In reality, she knew that was irrational. They had only declared their love for each other a month earlier, but Evie knew in her heart that theirs was a love that would last forever.

They sat down on the sofa opposite Evie's small Christmas tree. They had cups of hot chocolate and sugar cookies to enjoy before unwrapping their gifts to each other.

"Open this one first," Eric said as he handed Evie her first present. It was a large box, definitely too large for an engagement ring.

Evie smiled as she unwrapped the gift. Inside was a lovely baby-blue V-neck sweater.

"Do you like it?" he asked. "I thought it would match your gorgeous blue eyes."

Holding it up to her chest, she declared, "I love it! It's perfect. Now it's your turn," she added as she handed him his first gift. She watched as he opened the box. Inside was a CD of the Bee Gees' greatest hits.

He laughed heartily. "You may have thought this was a joke, but this is the best Christmas gift you could have given me. I have a CD player at home, and I'll wear this thing out playing it."

He looked sexy when he laughed. Evie felt herself falling more and more in love with him with each and every smile he flashed her.

"Your turn again," he said as he handed her another gift.

Upon unwrapping it, she discovered an expensive, shiny pink stethoscope. Her name and credentials were engraved on it. Her mouth dropped open. "Oh my goodness, I love it!" she exclaimed.

"You do? I wasn't sure. I didn't know if it was like buying your girlfriend a toaster or something." He laughed, as did Evie.

"Not at all. It's beautiful. Thank you," she said as she leaned over and gave him a kiss. "Your heart is the first one I want to hear with this," she added. She put the ear tips into her ears and placed the chest piece against his chest. His heart sounded strong and healthy. Evie smiled as she listened.

When she removed the chest piece, he asked, "So how did it sound, Doc?"

"It said that it loved me," she replied.

He grinned and pulled her to him. "That it does, baby doll. That it does."

They finished exchanging gifts, saving one each to open at her parents' home on Christmas morning.

Sitting in the dimly lit church next to her family and Eric, Evie couldn't imagine a more perfect Christmas Eve. She also couldn't stop thinking about maybe getting married in that church someday. She could envision it dimly lit with candles much as it was now.

Eric reached over and took her hand. Feeling as if he could see inside her head, Evie felt slightly embarrassed. She was glad when the church organist began to play. Her mind could finally shift focus from envisioning a wedding to celebrating the birth of her Savior, Jesus Christ.

When the intro began, they stood to sing the first Christmas carol of the night, and it happened to be Evie's favorite: "Angels We Have Heard on High." She gripped Eric's hand tightly and sang along with the heavenly sounding choir dressed all in white.

After several carols were sung, the congregation was treated to the pastor's reading of the Christmas story from the gospel of Luke in the Bible. Evie loved that passage, and she adored hearing her beloved gray-haired pastor read it.

At the close of service, they shared communion together, and then all the lights were dimmed, and each parishioner was handed a candle. Once all of their candles were glowing, they sang an acapella rendition of "Silent Night." Evie soaked in the serenity and sacredness of the moment. She was sad when the song ended and the candles were extinguished. She wished the service could have lasted longer.

In the car, as they headed for Evie's parents' home, Evie asked Eric if he had enjoyed the candlelight service as much as she had.

He chuckled. "That's not a fair question. I don't think anybody could enjoy Christmas as much as you do, Evie."

She laughed too. She knew he was right.

They all arrived home at the same time. Eric carried in Evie's and his overnight bags. After the hustle and bustle of taking off coats and wishing each other a good night, they headed off to their respective bedrooms. Evie showed Eric to the guest room, which was located directly next to her room.

"Do you need anything?" she asked quietly as they stood outside his door.

His face lit up with a mischievous and irresistible grin. "That's a loaded question, baby doll," he answered.

She giggled and punched him playfully on the arm.

"What's going on down there, you two?" Cloe asked as she reached the top of the stairs. "You're not up to no good, are you?"

They all laughed. "No, we're just saying good night," Evie replied.

"Okay then," Cloe said. "But don't worry. I won't tell on you." She laughed again as she went into her bedroom and closed the door.

"Well, good night, handsome," Evie said as she placed her hands on Eric's chest and gave him a quick kiss.

"Good night, baby doll," he said.

Sitting around the living room the following morning, dressed in their pajamas and armed with cups of coffee, they began opening their Christmas gifts to one another. Evie's favorite gift was the family's massive eight-foot Christmas tree. It was grand and gorgeous and was decorated with all of the family's old ornaments dating back to when Evie was just a baby. She could hardly take her eyes off it. It had been years since she had seen those ornaments. This was the first year since Clarissa's passing that her family had properly celebrated Christmas like this. Now that Cloe was clean and sober, things couldn't have been better.

Eric handed Evie her remaining Christmas gift. It was a small box wrapped in white-and-gold paper topped with a metallic gold bow. Evie's mind wandered. Surely he wouldn't propose to her in front of her family, would he?

"Go ahead and open it," he said.

As her family watched, she tore away the paper, revealing a square white box. She lifted the lid, and what she saw took her breath away. It was a stunning teardrop diamond necklace with matching earrings. They were splendid. Breathless, she took the necklace out of the box and held it in her hand.

"Here. Let me put it on you," Eric said as he took the necklace from her hand. He fastened it around her neck. "Do you like it?" he asked.

"Yes," Evie said, slightly overwhelmed with the extravagant gift. "You shouldn't have."

"Of course I should have," he said.

"Of course he should have," Cloe echoed as she jumped up to get a closer look at the necklace. "It's absolutely perfect. I approve," she said to Eric.

"Well, thank you, Cloe," he replied, smiling.

After all the gifts had been exchanged, everyone went back to his or her room to get dressed and ready to prepare Christmas dinner.

Standing in front of the mirror, Evie admired the incredible diamond necklace and earrings. She had never seen such impressive pieces. She gently touched the necklace and smiled.

Dressed in a red dress for Christmas, she pecked on the guest room door. Eric opened it, wearing the dark maroon sweater Evie had just given him. It fit him perfectly.

"You look great," she said happily. "Do you like it?"

"I love it," he said. "And you look spectacular." He pulled her to him and wrapped her in an enveloping hug.

She moaned and returned his Christmas morning embrace. *Could life possibly get any better?*

17

MELANCHOLY

The end of the holidays always made Evie feel a little bit blue. She and Eric had enjoyed a blessed and wonderful Christmas and New Year's together, and she envisioned many more to come.

Dressed in a pair of pink pajamas and a warm matching robe, she worked through her final tasks before going to bed. She took the last ornament off her little Christmas tree and placed it in the storage box. As she put the lid on the box, her cell rang. It was Eric.

"Hey, handsome," she said.

"Hi, baby doll," he said with a yawn. "I didn't wake you, did I?"

"No, I'm still up. Are you just now leaving the hospital?" she asked, somewhat surprised.

"Yeah, I had to cover a shift, so I pulled a few extra hours this evening. I'm beat. I'm just now driving out of the parking lot." He yawned again. "I don't have a specific reason for calling this late. I just wanted to hear your voice."

His sweet declaration made Evie's after-the-holidays blues melt away. "Well, that's a nice thing to say."

"It's the truth. I don't think I could sleep without hearing your voice before I go to bed."

Evie sat down on the sofa. "I swear, Eric, you say things that make me fall deeper in love with you with every passing day."

She heard him chuckle softly. "You shouldn't have told me that. That'll put a lot of pressure on me."

She laughed at his witty remark.

"Would you mind if I dropped by for a kiss before I head home?" he asked.

Evie felt herself fall a little deeper with his sweet request. "I would love it if you did," she replied.

"All righty then. I'll see you in a minute."

Seconds later, she heard the familiar sound of his car pulling into her driveway. She met him at the door with a huge grin on her face. He was smiling too—that captivating smile that caused her heart to skip a beat.

"Hey there," he said as he walked up to the door.

"Hi, handsome," she replied as she stepped aside so he could come in.

"It's cold out there. How about warming me up with that kiss you promised?" he said as he opened his arms to her.

She gladly stepped into his embrace. Standing on her tiptoes, she wrapped her arms around his neck, closed her eyes, and placed her lips against his. His beard and mustache tickled her skin as she kissed him. As their lips parted, their kiss deepened. He groaned as he pulled her closer to him. She could feel his excitement, which made her want him even more. Evie never wanted their kiss to end. It was finally Eric who ended it.

"Whoa!" he said. "That was some special kiss there, baby doll. I went from freezing to burning up in a matter of seconds."

Evie clung to his manly body. "I'm glad to oblige," she said.

"Man, I don't want to," he said, sounding reluctant, "but I'd better go. We both gotta get some sleep."

"I don't wanna sleep. I wanna play with you," Evie said, hoping to induce another one of his special smiles. It worked.

He chuckled sensually. "That's incredibly tempting, but you and I both need our rest. I'll see you tomorrow." He bent down and placed a tender kiss on her lips.

Sadly, she waved goodbye as he got into his car. As she closed the door and began walking toward her bedroom, her cell rang. Wondering who would be calling her at that time of night, she picked up her phone and looked at the screen. It was Eric. Curiously, she answered the phone. "What are you doing, you silly thing?" she asked.

"Check your right robe pocket," he replied mysteriously.

Following his instructions, she put her hand inside her pocket. She felt a small velvet box. Gasping, she pulled it out and slowly opened it. Inside was a magnificent diamond engagement ring. It was a brilliant stone in a solitaire setting on a delicate gold band and was the most elegant ring she had ever laid her eyes on. In tears, she raced back to open her door. There knelt the love of her life, gazing up at her expectantly.

"How about it, Evie? I know this may seem way too fast, but will you make me the happiest man on earth and be my wife?"

As she reached for him, he rose to his feet and walked back inside. He took her in his arms again.

"Yes, Eric. A thousand times yes. I would love to be your wife," she replied, sobbing.

Releasing her, he took the box from her hand. He removed the ring and asked for her left hand. She extended it to him. She trembled all over as he gently slid the ring onto her finger. He looked at her. "It fits perfectly," he said, appearing excited and happy.

Looking down at her hand, Evie couldn't believe it. It was like a dream come true.

"Do you like it, Evie?" he asked.

"Like it?" she asked as if he had taken leave of his senses. "I love it! I love it, and I love you," she said with tears streaming down her face.

"Don't cry," he said as he gently wiped away her tears. "I never want to see you cry."

"They're happy tears. I assure you," she said as she grabbed him in another clinging embrace. He chuckled softly as she held on to him. Realizing she didn't want to let him go, she asked him timidly, "Would you like to stay the night?"

He pulled back and looked at her with a shocked expression. "But I thought—"

"You can stay the night without us having to make love—can't you?" she asked. She could feel her cheeks turning pink.

He laughed again. "I honestly don't know if I can do that or not. I don't know if I can resist you," he said as he trailed his finger tenderly down her cheek. "But I would love to give it a try."

"Good," she replied, and hand in hand, they made their way to her bedroom.

The lights were off except for a small lamp in the corner of the room, which she left on. Evie turned her back when Eric began to undress. She waited until she heard him climb into bed before she removed her robe and climbed in with him. She rolled onto her left side, and they were face-to-face in her bed. Evie's heart thumped in her chest. She had such a gamut of emotions running through her mind that she didn't know what to think or do. She couldn't believe she was engaged. She lifted her left hand and looked at her ring.

"Do you really like it?" he asked in a whisper.

"It's the most exquisite thing I've ever seen," she replied.

"Were you surprised?"

"My goodness, yes! I was. I was most definitely not expecting that," she answered, smiling at him.

He smiled back. "I thought about doing it as a Christmas gift, but I changed my mind. I wanted to do it unexpectedly—in a way that you would always remember."

Tears rolled out of the corners of Evie's eyes. "Well, you accomplished that. I'll never forget your proposal—or this night," she said breathlessly.

"I won't either," he said while gazing into her eyes. He clasped her hand. "I want so much to make love to you right now. To hold you. To show you how much I care about you."

"I want that too, but ..." She paused, giving serious thought to abandoning her promise to herself to stay chaste until she was married.

"I know," he said as he leaned in and kissed her gently. "I know, baby doll." He smiled at her. "Now, how do you want to sleep—face-to-face or spoons?"

Evie giggled at her witty fiancé. "Definitely spoons," she answered as she turned her back to him. She was happy to feel that he was still wearing underwear. She snuggled the back of her body into the front of his. It was the first time she had ever been in the bed with a man. It felt exhilarating to be in bed with the man she loved.

He wrapped his arm around her and pulled her close to him. "Are you comfortable?" he asked softly.

His breath against her skin and words spoken into her ear sent an immediate quiver throughout her entire body. She snuggled even closer into him. She could feel his excitement against her. She felt good that he wanted her but bad that she was denying him.

"Yes, I am. I'm much more than comfortable. Are you okay?"

He chuckled sexily. "Yeah, I'm great, baby doll," he said. "But I tell you what: this is gonna have to be the shortest engagement in the history of the world."

She laughed, and he laughed too.

They lay there clinging to each other for half the night, talking and making plans for their future. Finally, they fell asleep wrapped in the warmth of the love they found in each other's arms.

18
PREPARATION

Since Evie's hectic and demanding schedule didn't allow for the planning of an elaborate wedding and extended honeymoon and since her residency wouldn't be over for more than a year, the couple decided on a simple but fairy-tale destination wedding at the Canaan Valley Resort and State Park, only four hours away from home. Nestled in the majestic mountains of Davis, West Virginia, the breathtaking setting offered all the amenities they could dream of, including a stunning view of the snow-covered mountains, a romantic venue space for the ceremony and reception, fabulous on-site dining, and, of course, the magnificent ski slopes.

The winter wonderland setting of Canaan Valley was a perfect choice because they could get married there on Saturday and then stay there and enjoy an extended weekend for their honeymoon. Although she wouldn't be getting married in her home church, as she had envisioned, her beloved pastor would officiate their wedding at Canaan. That sounded like the perfect compromise to Evie and Eric. Their wedding date was set for Saturday, the twenty-fifth of March—a little more than two months away.

To say that Evie was excited about her impending wedding day would have been a gross understatement. Eric seemed to be as anxious as she was, as were both of their families, especially Cloe. With a little help from a professional seamstress at church, Cloe would be designing and sewing Evie's wedding gown for her. When Evie first asked her to do her the honor, she wasn't sure if the stunned look on Cloe's face was from excitement or fear, but after a few moments, Cloe happily accepted the job.

After much deliberation, the sisters decided on a pure-white fit-and-flare wedding gown with lots of beading and embellishments. Cloe was all about the bling. Evie was skeptical at first, but when she saw Cloe's sketch of the gown, she immediately fell in love with it.

"It's just beautiful, Cloe," Evie said tearfully as she admired the drawing. She touched the paper with the tip of her finger, trying to imagine how it was going to look on her wedding day.

Her mother, who was also looking at the sketch, began to cry.

"Don't start crying, Mom. If you do, we'll all start," Cloe said with a laugh.

"I can't help it. It's my first daughter's wedding gown. How am I not supposed to cry?"

"Put on your big-girl panties," Cloe said.

They all laughed at Cloe's quip. It felt good to giggle with her mother and sister. There had been a time in the not-so-distant past when Evie had wondered if they would ever laugh together again like this.

After their laughter died down, Evie looked at Cloe and asked, "Have you thought about your maid-of-honor dress yet?"

Cloe's mouth dropped open. "You mean—you want me to be your maid of honor?" she asked.

"Of course I do. You're my sister, and I love you, and I can't imagine a better person than you to stand next to me while I marry Eric." Evie began to cry.

Cloe started to cry too, as did their mom. "I'd love to be your maid of honor," Cloe replied through the tears. "Now look at us. We're all crying again."

"Yeah, but it's a good cry, not a bad cry," Evie said, acutely aware of the difference.

About an hour later, the three Edwards women descended the staircase to find Dan and Eric seated in the living room, discussing the upcoming championship football game.

"So how did it go up there, my beauties?" her father asked.

"Just fine," Evie answered as she sat down close to Eric on the sofa and took hold of his hand. Looking to Eric, she said, "Since I'm too busy at the hospital, Cloe and Mom are going to handle the fine details of the wedding for us."

"I'm thrilled to help," Cloe said. "I never dreamed my first design job would be a wedding gown, but I'm excited." She bounced up and down the way she had when she was a child. It did Evie's heart good to see her sister so happy.

"And Cloe has graciously accepted our request to be my maid of honor," Evie said.

"Marvelous," her dad said as he threw his hands up in the air. "That'll give me two reasons to tear up on my daughter's wedding day—seeing both of my girls all dolled up and looking gorgeous."

Evie smiled at her father. He was laughing, but Evie had a feeling he was thinking of Clarissa. There was an unmistakable sadness in his eyes. She supposed that hint of heartbreak would be there until his dying day.

Cloe broke the silence. "I love your and Evie's idea of a light-blue-and-white color scheme—sort of a winter wonderland look," she told Eric. "That will be so beautiful. Oh! I hope it snows."

Evie laughed. "I'm so glad you're excited about our wedding, Cloe. I sure am going to be counting on you to help me."

"No problem," Cloe said. "What are sisters for? Just tell me what you need, and I'll get it done."

"Thank you, sis," Evie said. "We hired a wedding planner to make all the necessary arrangements up at Canaan—the catering, flowers, cake, and such—so that will help on that end. With you all at the helm on this end, I think we can pull off one heck of a wedding in such a short period of time."

Eric raised Evie's hand to his lips and kissed her fingers. "Personally, I don't think it's a short amount of time. I can't wait to make you Dr. Evie Edwards-Moses."

19

I TAKE THEE

With an unprecedented four days away from the hospital in a row, the eve of Evie and Eric's wedding day finally arrived. Her father had rented the Edwards family a two-bedroom cabin near the main lodge for the night before the wedding. Evie and Cloe wanted to share a room so they could spend some quality sister time together before Evie became a married woman. Evie could not have been more overjoyed at how close she and Cloe had become. Her heart overflowed with love for her beloved sister.

After hospital rounds on the Friday afternoon before their wedding day, the Edwards family had driven up to the gorgeous Canaan Valley Ski Resort. At that elevation, with the cold weather they had been having, there was still plenty of snow, so she and Eric planned on doing some skiing while they were there for their wedding weekend. Evie hadn't skied in years, but she looked forward to getting out in the snow with her brand-new husband.

After unloading the car, the family gathered in the living room. It was almost time for their dinner reservation at eight o'clock at the resort's main dining room, the Hickory Room. Eric and his parents would be joining them for dinner. It would be the first time the in-laws met. Evie was a bit nervous but knew she could do anything with Eric by her side.

Before dinner, her family sat around the rustic and charming living room area of the cabin. It had a fireplace, which they planned on stoking when they returned from dinner.

"We have a few minutes before we have to go," Evie's father said. "And I just want to take this opportunity to tell all of you how very much I love each of you. I don't know what I'd do without you, and I'm not sure how I'm supposed to give away my eldest daughter tomorrow. I'm really not sure if I can do that."

Evie went to her misty-eyed father and knelt down beside his chair. "You're not giving me away, Daddy. You and Mommy can't get rid of me that easily," she joked tearfully. "Besides, you'll be gaining a son—someone who enjoys talking about football with you."

"Well, there is that," her dad said with a smile.

"I'm excited to inherit a brother," Cloe said. "I couldn't have ordered a better one."

Evie was thrilled to hear her little sister's sweet comment. It meant the world to her that her family adored Eric.

Lorretta spoke up. "We'd better head off to dinner, or we're going to be late. We can light the fireplace and talk some more when we get back."

Evie looked forward to that—one last night as a single woman spent in the company of her cherished family. She felt blessed beyond compare.

The Moses family was waiting outside the restaurant when Evie's family arrived.

Evie watched Eric's face break out into his trademark smile when he looked up and saw her walking toward him. Evie couldn't help but smile back at him.

"I'm sorry if we kept you waiting," she told them.

"Nonsense, young lady," Eric's father said. "We just got here ourselves."

Evie had met Eric's parents on several occasions and liked them very much. His father, Joseph, was a robust man with a short gray beard and bald head. His mother, Katherine, was a bit taller than her husband, with a light brown complexion and short black hair. She had dark brown eyes like her son's.

"Well, let's make the introductions, shall we?" Eric said, and he introduced Evie's family to his parents. When all the salutations and shaking of hands were finished, the group walked up to the hostess stand. After Evie's father stepped up and gave the young woman the name on the reservation, the hostess led them to a large, round table next to the window. Everyone took his or her seat. Evie was seated with Eric on one side and her sister on the other.

Looking around her, Evie couldn't believe how opulent the place was. There was a huge fireplace in the center of the room, and the entire glass-walled restaurant overlooked the snow-covered mountains and valleys. "Oh my gosh! It's gorgeous in here," she said breathlessly.

"It is now that you're here," Eric said as he kissed her hand.

"Aw, that's so sweet," Cloe said. "Do you have any cousins or anybody you could introduce me to?" she asked jokingly.

"As a matter of fact, I do," Eric replied.

"Hold up!" Evie's father said, laughing. "One girl leaving the nest is enough for this old man to take right now. You're just going to have to wait for a bit there, Cloe."

Pretending to pout, Cloe replied, "Okay, Daddy."

After scanning the mouthwatering menu, the group placed their orders.

While waiting for their dinners to arrive, they made pleasant and easy small talk. Eric's father had an engaging wit, just as his son did. He kept the crowd entertained until their meals arrived.

The waiter set an artfully presented plate of salmon in front of Evie and a New York strip in front of Eric.

They looked into each other's eyes. Evie swallowed hard, amazed that she had found the love of her life in Eric.

He squeezed her hand and leaned over next to her ear. "I love you," he said softly.

"I love you too," she whispered.

"If you all don't mind, I'd like to say grace over our meal," Evie's father said.

"We would very much appreciate that," Joseph replied.

Dan cleared his throat and said quietly, "Dear heavenly Father, we thank You for the food that is set before us. Please bless it for the nourishment of our bodies, and please embrace each of us with Your deep and unconditional love. And please be with Evie and Eric as they get married tomorrow, and bless them with a long and happy marriage. In Jesus's name we pray. Amen."

A chorus of "Amen" was uttered around the table before everyone dug into his or her dinner.

The Edwards family returned to their cabin after enjoying a delightful meal and fellowship with the Moses family. Evie could feel herself glowing from the kiss Eric had given her outside the restaurant— their last kiss as a single couple. She couldn't stop smiling.

"You're grinning like the Cheshire Cat," Cloe said, laughing.

Evie punched her sister playfully on the arm. "Shut up, Cloe." She giggled.

"You kind of are," her mother said, joining in the laughter.

"I agree," her daddy said as he lit a fire in the fireplace.

Evie sat down on the sofa between her mother and sister. "All of you are ganging up on me," she said happily.

"Sorry," Cloe said. "I couldn't resist."

"How about we have a glass of sparkling juice to commemorate this last night of Evie's single life?" her father asked.

"Hear! Hear!" her mother replied. "I think that's a grand idea."

Her father opened the bottle and handed each of them a bubbly fluted glass of juice.

They stood in a group together.

"Here's to Evie and Eric," Lorretta said.

"To Evie and Eric," Cloe and Dan repeated.

They tapped their glasses together and took a sip.

"So how does it feel to be an almost-married woman?" Cloe asked. "I want to know what I have to look forward to."

Evie sighed. "It feels absolutely indescribable, Cloe. It feels magical. It feels spiritual. I can't believe that God led me to my soul mate." To her surprise, a happy tear found its way down her cheek.

"I'm so happy for you," Cloe said, tenderly hugging Evie.

The hours passed like minutes as the small family talked about the wedding and their hopes and dreams for Evie and Eric and for themselves. Before Evie knew it, it was after midnight.

"We'd better get you to bed, young lady," Evie's mother told her. "You too, Cloe. We can't have you girls with puffy, sleep-deprived eyes tomorrow."

"Okay, Mom," Evie said. "You're right. It's getting late."

Everyone retired to his or her respective bedroom. Evie and Cloe changed into their pajamas and climbed into separate beds. As they lay face-to-face, Evie felt as if they were children again. Evie had been twelve years old when Cloe and Clarissa were born. Back then, she'd played with her baby sisters as if they were dolls. Now Evie and Cloe were both adults, and Evie's life was about to change forever.

Not wanting to cause any pain or sadness, Evie couldn't help but bring up her missing sister's name. It didn't feel right to leave her out.

"I wish Clarissa was here," she whispered in the semidarkness.

"I do too," Cloe said. "She would be as blissfully glad for you as I am."

"Thank you, sis," Evie said softly. "I'm so happy in my heart that you are with me and that you love me again."

Cloe rose up on her elbow. "Now, you listen to me, Evie. Even in my darkest time, I never stopped loving you." Evie could hear the heartfelt emotion in her sister's voice. "Even though I didn't show it, I always loved you, and I always will."

"I love you too, sweet Cloe."

They talked and giggled well into the wee hours of the morning. Finally, their mother knocked and opened the door. "We can hear you girls all the way down the hall. If you don't get some sleep, you're going to drop dead during the ceremony."

The sisters laughed and agreed and finally went to sleep.

It seemed as if Evie's head had just hit the pillow when her mother tapped on the door. "It's time to get up, girls," she said quietly. She pulled back the curtain to reveal a bright and breathtaking view of the snow-laden valley below. "We got some more snow last night."

"Yea!" Cloe squealed. "I wanted it to snow for my sister's big day. You'd better get up, Evie. You're a bride today. We gotta get you ready," she said happily.

"Oh my gosh!" Evie exclaimed. "I'm getting married today!"

"Yes, you are," Lorretta said. "In just a few hours. Now, come down and have a little breakfast before you girls start getting ready."

"Okay," they said in unison as they put on their robes and headed downstairs to the kitchen.

Evie's mother had prepared a large breakfast, but Evie only had a blueberry bagel with cream cheese and a cup of steaming-hot coffee. She couldn't wait to start getting ready.

Shortly after Evie and Cloe finished their breakfast and showers, the hairdressers arrived. The wedding planner had made the arrangements to have their hair done professionally, but Evie and Cloe had opted to do their own makeup.

As they sat side by side, the hairdressers styled the sisters' hair. Evie planned on some curls and a partial updo, while Cloe chose to wear her shoulder-length locks straight.

Chatting with Cloe while she applied her makeup helped to steady Evie's trembling hand a bit; still, she found it difficult to get her eyeliner on straight.

Obviously noticing that Evie was having some trouble, Cloe asked, "Can I do your makeup for you, sis? I would really like to do it, if you don't mind."

"I don't mind at all," Evie replied as she happily relinquished her tube of eyeliner to her sister.

She sat in the chair while Cloe removed and then began to reapply her makeup. Cloe's hand moved steadily and swiftly from various tubes and brushes as she gently tended to Evie's face.

Growing concerned that Cloe might be getting a little heavy-handed, Evie said, "Be careful, sis. I don't wanna look like a clown on my wedding day." She giggled.

"I'm insulted," Cloe said playfully. "I'm not going to make you look like a clown." She stopped what she was doing and looked down at Evie. "Don't you trust me?" she asked.

"Of course I do. I'm sorry," Evie replied.

"All right then. I'll get back to my job."

After several minutes, Cloe stopped and stood back. "Now close your eyes while I get a mirror." Placing a handheld mirror in Evie's hand, she said, "Now open."

Evie opened her eyes and gazed into the mirror. She couldn't believe her reflection. Her makeup looked flawless. It was natural looking but elegant at the same time. She liked Cloe's choice of a smoky nude eye shadow base with a hint of a baby-blue accent. Her eyeliner was dramatic but tasteful. Her lashes were curled and lush. A stroke of barely there shimmering pink blush highlighted her cheekbones, and her lips were lined and tinted with a rosy pink. She turned her head from side to side and looked at herself.

"Gosh, Cloe," she said as she stared at her reflection, "I feel so beautiful."

"You are beautiful, sis—both inside and out."

"Thank you, Cloe. Thank you for everything."

Before Cloe could respond, their mother pecked on the door and came inside. "I just wanted to see how you girls were doing," she said. "And I can see that you both look absolutely gorgeous. You're going to make me cry."

"Don't cry, Mom," Evie said. "If you do, then I will, and I'll ruin Cloe's makeup job. Let's see how you look, Mom."

Lorretta came in and did a slow twirl. She was wearing a light blue skirt and jacket with a white silk blouse.

"You look lovely, Mom," Evie said as she went to give her mother a hug.

"Thank you, sweetheart. Now, you two had better get into your dresses," she said. "Do you mind if I stay in the room with you?"

"Not at all, Mom. We would love to have your company," Evie answered.

Cloe got dressed first so she could help Evie into her gown. She came out of the bathroom wearing an ankle-length, fitted baby-blue silk dress. It had a sweetheart neckline, spaghetti straps, and a short train.

Evie clapped her hand over her mouth.

"My goodness, Cloe, you look so beautiful," their mother said.

"Yes, you do!" Evie exclaimed. "I can't believe you made that dress along with my gown too. You are truly gifted, my sister."

"Thanks," Cloe said. "I had a lot of help, but I'm thrilled with how the dresses turned out. Now let's get you into yours," she squealed happily. "I'm so excited to see how you look all dolled up."

Evie stood and let her sister help her into her gown.

"Just step into it, and I'll pull it up," Cloe said.

Doing as her sister said, Evie stepped into her wedding gown. She was practically breathless in anticipation. She had tried the dress on a few days earlier, but that had been before Cloe's final embellishments and alterations. She trusted her sister's unique fashion abilities; still, she was a bit nervous.

After pulling the dress up, Evie waited while Cloe buttoned up the back. Then Cloe smoothed the gown at the top and fluffed up the bottom.

"Now, let's have a look in the mirror and see what you think," Cloe said.

Taking a few steps toward the full-length mirror, Evie looked at herself. She gasped at her own reflection. The gown on Cloe's initial sketchpad had come to fruition. The strapless fit-and-flare dress fit her body perfectly and was astonishing. It clung to her curves and accentuated her womanly figure. The beading and embellishments at the bodice and down to below her hips were dazzling. The lower part of the dress was soft and billowy.

"I still can't believe you made this, sis!" she exclaimed. "I feel like a princess. That's exactly the way I wanted to feel on my wedding day. Thank you for making that happen." Evie was on the verge of tears but tried to hold them in.

"You're a knockout," Cloe said proudly as she snapped a picture with her cell phone. "You are going to take Eric's breath away."

"You sure are," Lorretta said as she dabbed her eyes with a tissue.

"Now let's get your diamond necklace and earrings on you, and then we'll put on the veil," Cloe said. "Then you'll be all set."

After putting on her sparkling Christmas gifts from Eric, Evie stood still while Cloe attached the long white veil to her head. Once her sister had finished fussing with the translucent accessory, Evie turned back to the mirror again.

The shimmering veil was attached to a small, sparkling band of faux diamonds. Evie gently touched it. "It's so pretty, Cloe. Thank you."

"You're welcome. Now we have to make sure you have everything you need," Cloe said while opening her overnight bag. "Something blue—your garter has a blue bow." She giggled as she handed the dainty piece to Evie. "Something old—Mom has one of Grandma's old hankies for you to put in your bra in case you need it."

Evie turned to her mother and received the handkerchief.

"Something new—your gown, of course, which your sister so graciously made for you," Cloe said while curtseying. "And something borrowed." She pulled a tiny ring off her pinkie finger. "You gave this to me when I turned twelve years old. Do you remember? I never take it off. I will always wear it." She handed it to Evie, and Evie slipped the pearl-studded ring onto her pinkie finger.

"Yes, I remember giving this to you. I'm so glad you still wear it." Evie grabbed her sister and hugged her tightly. Seeing her mom standing off crying, Evie said, "Come on, Mom. We're having us a hug fest."

"Never let it be said that I turned down an opportunity to hug my girls," her mother said with tears in her eyes.

Just outside the doorway to the wedding ceremony space, Evie, her father, Cloe, and the wedding planner stood ready for the event to begin. Her mother had already been seated, and the music for Cloe's entrance was about to start.

Cloe fussed with Evie's veil. "You look amazing, sis," she whispered. "You're gonna knock Eric out when you walk down that aisle."

"Thank you, Cloe," Evie said. "I love you very much."

"I love you too," Cloe said.

The wedding planner motioned for Cloe to take her position. As the music began to play, while clutching a lovely bouquet of assorted white flowers, Cloe started her long walk down the aisle.

"How about it, Daddy? Are you ready?" Evie asked.

"No," her father answered softly, obviously fighting back tears. "You are my first baby girl, and I love you more than words can express. I'm so proud of the woman you've become, Evie. I hope you know that."

With misty eyes, Evie replied, "I know, Daddy. I love you too. You and Mom are the best parents any girl could ever hope for, and I will always be your first baby girl."

Her father released a deep breath. "Okay then. Let's get you married. Your mother and I are looking forward to inheriting us a son."

The wedding planner handed Evie her bouquet of cascading white roses with baby-blue accents. It was the most splendid floral arrangement Evie had ever seen. She looked down to find the bouquet shaking slightly in her trembling hand.

The planner motioned for the bride's entrance music to begin. Elegant string music began emanating from the ceremony room. It was time for Evie to get married, and she was on top of the world.

She and her father took their places at the door of the room. The intimate party of seventy-five people stood as the bride and her father began their slow walk down the aisle.

Evie saw Eric standing at the other end of the long white floor runner. He looked handsome dressed in a black suit with a baby-blue tie. The fireplace behind him was draped in crystal-clear glowing lights. The mantel, which was lavishly decorated in white and soft blue flowers, flickering candles, and flowing fabric, completed the ethereal ambiance. Everything looked captivating, but at that moment, all Evie could see was Eric. He was gazing at her and crying. She could feel the tears trickling down her own cheeks.

When Evie and her father reached the end of the runner, they stopped.

The pastor asked, "Who gives this woman to be married to this man?"

Evie's father replied, "Her mother and I do." After saying that, he lifted Evie's veil slightly and kissed her on the cheek. He took her hand and placed it in Eric's. "Take care of our baby, son," he whispered.

"I will," Eric said as he grasped Evie's hand.

Cloe took a step forward and received Evie's bouquet. Then, hand in hand, Evie and Eric stood together, facing the pastor. He read from one of her favorite books of the Bible: 1 Corinthians. He spoke about what true, pure love was and what it wasn't. Eric clutched Evie's hand during the entire ceremony, making her feel loved and secure.

Finally, the pastor had the couple face one another. After exchanging rings, they repeated their heartfelt vows to each other. The entire time their hands were clasped tightly together, Evie made Eric a silent promise that she would never let go.

With tears streaming down both of their faces, the pastor told Eric that he could now kiss his lovely bride.

Eric smiled that dazzling smile of his. He carefully lifted the veil and stared into Evie's eyes. "You are so exquisite. You take my breath away," he said, and they kissed for the first time as husband and wife.

The kiss was deep and meaningful. They clung to each other lovingly as they embraced. If Evie could have stopped time, that would have been the moment she chose.

As the DJ announced them for the first time as husband and wife, Evie and Eric walked out onto the dance floor for their first dance together. As he took her in his arms, the first few notes of the song started. Evie immediately recognized it as the Bee Gees' "How Deep Is Your Love." She smiled while wrapped in Eric's warm embrace.

"I specifically selected our song. I hope you don't mind," he said.

"Are you kidding me?" she asked softly. "I love it, and I love you."

Gazing into her eyes, he said, "I love you too, baby doll, and I always will."

They held each other as they swayed to the melodious music. With her head resting against Eric's chest, she could feel his heartbeat. Closing her eyes, she relished the moment. She was in total disbelief. She couldn't believe this fairy-tale night was actually real.

Leaning her head back, she looked into Eric's eyes. "How did I get so blessed?" she asked.

Eric smiled. "I think you have it backward. I'm the one who's blessed. I have an angel for my wife."

She smiled back at him.

As their song came to an end, he gently dipped her and bent down and kissed her on the lips. The guests clapped in response.

From then on, Evie was lost in the euphoria of the evening. Side by side at the sweetheart table and surrounded by family and friends who wished Eric and her nothing but the best, they enjoyed a fantastic white-glove-served meal of filet mignon and chicken breast accompanied by grilled asparagus and decoratively piped mashed potatoes. Evie took a few bites but couldn't seem to concentrate on the delicious food before her.

"Are you too excited to eat?" Eric asked.

She looked over at her husband. He looked strikingly handsome. She couldn't believe he loved her and had just married her. "I feel like the luckiest woman in the world," she told him.

"And I feel like the luckiest man alive," he said as he leaned over and kissed her.

After dinner, they cut and served each other their luscious red velvet wedding cake and then danced the evening away with their family and friends.

Elizabeth and George chatted with the newlyweds briefly between songs.

Evie looked her two friends up and down. "You two make a nice couple," she said jokingly.

"Shut up." Elizabeth laughed.

As hard as Evie tried to stay in the moment, the evening seemed to pass in a blur. All too quickly, the wedding and reception were over. After making their official exit from the venue, they walked through the lobby and to their honeymoon suite.

"I can't believe we're married," Eric said as he unlocked the door.

"I can't either," Evie said breathlessly. She was slightly apprehensive about her honeymoon night. Eric must have picked up on her uneasiness.

"You nervous?" he asked softly.

She nodded. "A little."

"Don't be. Not with me." He flashed her that warm smile of his, which immediately dissolved her inhibitions.

He kissed her as he picked her up in his arms and carried her over the threshold.

Once they were inside their inviting suite, Eric carried Evie into the bedroom and put her feet down on the floor. Smiling, he looked at her. "You look astonishingly beautiful," he said as he tenderly touched her face. "I couldn't believe my eyes when I saw you walking down that aisle. You took my breath away and turned me into a blubbering fool."

"I know what you mean," she said. "The moment I saw you standing there waiting for me, I couldn't stop the tears. It was a very emotional and magical moment that I will never forget for as long as I live."

"I won't forget it either, baby doll." Looking down at her gown, he said, "Cloe sure outdid herself on that dress. It's unbelievable."

Evie did a little twirl. "She did, didn't she?"

"She sure did, but you are what made it a stunner," he said with a wink. "Would you like something to drink? I put some champagne and sparkling juice in the refrigerator when I brought our bags up to the room this morning."

"I think I would love a sip of champagne," Evie said. "An enchanting honeymoon wouldn't be complete without champagne."

"You're right about that," he said as he took off his jacket and tie and laid them on the chair. Following him into the kitchen, she watched as he expertly opened the champagne bottle. She jumped when the cork popped. Grinning, he poured each of them a glass of the bubbly wine.

"May I make the toast?" he asked.

"Please," she answered.

"To the most gorgeous wife in the world and to many, many years filled with love and laughter and living life to its fullest."

"That was beautiful," Evie said as they clinked their glasses together.

They each took a sip.

The bubbles tickled Evie's nose. "This is delicious," she said as she took another tiny drink.

"It is, isn't it? I haven't had champagne in forever," he said. "Do you want to sit down in the living room?"

"No," Evie said as she set her glass down on the table. "I would like one more dance with my husband."

Smiling, he retrieved his phone and turned on some music. Evie giggled when she heard that it was their Bee Gees song again. "I just want you to always think of me when you hear this song," he said.

As he took her in his arms, she replied, "I will, but I don't need a song to make me think of you."

He groaned. "That was a sweet thing to say."

Wrapping her arms around his neck, she laid her head against his chest. They swayed to the familiar song as they kissed and caressed each other's body. Evie's entire being was excited at the sensation of Eric's gentle and roaming hands. Down her back and lower, he touched her in places she had never been touched by a man before. She sighed and moaned as he explored her body. She could feel his excitement pressing against her.

"Eric?" she asked breathlessly.

"Yes, baby doll?" he answered as he nibbled on her ear.

"Would you make love to me now?" she whispered.

He moaned his response while picking her up and carrying her to the dimly lit bedroom.

"Do you want me to help you out of your dress?" he asked. "There are a lot of buttons."

"Yes, please." She turned and waited as he slowly unfastened the many buttons down the back of her dress. Once he did, the white fabric pooled at her feet in a large pearly puddle. He offered her his hand, and she took it and stepped out of her gown. She was dressed only in her strapless, white lace bra and panties. She looked at him while he looked at her. She was fearful, wondering if she was enough to satisfy him.

"You're the most splendid woman I've ever laid my eyes on," he said. "You are truly a vision."

"Thank you, Eric," she said softly.

He came to her and took her in his arms again. He kissed her passionately. As their lips parted, their kiss became more urgent.

Putting her hands on his chest, she unbuttoned his white shirt. As she did, she planted wet kisses down his chest. He moaned his approval as she slid his shirt down his arms and off his body.

With nothing but the sounds of their heavy breathing, sighs, and moans, they touched each other's trembling body.

When his fingers unfastened her bra in the back, Evie gasped softly as the dainty garment dropped to the floor at her feet.

"Are you all right?" Eric asked. His voice sounded raspy and sensual.

"Yes," she whispered.

He began kissing her neck and shoulders as his deft hands slid to the front of her body and found her breasts. He gently squeezed her breasts in his hands, causing her to moan loudly in response.

"You are so perfect," he said. Once again, his voice was wrought with emotion and desire.

His kisses made their way down her body until his mouth found her breasts.

The sensation of what he was doing to her caused her to quiver all over. She had never experienced this level of arousal before. "I'm sorry," she whispered.

He raised his head and looked at her. She could see the fire of desire burning in his dark eyes. "You have nothing to be sorry for, Evie. Would you like to slow down?" he asked.

"No. Would you?"

"No, I wouldn't," he answered as he placed his lips against hers. Once again, his hands roamed around her body. He slipped her out of her panties. Standing before him completely nude, she had never wanted a man more.

Following his lead, she allowed her hands to explore his body. The feel of his warm skin and muscular arms and back fueled her. Her fingers found their way to the waistband of his pants. She unbuckled his belt and slowly lowered his zipper. His pants dropped to the floor, and he quickly stepped out of them. After picking her up, he gently laid her nude body on the bed. His eyes never left hers as he slipped into bed with her. Lying side by side, they continued to kiss and caress each other, until finally, he lowered his body on top of hers.

"I love you, Evie," he said as their bodies joined.

She moaned loudly at the sensation. "I love you too, Eric," she said breathlessly as an emotional and tantalizing night of lovemaking began.

Evie awakened the following morning depleted and happy. Face-to-face, she and Eric were wrapped snugly in each other's arms.

"How do you feel?" Eric asked.

Evie purred softly. "I feel indescribably happy. How about you?"

"I feel the same way, my wife. I've never been happier in my entire life."

They gazed into each other eyes without saying anything for a few moments. Their smiles said it all.

"I'm almost afraid to ask this," he said, "but did I disappoint you last night?"

Evie smiled and stroked his handsome face. "In no way did you disappoint me, Eric. Last night was far beyond my wildest dreams."

He grinned. "I'm glad to hear that—really glad."

"How about me? Did I disappoint you?" Evie asked timidly.

"Not in the least," he said while gazing seriously into her eyes.

"But a little more practice wouldn't hurt, would it?" she asked, grinning.

Laughing, he grabbed her and pulled her firmly against his excited body.

20

BACK TO REALITY

Going back to the hospital on the following Wednesday morning was not going to be an easy feat. After spending a blissfully enchanting honeymoon with her husband, Evie showered, dressed, and got ready to report for morning rounds. She came into her kitchen to find that Eric, wearing only his boxer shorts, had prepared her favorite breakfast: a blueberry bagel with cream cheese and a cup of black coffee.

"Aw, you didn't have to get up early for me," she said as she kissed her sleepy-looking husband before taking a bite of her bagel. "Don't feel like you have to do this. You could have slept in for a couple more hours."

"I'll go back to bed after I see my sexy wife off," he said. "And I know I don't have to. I want to. Now, eat while I ogle you." He laughed.

She laughed too. He said the funniest things. She loved his quick wit. It made him irresistible.

"So what are you going to tell your friends about our honeymoon? Are you going to tell them that we were too busy to go skiing?" He laughed again.

She blushed and poked him playfully on the arm. How was she going to tell her friends that she and Eric hadn't left their room except to go down to the dining room for dinner once? For the rest of their meals, they'd ordered room service. They had taken baths together in the large Jacuzzi tub. They'd spent hours upon hours holding each other and talking about their bright and wonder-filled plans for the future. And they'd made glorious, passionate love to each other over and over again.

"My friends will most definitely get a very G-rated version of our honeymoon," she said while taking another bite of her breakfast. "What are you going to tell your friends?"

"Oh! Men are completely different creatures, honey. We give all the specific, erotic, and intimate details." He chuckled sexily.

"Eric Joseph Moses, you'd better not," Evie said, laughing.

He grinned and pulled her into a hug. "I won't, baby doll. I'm just messing with you."

She wrapped her arms around his neck. Face-to-face with him, she gazed into his inviting dark eyes. "I wish I didn't have to go. It's our first day back home as man and wife, and I want to stay here and enjoy it with you."

"I wish you could stay with me too," he said, sighing. "But you gotta go, or you're gonna be late, and then your cohorts will most definitely give you grief for sure." He winked sexily at her, causing her to giggle like a silly teenager.

"Well, if it isn't Dr. Evie Edwards-Moses," Elizabeth said as Evie met her fellow group of residents at the nurses' station.

"How was the honeymoon?" George asked with a mischievous smile.

Linda and Lonnie just stood back and grinned at her.

"Okay, you nosy bunch of residents," she said, laughing. "My honeymoon was wonderful. Thank you very much for asking. Now, where's Dr. Stone?"

"Right here," Dr. Stone said from behind her. "How was the honeymoon?" he asked, laughing.

Evie rolled her eyes in defeat.

Two doors down from the nurses' station, the group walked into the room of a little girl. The toddler was sleeping in her mother's lap.

"Dr. Stewart, would you mind giving us an update on our patient?" Dr. Stone asked quietly.

Elizabeth stepped forward and answered in a hushed voice. "Two-year-old Nevaeh Nelson was admitted to the hospital on Monday morning, presenting with ongoing complications of a congenitally defective mitral valve. She is scheduled for a laparoscopic ring annuloplasty surgery at ten o'clock this morning to repair the valve. Her vitals remained stable and without further complaint or complications overnight."

"Thank you, Dr. Stewart," Dr. Stone said. Addressing the mother, Dr. Stone asked if she had any further questions or concerns about the surgery. Shaking her head, the mother began to cry. Evie's heart went out to her.

"Nevaeh is a lovely name," Evie whispered.

"Nevaeh is *heaven* spelled backward," the mother replied tearfully.

The child awakened. Being surrounded by people in white lab coats obviously frightened her. She immediately grabbed on to her mother and began to whimper.

"Dr. Stewart will be assisting Nevaeh's cardiothoracic surgeon, Dr. Jones, with her surgery this morning, and I assure you that your baby will be very well taken care of," Dr. Stone told the mother.

The tearful baby girl looked at Evie and pointed.

Her mother smiled softly. "She's admiring your pink stethoscope around your neck. Pink is her favorite color."

"Oh," Evie said with every intention of letting the little girl touch the instrument.

Dr. Stone interrupted. "Would you mind placing Nevaeh on the bed so that Dr. Stewart may listen to her heart?" he asked.

"Of course," the mother answered while doing as he requested.

In an attempt to calm the whimpering baby during Dr. Stewart's examination, Evie let the child hold her pink stethoscope. She smiled a toothy grin at Evie, which instantly stole Evie's heart.

After the examination was complete, the doctors walked out of the room.

"Dr. Stone?" Evie asked.

"Yes?"

"Do you think it would be all right if I scrubbed in on Nevaeh's surgery this morning?"

Elizabeth looked at her quizzically.

"Just to observe," Evie added quickly.

"I don't see why not, but that's up to your attending and Dr. Jones. You'll have to clear it with them."

"Okay, thank you," Evie said.

"So how was your day?" Eric asked as Evie walked through her apartment door. Eric was standing behind a tall stack of brown moving boxes. The following day, he and Cloe were going to move Evie's things into Eric's charming cottage-style home on the west end of Ritter Park.

"Aside from getting my heart stolen by a two-year-old little girl this morning, my day was okay," she answered. "How was yours?"

she asked as she walked toward him to give him a kiss. He looked attractive still dressed in his navy-blue scrubs.

"My day is great now that you're here," he said as he grabbed her and pulled her into a warm embrace.

All of her cares of the day disappeared when she was in his arms. She moaned and clung to him as they kissed. Feeling his warm body pressed against hers left her wanting more.

After their passionate kiss ended, Evie whispered, "Would you make love to me, Eric?"

He answered her question by silently picking her up and carrying her off to her bedroom.

Their welcome-home lovemaking session lasted well into the evening. Afterward, while they sat at the kitchen table for a late-night breakfast dinner of pancakes and scrambled eggs, Eric said, "Now tell me about your day. What about this little girl? Did she happen to help you make your final decision about if you want to specialize or not?"

Evie smiled while thinking of little Nevaeh. Her surgery had gone flawlessly, and she was recovering well. "This little girl was absolutely adorable, and yes, I think she did help me to decide for sure about which specialty I would choose. I would choose pediatric surgery for sure. I will always have an affinity for the elderly, but I think my heart is in pediatrics."

"I think so too, baby doll. I think you would be making a wise decision should you decide to fellowship and specialize rather than going directly into practice with your father's group. You still have that decision to make, but you have plenty of time." He grinned at her.

She couldn't help but laugh. She covered her face with her hands.

"What are you doing, my silly wife?" Eric chuckled.

"I can't look at you," she replied. "When you smile at me like that, all I can think about is how sexy you are and how much I want you."

He got up and gently pulled her hands away from her face. He wasn't smiling anymore. "So what's wrong with that?" he asked as he picked her up again and carried her off to the bedroom, abandoning their half-eaten meals.

21
FINALLY

A year and a half later, Evie had finished her fifth and final year of residency. While she and Eric had joyously settled into married life, time had seemed to pass by like a whirlwind.

The big day in her career finally arrived. After much time and deliberation, Evie had changed her mind and decided not to pursue a fellowship in pediatrics right away. At that moment in time, the thought of three more years of residency didn't appeal to her in the slightest. She could pursue her pediatric specialty at another time. At present, she was happily going directly into general surgery practice with her father's group. Full of excitement, she was ready for her career to begin.

Following an afternoon hospital reception with congratulatory cake and finger foods, the Edwards family and the Moses family were meeting at a steakhouse in Charleston for a celebration dinner. Evie and Eric were about ten minutes away from the restaurant.

"You've been smiling all day," Eric said as he reached over, took Evie's hand, and kissed it. "You're so beautiful but even more so when you're smiling."

"Thank you, my love," she said. "I feel the same way about you."

He glanced at her from the driver's seat. He was grinning and looked striking in a navy-blue suit and tie. "You look pretty in your summery pink dress," he told her.

"Thank you. Cloe made it for me. I like it too."

"Speaking of Cloe," he said. "I don't know how you'd feel about it, but I was thinking maybe we could set her up on a date with my cousin Nathaniel."

"You mean Nate? The tall, dark, and handsome Nate?" Evie asked. She had met Eric's cousin in December at the Moses family's Christmas dinner.

"Yes, that's the Nate I'm talking about—the handsome one." Eric laughed heartily.

Evie laughed too. "Well, he doesn't hold a candle to you, my fabulous husband." She reached over and caressed his face.

He leaned his cheek into her hand. "I love it when you touch me," he said softly.

She continued to stroke his smooth cheek; neither of them said a word.

Several moments later, he chuckled. "Now, what were we talking about before you distracted me with your gentle fingers?"

"We were talking about fixing up Nate and Cloe. I think it would be a grand idea. I think Cloe would like Nate. He seems like a very nice guy."

"I think he would like Cloe too. She's very pretty, like her big sister, and she's interesting and very likable."

Evie nodded. "Good then. We'll see if they're open to it. You ask Nate, and I'll ask Cloe. Hey! How about we go out on a double date with them next Saturday night?"

He seemed reluctant to answer at first. "Hmm, I love that idea. That would be a blast," he finally replied. "We're here," he announced as they pulled into the parking lot. After turning off the engine, he looked over at her. "I am so proud of you, my wife. Dr. Edwards-Moses—that has a very nice ring to it." He leaned over and planted a sweet kiss on her lips.

Both families were already seated in the restaurant when Evie and Eric arrived. As soon as Evie walked up to the table, everyone raised his or her glass and saluted her.

On the verge of happy tears, she smiled and thanked them as Eric pulled out her chair for her. He sat down next to her, put his arm around her, and kissed her on the cheek.

She looked at the love of her life through misty eyes. "I love you," she whispered.

Although a happy day, it had been an emotional one for Evie. She had studied so diligently and worked so hard for so many years to get where she was this day. It was quite overwhelming.

"Speech!" Eric's father said loudly.

"Yes, speech!" Evie's father repeated.

"Okay," Evie said softly as she rose to her feet, "but you all are going to make me cry. I don't have anything to say except thank you. Thank you, Mom and Dad, for all of your support and for guiding me to a vocation that I love." She placed her hand on her heart. "Thank you, Cloe, for being the best sister anyone could ever ask for, and thank you, Joseph and Katherine, for creating my soul mate." She turned to look at Eric. Tears trickled down her face as she gazed at her husband. "And thank you, Eric, for everything. Thank you for loving me and for supporting me and for always being there for me. I will love you forever and for always."

After she sat back down, Eric leaned toward her and placed a tender kiss on her lips. "I love you too, Evie," he whispered, sounding emotional.

Turning back to her blended family, she wiped away her tears. "That's all I have to say—just thank you, and I love all of you."

Her declaration of love was repeated back to her from around the table.

After enjoying a delectable steak dinner, Evie and Eric chatted all the way home.

"Can you believe I don't have to be at the hospital at five o'clock in the morning anymore? I can sleep in and make love to my husband," she said.

Eric chuckled. "Now, that sounds like the best perk of all. Can I get a promise that you'll always wake me up like that every day for the rest of our lives?"

"You sure can," Evie said. "I promise."

After they pulled into the driveway of their home, Evie waited while Eric came around to open her car door.

When they reached their front door, Eric unlocked it and said, "Would it be all right if I carried the new surgeon over the threshold?"

Touched by his sweet sentiment, Evie answered, "I would love that."

He picked her up, carried her into the foyer, and set her down. The first thing she noticed was a collection of luggage at the side of the stairs. Looking quizzically at Eric, she asked, "What's this? Where are you going?"

He laughed and pulled her to him. "I'm not going anywhere. We're going to Paris for one entire week. Our flight leaves at six in the morning, so you'd better get some sleep."

Shocked and pleased, she jumped up and down in his arms. "What are you talking about?" she asked disbelievingly. "I can't be ready that quickly. I have to pack and everything."

"Cloe has already packed for you," he answered. "All you have to do is gather your last-minute girlie things, and we'll be on our way to Paris—the City of Love."

Evie couldn't believe her ears. She couldn't believe how blessed she was to have Eric in her life. "The City of Love," she repeated. "That's the perfect place for us because I love you, Eric Joseph Moses. I know you might get tired of hearing it, but I love you with all of my heart and soul."

He cupped her face gently in his hands. "Now, you listen to me, baby. I will never, for as long as I live, ever get tired of hearing you tell me that you love me. Please don't ever stop saying those words to me."

Pressing his lips against hers, he kissed her passionately. He took her breath away. She knew in her heart that he always would.

22
PARIS AT LAST

After a long but uneventful fifteen-hour trip, Evie and Eric arrived in the lovely city of Paris, France. Evie couldn't believe that after all these years, she had finally made it to Paris. Although she was there for a different reason, Evie knew Paris wouldn't disappoint, especially with Eric by her side.

After gathering their luggage and hailing a taxi, they climbed into the backseat. It was after three in the morning, and the city was aglow with streetlights. What she could see of the astounding scenery left her speechless. With her hand clutching Eric's, she gaped out the window at the City of Love and Light. Off in the distance, she could see the massive Eiffel Tower standing tall. It was brightly lit from top to bottom.

Finally finding her voice, she whispered excitedly, "Look, Eric. It's the Eiffel Tower."

He chuckled at her. "I know, Evie. I can see it."

She laughed too. "I know I'm being silly. I'm sorry."

"You don't ever need to apologize to me, Evie," he said.

She looked at him sitting next to her. Reaching over, she wrapped her arms tightly around his neck. "Thank you for bringing me here," she said.

"You're welcome, baby doll. It's our long-overdue honeymoon. I hope you have a wonderful time."

"*We* will have a wonderful time," she said.

Moments later, their taxi deposited them in front of a lavish-looking hotel. Evie looked through the taxi window. "We're staying here?" she asked in disbelief.

"We sure are," Eric answered.

After paying the driver, Eric exited first and held the door open for Evie. Taking his offered hand, she stepped out of the taxi, feeling as if she were stepping into a whole new world.

The hotel doorman held the door while a concierge attendant loaded their luggage onto a cart and escorted them into the lobby, which was glowing and lushly decorated in antique white and gold. The floors were mirror-polished and reflected row after row of sparkling, cascading chandeliers. The furniture and decorative statues were also done in antique white and gold.

"This is the most luxurious hotel I've ever seen," Evie said.

"I know," Eric replied, "but I have an idea that we haven't seen anything yet."

After checking in at the desk and being led to their room, Evie and Eric walked into their suite. Evie headed toward the window while Eric tipped the attendant. Pulling back the curtains, she found they had a bird's-eye view of the Eiffel Tower. The stunning sight instigated an emotional response inside her.

"What do you think?" Eric asked as he wrapped his arms around her from behind. "I wanted you to have the perfect view while we're here."

She turned in his arms to face him. "I can't believe you did this for me. I truly can't," she whispered tearfully.

"I know you've always wanted to come here to immerse yourself in your dream of the arts. I'm sorry you didn't get to do that," he said, holding her tightly.

"I'm not sorry at all," Evie said. "I thank God every day that He led me into medicine instead of art. If He hadn't, I would never have met you." She fought back tears. "You are my dream, Eric."

They gazed into each other's eyes before they kissed. With her eyes closed and her lips pressed against her husband's, Evie thanked God for all of His immeasurable blessings but especially for Eric.

After only a few hours of sleep, Evie awakened early the next morning. From the bed, she looked around at the lovely hotel suite. It was spectacularly decorated in Victorian blue, cream, and gold, with matching carpet. The bedroom had a sitting area with fabric-covered seating facing the windows. Three steps down from the bedroom was a large two-person Jacuzzi tub. That was all Evie could see without getting up. Eric was still sleeping, and she didn't want to wake him.

Turning onto her left side, she could see the Eiffel Tower looming in the distance through the window, but she couldn't seem to stay focused on it. She didn't want to take her eyes off her sleeping husband.

Moments later, he opened his captivating dark eyes.

"Good morning, handsome," Evie said.

"Hi, baby doll. How long have you been awake?" he asked sleepily.

Evie smiled at him. "Just for a few minutes. You looked like you were sleeping soundly. Did you have a good few hours of sleep?"

"Yes, I did," he answered through a yawn and a stretch. "How about you?" he asked as his stretch ended, and he pulled her into his embrace. "Did you sleep well?"

"I absolutely did," she said as she moaned and snuggled up next to his warm body.

"What would you like to do first?" he asked while kissing her on her forehead.

Evie giggled. "Well, first I want to step into that Jacuzzi tub with my sexy spouse."

"Now, that sounds like just the ticket to me," he said with a huge grin. "It's hard to tell where that will lead, though."

"I know," she whispered while staring into his eyes. "I hope it leads us back to bed."

"Your wish is my command, my dear," he said before he covered her face with playful kisses.

After a luxurious bath and a morning of sensual lovemaking, Evie and Eric decided to get dressed and go out for lunch and then do a little sightseeing.

The Eiffel Tower was within walking distance of the hotel, so they decided to make it their first destination to visit. On the way, they stopped by a quaint little French bistro. They opted to sit outside in the balmy summer air, where they could admire the sights of the city.

After perusing the tempting menu, they settled on cheese soufflés served with flaky croissants. The meal sounded French, decadent, and delicious.

"I'm starving," Eric said. After the waiter had disappeared with their menus, Eric leaned toward her. While wearing a sly smile, he said, "You made me work up an appetite this morning."

"Sorry." She laughed.

"I'm not," he said.

While talking and taking in the sights around them, they sipped on their cups of coffee. A few minutes later, the waiter brought out their food and set it before them. It looked and smelled divine.

When he asked if they needed anything else, Eric told him, "A little more coffee, please, and thank you so much."

Evie took her first bite of the billowy soufflé. "Oh my gosh! This is to die for," she said.

"Mm, yes, this is fantastic," Eric agreed. "I think I could eat ten of these at one time."

"And I could eat ten croissants," Evie replied.

After enjoying their late lunch, they began their leisurely hand-in-hand walk toward the magnificent Eiffel Tower.

Once they reached the base, they saw that it was overly crowded. The line to board one of the packed elevators to the top was extensive.

"What do you think, baby doll? Wanna ride to the top?" Eric asked.

Evie looked around at the throng of people. "Would you be terribly disappointed if we didn't? The crowds don't look very appealing to me."

"Whew!" Eric said, laughing. "I was hoping you'd say that. I don't dig that many people in one overstuffed elevator either." He looked around them. "So where do we go from here?"

"What about the Musée d'Orsay?" she asked.

"Whatever you orsay," Eric answered, smiling.

Evie laughed at his witty comeback. Getting out their tourist map, they headed toward the Musée d'Orsay, which was only a few blocks away. "This is the museum that has always called to me," Evie said. "I've always wanted to see it and see the original works of art of the greats hanging in one place—Monet, Gauguin, Renoir, and Van Gogh, to name a few."

"Then see it you shall," Eric said while raising her hand to his lips and kissing it. "Cloe told me you wanted to see this place, so I bought our tickets online when I booked the trip."

Evie was touched that he had gone to so much trouble just to make her happy. "Thank you so very much, my considerate husband."

"You're welcome, my lovely wife," he said as they walked toward the entrance of the museum.

Evie looked down at her watch and noticed they had been wandering around the museum for hours. "I'm so sorry, Eric," she said. "You must be bored to tears watching me look at art all this time."

"Don't worry your pretty little head about it," he replied. "I'm enjoying myself watching you enjoy yourself. After four years of medical school and five grueling years of residency, you deserve it."

"Thank you very much," she said. "Now, let's go get something delicious to eat."

"Now you're talking, woman," he said, laughing.

They walked out of the museum the same way they had walked in: hand in hand.

"I wish you would start painting again now that you'll have more time," Eric told her. "I can see your passion for it shining in your eyes."

"I just might do that," she said.

"So what is your forte?"

"Landscapes mostly. I especially like sunrises and sunsets." She felt herself blushing slightly. "Looking at all of these masterpieces, I can see that I wasn't very good."

"Nonsense. I've seen some of your paintings."

She stopped and looked quizzically at him. Knowing she had left that part of her life behind and had stored her paintings away in her parents' attic, she wondered how he had seen any of them.

"Cloe showed me some of them on her phone. I didn't get to see the real thing, but they're lovely, Evie. You have a gift. You shouldn't waste that gift."

"Thank you, Eric. Maybe I'll start painting again someday soon."

Sitting down to a dinner of coq au vin served with caramelized roasted vegetables, Evie and Eric decided to splurge and have a glass of red wine to go with their meal.

"This is the best fancy chicken I've ever eaten in my entire life," Eric said. "Present company's fancy chicken excluded, of course."

Evie laughed, knowing that her cooking was subpar, to say the least. Hopefully she would improve now that she would have more time to devote to preparing dinner for her husband, she thought.

Looking around the romantic bistro in Paris, sitting next to her soul mate, Evie couldn't believe she was really there. It seemed like a dream—a wonderful dream she never wanted to awaken from.

"What are you thinking about?" Eric asked as he took a sip of wine.

Evie shook her head. "I was just thinking about how perfect this time is with you—how precious it is to me."

"I feel the same way, baby. We have the rest of our lives to spend together, but I try to be in the moment and enjoy every single second and every experience I get to share with you." He smiled. "I'm one lucky man, and I know it."

Evie shook her head. "I would have to beg to differ with you on that. I think I'm the lucky one in this marriage."

They clinked their glasses together and took another sip of wine.

"So what would you like to see tomorrow?" Eric asked as he took another bite of his dinner.

"Well, there's the Louvre, of course; the Musée Marmottan Monet; the Musée Picasso; and, if we have time, the Palace of Versailles," she answered excitedly.

Eric pretended to choke on his food. "Is that all?" he asked, laughing.

"Yes." She giggled. "How about you? What would you like to see?"

"Sadly, because of the fire, Notre Dame Cathedral is still closed. I would have loved to see that, but there is the Basilica of Saint-Denis. I would like to go there. I love old churches."

"I do too," Evie said. "Let's do that tomorrow."

"Sounds like a plan to me," Eric said.

Their waiter returned to their table and asked if they would like a cheese course or dessert.

"What is your specialty dessert?" Eric asked.

The waiter smiled as if proud of what they had to offer. "That would be our crème brûlée, sir. Also, our caramel profiteroles filled with pastry cream are delightful as well."

"What will it be, Evie?" Eric asked.

"How about we get one of each and share?" Evie answered.

"That's very diplomatic of you," Eric said, and he gave the waiter their order.

While they waited for their dessert to be served, they drank the last of their wine.

Eric looked at Evie with a mischievous look on his face. He had an expression sometimes that made him look like an ornery young teenager. "What's say we scarf down our desserts so we can get back to that Jacuzzi tub and big, soft king-sized bed?"

Evie giggled at him. "I would love nothing better, my husband," she answered honestly.

23

PROMISES

Their week in Paris passed much too quickly. It seemed that no sooner had they gotten there than they had to leave. Evie was on the verge of tears as she looked around the lovely room she had shared with Eric for the past seven days.

"Don't look so sad, baby doll," Eric said as he held her. "We'll come back here again. We'll come back to this very same hotel if you would like. I promise you that."

Wrapped safely in her lover's arms, Evie took solace in her beloved's promise.

Able to bury the sadness she felt at having to leave Paris, Evie enjoyed a long but pleasant return flight home with Eric. They passed the time by looking at pictures on their phones and reminiscing about their trip.

Before she knew it, they were walking into their cozy house, the sight of which made Evie happy. She loved their two-story cottage-style home. She had changed little of the decor from when

Eric had lived there as a single man. He had impeccable taste. The warm and inviting home had a vintage feel, with a diverse but coordinating style of furnishings. The color scheme was light taupe with creamy white trim and ornate crown molding. A splattering of colorful pillows on the sofa and tasteful artwork throughout the house added just the right splashes of color. Their home was striking. Evie loved it.

As they carried their luggage in, Evie noticed it was beginning to get dark outside. She was glad. She was tired. Going to bed early sounded like a great idea, but she was also hungry and assumed Eric was too.

"Would you like for me to fix us something to eat?" Evie asked.

Eric looked at her with a concerned expression on his face. "Now, don't take this the wrong way, but you look tired, baby. Why don't you sit down on the sofa while I fix us something to eat?"

"Would you mind?" Evie asked.

"Of course not. Come on into the living room," he replied as he took her hand. "Stretch out on the sofa, and I'll have our dinner ready tout de suite." He chuckled. "My French accent leaves a lot to be desired, huh?"

Evie laughed. "I find your French accent very sexy."

"Oh, *mon chéri*, I've only just begun." He laughed as he headed off to the kitchen.

Moments later, Evie felt Eric's gentle hand on her shoulder.

"You fell asleep on me," he said. "Come on into the kitchen, eat your dinner, and then we'll get you off to bed." He helped her to her feet. He appeared anxious. "You're feeling all right, aren't you? Just tired?"

She smiled at him. She felt exhausted but didn't want to worry him. "I'm fine," she assured him. "It's just jet lag."

Eric didn't seem convinced. "I don't think my humble dinner of tomato soup and grilled cheese is going to measure up to the delicious French cuisine we've been accustomed to this past week, but I did my best."

"Well, it smells delicious," Evie lied. Actually, the sight of her dinner made her sick to her stomach, but she wasn't about to let him know that. She would eat his generous offering or die trying.

Once they had finished eating, they headed off to bed. "We'll worry about unpacking tomorrow or even the next day. Life is our oyster, Evie," Eric said.

Evie's stomach wished he hadn't mentioned oysters.

The following morning, Evie awakened before Eric. She loved it when that happened. She enjoyed watching him sleep. He looked so quiet and peaceful. She wondered if he was having sweet dreams, because every so often, he would smile slightly in his sleep.

All too soon, his brown eyes slowly opened. He smiled at her. "You were watching me sleep again, weren't you?"

"Guilty as charged," she answered softly.

"So how are you feeling this morning?" he asked. "Well rested, I hope."

She loved how kind and considerate he was. "Yes, handsome. I feel much better this morning. In fact, I'm feeling rather naughty and rambunctious," she replied as she climbed on top of his sensual body.

"Whoa!" he said, chuckling. "At least kiss me first, you little vixen."

Evie laughed at her fun husband.

24
NEWS

One week later, Evie lay on her doctor's examination table. She was staring up at a white ceiling with a plethora of thoughts running through her mind.

"You may sit up now, Dr. Moses," Dr. Simpkins said as she walked over to the sink, snapped off her gloves, and washed her hands. "Everything appears to be just fine. Your vitals are great. Your heart sounds strong, and your lungs are clear."

Dressed in a paper gown, Evie sat up on the side of the table.

The nurse returned with a sheet of paper and handed it to Dr. Simpkins. The doctor smiled. "It appears that congratulations are in order, Dr. Moses. You're pregnant. I suspected from your exam, but these labs confirm it. Based on the dates you gave me earlier, I'd estimate your due date to be the fifth day of April."

It was a good thing Evie was sitting down, because she felt as if she might faint. Even though the in-home pregnancy test she had taken had been positive, she still couldn't believe it.

Getting pregnant at this time had not been part of Eric's and her plan. While she'd been a busy resident, it had not made good sense, so she had taken great care to choose a reliable birth control.

Even now that the craziness of her residency had come to an end, she was just starting this new phase in her life, so how could this be? She felt conflicted. What was Eric going to say? Would he be happy? She didn't know. She didn't even know how she felt at the moment.

Looking down, she placed her hand on her flat abdomen. As she gently rubbed it, the paper gown made a rustling sound. Evie sighed, allowing herself to absorb the fact that she was pregnant. She was carrying Eric's baby. A tiny part of her soul mate was growing inside her. Once that revelation sank in, she immediately began to cry.

Dr. Simpkins came over and placed a hand on Evie's shoulder. "I hope those are tears of joy," she said.

"They are," Evie said. "I'm overwhelmed but very happy."

Eric had taken the day off and gone up to Charleston to play golf with his father. He wasn't due home until around six o'clock, so Evie had all day to prepare.

She racked her brain, trying to come up with an ingenious way to tell Eric the news of their pregnancy. She thought of the usual things—balloons, a bun in the oven, an announcement cake—but those ideas didn't seem right for the two of them. Romance was such a significant part of their lives that she decided to tell him in a romantic way. She would need a lot of red roses and candles and a delectable dinner, so she stopped on her way home to gather the things she would need. After deciding to make spaghetti and meatballs, a meal she was actually good at, and store-bought crème brûlée for dessert, she paid for her purchases and headed home.

She smiled all day while preparing her intimate announcement party. She wanted to tell her parents and Cloe the unexpected and blessed news, but she had to wait to tell Eric first.

She created a walkway of red rose petals and candles from the front door to the dining room. She would light the candles at the last minute.

At a quarter past five, Evie's phone rang. It was Eric. It took all the willpower she could muster not to answer the call by squealing that they were pregnant.

"Hey, handsome," she said while bouncing up and down.

"Hi, baby doll. I'm just calling to tell you that I'm just now leaving my parents' house. I should be home by six o'clock if I don't get stuck in traffic."

"Okay," Evie said as calmly as she could. "I made you some spaghetti and meatballs for dinner."

"Baby, that sounds great. I'm starving," he said.

"Me too," she said. "And I can't wait to see you."

"Evie?"

"Yes, handsome?"

"I love you, Evie," he declared softly. "I love you more with every day that passes. I wish you could know how deeply in love with you I am."

Happy tears filled Evie's eyes at his sweet and impeccably timed affirmation. "I love you too, Eric—more than words can express. I will love you forever and for always. I hope you know that."

"I do," he whispered. "I'll see you in just a bit, baby doll."

"I'll be waiting," she said just before they said their goodbyes.

The ensuing forty-five minutes seemed to drag by. Just before six o'clock, Evie lit all the candles in the foyer leading to the dining room. The table was set with their best china. Long, tapered white candles glowed atop a crystal candleholder. The white tablecloth was adorned with red rose petals.

Wearing a pure-white dress, Eric's favorite, Evie paced while waiting impatiently for the sound of his car pulling into the driveway. She became more and more anxious as the minutes passed.

She was hesitant to call him, because he was driving. Even though he talked hands-free in his car, she didn't want to distract him. Finally, at seven o'clock, she couldn't stand it any longer. She dialed his number. The phone rang several times before the call went to voice mail. She left a tearful message for him to call her back.

Evie looked down at the candles in the foyer. They had burned out. Sighing, she pulled back the curtain to the window that looked out onto their driveway. Still no Eric. Her mind raced as to what she should do. Whom should she call?

She gave a silent prayer of thanks when she saw headlights pulling into their driveway. However, as she watched the car pull in, the realization of what she was seeing overcame her. The headlights were not from Eric's car. They were the bright lights of a police cruiser.

Immediately, her tears began to flow. She fumbled for the door handle, nearly forgetting how to operate it. She opened the door to the face of a somber and sad-looking police officer. He didn't need to say it. Evie already knew what he was going to say without a word crossing his lips. Her Eric was gone.

"Are you Mrs. Eric Moses?" the officer asked.

She nodded dutifully as tears streamed down her cheeks.

"Ma'am, may I come in?" he asked.

Evie couldn't speak. Sobbing, she nodded again and opened the door wider for him to enter their home.

"Ma'am," he said. He hesitated. "It would be best if you sat down."

As the gravity of what was happening hit her, Evie screamed, "No, no, no!" She crumpled into a sobbing heap on the floor. "Where's Eric? I want Eric!" she cried.

The officer didn't reply. As if in a fog, she felt him help her to her feet. He assisted her to the sofa, where she sat down.

Standing beside her, he said the words that dropped like a bomb, shattering Evie's heart into a million irretrievable pieces.

"I'm sorry to inform you that your husband was in a serious car accident on Interstate 64, just east of town." The officer hesitated again before continuing. "I regret to have to tell you this, but he didn't make it."

"No!" Evie shouted again. "He can't be gone! He can't be!" In a moment of sheer desperation, she asked, "Are you sure it was him? Are you positive it was Eric?" She wrung her hands, hoping a dreadful mistake had been made.

"I'm so sorry, but yes, ma'am, I am sure."

Sobbing uncontrollably, Evie put her face in her hands and began rocking back and forth on the sofa. "Oh my God!" she repeated over and over as her distraught mind struggled to comprehend what was happening. Visions of her Eric lying dead on the highway accosted her. Had he died instantly? Had he suffered? She wrung her hands again as tears poured down her face.

"Ma'am, is there anyone I can call for you?" the officer asked softly.

Evie's mind was so clouded with disabling grief that she could barely think. Finally, between gut-wrenching sobs, she answered the officer. "Cloe," she said softly and tearfully. "I want my sister."

"Yes, ma'am," the officer said.

After making the call, the officer slowly paced from the doorway to the sofa as if standing guard over Evie. Moments later, Cloe arrived. She ran in and sat down next to Evie on the sofa. Evie looked to see that her sister was crying as well.

Cloe grabbed hold of Evie and held her tightly. "I'm so sorry, sis," she said as she rocked Evie in her arms. "What can I do?"

Evie's words were muffled by sobs. "He's gone, Cloe. Eric's not coming back. I want to die too. I can't—" She couldn't speak anymore. She was afraid of what she would say.

"Don't say that, Evie. You'll get through this," Cloe said softly. "Mom and Dad and I will help you. Just hold on for one more minute. That's all. Just focus on one minute at a time."

Evie didn't want to. She didn't want to live even one second in a world without Eric in it. "I can't, Cloe," she whispered. For the life of her, she couldn't stop crying. She wondered if she ever would.

Cloe continued to hold her and rock her gently in her arms.

The front door burst open, and her parents rushed into the room. They joined Cloe and surrounded Evie and held her for what seemed like an eternity, just letting her cry.

Finally, her mother spoke. Quietly, she said, "Evie, honey, someone has to notify Eric's parents. Would you like for your father to do it?"

Evie had been so wrapped up in herself that she hadn't thought about Eric's mom and dad. They would be devastated at the loss of their only son. Sniffling, Evie raised her head from Cloe's shoulder. Wiping away her tears, she answered. "Yes, Mom. If Daddy wouldn't mind, would he please call Joseph and—" She stopped and cleared her throat. "And tell him what's happened. I can't do it," she whispered. "I can't break their hearts."

"Of course I'll make the call for you," her father said. "Don't worry."

Evie sat there. She could hear her mother's and father's muffled voices coming from the kitchen. She turned and looked into her sister's caring eyes. "I warned Eric that he drove too fast, Cloe. He felt invincible in that stupid car." Evie put her face in her hands and began to cry again. "I hate that car," she said.

25

GONE

The preceding two days had been a walking nightmare. Funeral arrangements had to be made, and Evie would not allow anyone else to make them but her. It was the last thing she could do for her Eric, and she wanted to do it herself.

She would be having a closed-casket service but took Eric's navy-blue suit to the mortuary for him to be buried in. She also took the baby-blue tie he had worn on their wedding day.

With Cloe by her side on the sofa, Evie cried as she scoured the pictures in her phone, searching for the perfect one to be placed on his casket during the service. Evie finally chose her favorite shot of Eric. It was a candid photo of him wearing a maroon sweater she had bought him for Christmas, and he was flashing her that smile he had—just for her. It shattered her to know she would never see that smile again. She put her phone to her lips and kissed the picture of her beloved.

"Let me take that and get it enlarged, printed, and framed for you, sis," Cloe said. "I would like it if you would lie down and take a short nap. Tomorrow will be ..." She trailed off. "You're going to need your strength."

Evie swallowed hard. Unreasonably reluctant to let go of her phone containing the picture of Eric, she finally relinquished it to Cloe's hand.

"Come on, sweetheart," her mother said. "Let me walk you upstairs and get you into bed."

Evie looked around the room at the grieving group of people mourning her Eric. Her parents were spending the night with her, as were Eric's. Evie attempted a grateful smile at all the eyes focused on her, but she couldn't. She doubted she would ever smile again.

On shaky legs, she climbed the stairs and entered their bedroom. Her knees almost buckled when she looked at the bed that she would never again share with Eric. She would never again have the privilege of waking before him and watching him sleep. She would never again feel his arms around her as they talked, laughed, and planned their future together. She would never again enjoy the intimacies of being in bed with her husband.

She watched as her mother turned down the covers. Trembling and sobbing, Evie climbed into the bed. Her mother covered her with a sheet and kissed her on the cheek.

"Try to get some rest, sweetheart," she said.

Evie couldn't speak. She didn't want to talk. She wanted to die.

Services began at eleven o'clock the following morning at Evie's home church. She rested in the knowledge that her loving pastor would deliver a eulogy worthy of her Eric.

Evie sat in the front row with Cloe, her parents, and Eric's parents alongside her. She stared at Eric's picture atop his bronze casket, which was adorned with a cascading arrangement of white roses. Baskets of flowers were scattered abundantly around the altar and the front of the church. Eric had been loved by many people.

Elizabeth and George were there, as were many of Eric's and her friends and coworkers from the hospital. Evie did her best to maintain her composure upon accepting their condolences but failed miserably. The only time she could stop sobbing was when she was staring at Eric's gorgeous smile staring back at her from the picture. She did her best to stay focused on his smile.

As she'd requested, Evie listened to her pastor read from the book of 1 Corinthians in the Bible—the same verses he had read at their wedding ceremony. She heard the pastor's soft words as he spoke about the attributes of love while knowing deep down in her soul that she would never love again. Her heart belonged to Eric, and it always would.

After the service, the funeral procession drove slowly to the cemetery. Evie stared blankly out the window and sobbed the entire distance as the limo carried her to the place where Eric would be laid to rest.

After finally arriving at their destination, Evie took a deep breath. She reached out for her father's hand as he helped her out of the car.

She had chosen a plot beneath a massive oak tree. It was a sunny summer day, so the tree provided cool shade for the bereft attendees while the pastor said his final graveside words. He ended the service with a prayer.

Evie stepped forward with a single long-stemmed red rose and placed it lovingly on top of Eric's casket. She lingered there, wishing she had the fortitude to say a few words about her cherished husband, but she couldn't. The only thing she could manage was a silent promise to him that she would love him forever and for always.

26

GRIEVING

It had been four weeks, and Evie had not left the home she and Eric had shared. Overcome with darkness and despair, she couldn't seem to find her way out of her grief. She couldn't bring herself to go outside; it felt disrespectful and wrong to go on with life without Eric. She just couldn't do it.

Evie's father had been understanding in letting her renege on their plan for her to join him in his practice for now.

Her devoted Eric had made generous provisions for her. He'd left her everything in his will and life insurance policies. She had need of nothing, except for Eric.

It was her tenth week of pregnancy, and Evie still had not told anyone about the baby growing inside her. She hadn't even told Cloe, who had been her rock through all of this, checking on her every single day and providing some comfort through all the pain.

It was time for her second appointment with her obstetrician, Dr. Simpkins. Evie stood in the doorway of her home with her car keys in hand. She was dressed in a pair of jeans and a pink T-shirt. It was the first time she had been out of her pajamas for a month.

Her eyes were red-rimmed and swollen. She looked terrible, but she didn't care.

Feeling a little nervous in her stomach, she willed herself into her car and drove herself to her appointment.

After waiting only a few moments in the doctor's waiting area, Evie was shown to the back.

"I'm Caroline," the nurse said as they walked down the hallway to where a tall scale was tucked into a quiet corner. "You can set your purse on the chair over there, and then please step up onto the scale for me."

Evie did as she asked.

"You've lost three pounds since your last visit." Caroline smiled sweetly at Evie. "Don't worry, though; you'll be putting on some weight here in the next few months." Gesturing to her right, she continued. "We need a urine sample, so if you can, you may use this restroom. There are instructions on the wall. When you're finished, please take a seat on the table in the room directly across the hall. The doctor will be with you momentarily."

Evie thanked her, and the nurse promptly disappeared down the hallway.

No sooner had Evie sat down on the table than Dr. Simpkins appeared. The doctor walked silently over and took Evie by the hands. "I am so very sorry to hear of your husband's passing, Dr. Moses. Please accept my deepest condolences."

As hard as she tried not to, Evie began to sob. The doctor just stood there quietly holding Evie's hands.

"I didn't even get to tell him we were pregnant," Evie cried.

"I'm so sorry," the doctor said as she squeezed Evie's fingers.

Looking into Dr. Simpkins's compassionate eyes, Evie could tell her sympathies were heartfelt. She held Evie's hands tightly without saying a word, as if allowing her patient time to collect herself. Finally, Evie was able to stop sobbing. She wiped her face and looked up at the doctor.

Dr. Simpkins spoke softly. "I see that you've lost a few pounds. That can be very common in the first trimester, due to food aversions and morning sickness, but I know it can also be brought on when you are not eating due to grief. You have been eating, haven't you? And taking your prenatal vitamins?"

"Yes, I have." Evie paused. "Well, I've been trying to."

"Let's take your blood pressure and have a listen to your heart and lungs," Dr. Simpkins said.

Evie wiped her face again with a tissue and sat quietly on the table while her doctor carried out her examination.

"Everything seems to be in order," the doctor said. "I'll see you back here in a month for your next checkup." Dr. Simpkins met and held eye contact with Evie. "If you need me in the meantime for anything, please don't hesitate to call. I don't mean to talk down to you. I know you're a doctor as well, but the first trimester in a pregnancy can be very sensitive. Please try to eat properly, get your rest, and take your vitamins."

Evie answered. "I'll try. Thank you, Doctor."

Returning home, Evie found Cloe pacing in her driveway, looking frantic. "Where've you been?" she asked while Evie was getting out of her car. "You didn't answer your phone. You scared me, sis." She reached out and squeezed Evie tightly in a hug.

"I'm sorry. I had my phone turned off. I was …" Evie trailed off.

"You were where?" Cloe demanded as she released her.

Sighing, Evie was unsure what to do. Muggy afternoon heat radiated off the paved driveway. "Come on inside. It's hot out here."

Looking skeptical, Cloe followed her inside the house. When Evie opened the door, it was as if the foyer of the home she had shared with Eric enveloped her. "Come into the living room. Let's sit," Evie said.

Once they had sat down, Cloe asked if Evie needed something cool to drink.

"I have some sodas in the fridge. I'll get us a glass."

"You stay put," Cloe said. "I'll get our drinks."

While Cloe was getting their sodas, Evie tried to decide what she should do. She knew the time would come when she had to tell everyone about the baby, but telling her family the news that she had never gotten to share with Eric somehow felt like a betrayal. Still, she couldn't put it off much longer. She quickly decided it was best to break the ice by telling her sister first.

Cloe returned with their drinks and handed one to Evie. Evie thirstily took several large swallows of the cool soda. Looking up at Cloe, she began to tear up.

"Don't cry, honey," Cloe said as she sat down and wrapped Evie in a hug. "Where have you been today?" she asked softly, as if trying to distract her distraught sister.

"I was at the doctor's office," Evie answered.

Cloe pulled back, looking panicked. "What's the matter? Are you sick?"

Evie shook her head. "No, Cloe, I'm not sick. I'm pregnant. Eric and I are going to have a baby," she cried.

Cloe's jaw dropped. As if unsure what to say, she just sat there holding Evie's hands until they collapsed together in a heap of tears.

Finally, Cloe spoke. "How long have you known?"

"Since the night Eric …" Evie hesitated. "I was going to tell him when he got home that night."

Cloe nodded as if she understood. "That's the reason for all the candles and the rose petals."

Evie nodded. "I wanted to surprise him."

"Oh, Evie, he would have been over-the-moon happy," Cloe said. "And he would have made a wonderful father—just like you'll make a wonderful mother."

"I was hoping he would be happy," Evie said tearfully. She reached for her glass on the table and took another drink of soda. The condensation droplets from the glass dripped onto her jeans, as did the tears that were rolling down her cheeks.

The two sisters sat in silence for several minutes.

"Why don't you come home with me and have dinner with Mom and Dad and me?" Cloe asked softly. "You can tell them your news and maybe stay the night with us."

Evie sighed deeply. "I'll go over so I can talk with them, but I don't think I can stay overnight. I don't think I can sleep in another bed. I have to sleep in Eric's and my bed." She looked at her sister. "I sound foolish, don't I?"

"No, you don't. Not at all, but how about I come back and spend the night with you? Would that be okay?"

Evie nodded. "I would like that," she whispered. "Thank you, Cloe."

Cloe smiled. "That's what sisters are for."

After a short ride in Cloe's car, they arrived at their parents' home. Cloe had called ahead, so their mother and father were waiting at the door when they arrived. They both seemed happy to see Evie.

"Hi, girls," Lorretta said. "Come on in. Dinner is almost on the table."

With an arm around Cloe and Evie, their dad led them into the dining room.

"It smells great in here, Mom," Cloe said.

"Thank you, sweetheart. It's beef tenderloin with your favorite twice-baked potatoes. Are you hungry, Evie?" her mother asked, sounding hopeful.

"To be honest, Mom, I hadn't given it much thought, but after smelling the delicious aroma in here, I think I may be," Evie answered quietly. She knew she needed to eat, if for no other reason than for the sake of the baby.

"Everybody take their seats, and we'll say grace so we can eat," her father said.

While her dad was talking briefly to God, Evie wondered how she felt about her relationship with God. For the life of her, she couldn't understand how a loving Father could take away the love of her life the way He had. She wasn't angry with God per se, just disappointed that He would hurt her so badly.

The prayer was over, but Evie was still deep in thought. Her mother prepared her plate for her and set it down in front of her. "Here you go, sweetheart. You need to eat. You look thin."

Evie placed her hand lovingly on her flat stomach before she picked up her fork and took her first bite of food. She chewed it slowly. It was tasty, and she realized she was famished.

"This is wonderful. Thank you, Mom and Dad, for letting me come over," she said, unable to stop the tears that were filling her eyes.

"What are you talking about, Evie? You're always welcome here for dinner or otherwise. You know that, don't you?" her father asked tenderly.

Evie nodded as a tear rolled down her cheek. Maybe she was just feeling sorry for herself, she thought, but she cried the entire time she ate—and her family let her. They comforted her with sympathetic glances and smiles, but they allowed her to cry all she wanted.

At the end of their meal, she apologized for her tears.

"Your apology is not accepted here," her father said, "because it is not needed."

Evie nodded her thanks.

Cloe looked at her as though willing her to tell them her news.

After clearing her throat, Evie said faintly, "Mom, Dad, I have something I need to tell you."

They didn't say anything. They just looked at her expectantly.

"I wanted this announcement to be so different," she said tearfully. "But here it is anyway." She looked from her mother to her father as she said the words. "Eric and I are going to have a baby. I'm pregnant."

Her parents looked shocked at first and then smiled. Neither of them responded. They seemed unsure what to say to the unexpected news.

After a few moments, her mother spoke. "How do you feel?" she asked. "Is the baby okay?"

"I'm all right, and so is the baby. I saw my doctor today, and we both checked out just fine," Evie said as she looked down and placed her hand against her stomach.

"How far along are you?" her father asked.

Evie looked up at him. He had tears in his eyes. "Ten weeks," she whispered. "I hope it's a girl. Eric would have loved a baby daughter."

"Did he know about the baby?" her mother asked timidly, looking at Evie as though she might break if she spoke too loudly or said the wrong thing.

Evie shook her head. "I didn't get to ..." She paused and tried to compose herself. "I was going to tell him the night I lost him." Tears continued to roll down her face.

Evie's mother came to her. She knelt down beside Evie's chair and grasped her hands. "I am so very sorry, sweetheart. I know that means little, but my heart is broken for you. I wish I could absorb your pain. I would if I could."

Her mother's sweet declaration touched Evie's heart. She gripped her mother's hands. "I know you would, Mom, and I appreciate that."

Evie glanced at her father. He seemed anxious, as if he didn't know what to say or do. "Let's go into the living room and have our dessert. We'll be more comfortable there," he said.

Without answering, they all stood up and walked into the living room.

"Who would like a slice of lemon pound cake and a cup of coffee?" Lorretta asked.

"None for me. Thank you, Mom," Evie answered.

The rest of the room declined dessert as well. Everyone seemed nervous and at a loss for words. It was her father who spoke first. "Evie, honey, you know you can come back home and live here with us. We would love to have you."

Evie bristled at his heartfelt invitation. There was no way she was going to abandon Eric's and her home. Leaving it would have broken her heart even more so than it already was. It would have been like leaving Eric behind, and she couldn't do that. "I appreciate the offer, Daddy. I truly do, but I can't. I won't leave our home."

He looked at her with empathy in his eyes. "I understand, honey. I just wanted you to know that you are always welcome here."

Evie managed a forced smile at her caring father. "I know, Daddy, and I thank you and Mom for making me feel loved and wanted."

"Aw, you're welcome, sweetheart," her mother said.

Cloe, who had been quiet for the majority of the evening, spoke up. "I'm going to stay the night with Evie tonight," she told her mom and dad. Turning her head toward Evie, she said, "I can move in with you if you would like. I can stay with you for as long or as little as you want me to."

Evie was caught off guard by Cloe's unselfish and kind offer. It made her start to cry again. At first, she didn't know how to feel about it, but after only a minute's thought, she answered. "Cloe, I would love to have you as a houseguest for a while. Are you sure it won't interfere with your design work?"

Cloe appeared relieved and happy. "No, it won't affect anything at all. My classes are all done online, so if you don't mind my sewing machine and other paraphernalia in your guest room, I'll be just fine working from your home."

"I won't mind. You're welcome to do whatever you would like in your room. Our house is your house."

Evie's father smiled. "Now, that's a compromise I can live with," he said, appearing pleased.

27
SISTERS

Cloe had been living with Evie for a month. Things were working out well between them. Cloe was busy for most of the day, which gave Evie the time she needed to think and to grieve. She missed Eric so much that she was in physical pain. She missed everything about him. She even missed the way he sometimes had left the house messy or hogged all the bedcovers. She missed his smile and the way he had made her laugh. Most of all, she missed his touch, his embrace, and the feeling of being cherished and loved by someone. Oh, how she missed making love with him. She ached to feel him—to feel his body intertwined with hers in an absolute expression of pure and devoted love. He was never far from her thoughts, and she planned on keeping it that way.

It was time for her second prenatal doctor visit. It was a brisk early fall morning, so Evie dressed in a pair of jeans and a long-sleeved yellow-and-black-print button-up blouse. She stood in the kitchen, having a cup of tea and a slice of toast with peach preserves. She had switched from coffee to herbal tea for the sake of the baby.

Cloe came out of her room as if on a mission. Evie had just brewed her sister a pot of coffee.

"I can smell fresh coffee," Cloe said before giving Evie a quick kiss on the cheek. She thanked her for making the coffee. Pouring herself a cup, she said, "I wish you'd let me go to the doctor with you. I wouldn't mind at all."

"I know you wouldn't, but you have your classes, and this is just a routine checkup." Evie finished her breakfast and placed the dirty dishes in the sink. "You can come with me the next time, sis. I'll be getting an ultrasound of the baby on my next visit, so you'll be able to hear the heartbeat, and hopefully we'll learn the gender."

Cloe's face lit up. "You promise you'll let me go with you next time?"

"I promise," Evie said. "Now, get back to your classes, and I'll see you in a bit."

After a quick hug, Cloe disappeared into her room.

Evie arrived at Dr. Simpkins's office and signed in. She sat down and picked up a baby magazine. An article caught her attention. It was about the mind-and-body connection between a pregnant mother and her baby. Just as she was getting interested in the article, Nurse Caroline called her name. Taking the magazine with her, Evie followed the nurse to the scale. Laying her purse aside, Evie stepped onto the scale.

"One hundred and five pounds," Caroline said. "You've lost another two pounds."

Evie immediately became anxious about her additional weight loss.

After giving a urine sample, Evie followed Caroline to an examination room. Upon entering the room, Evie sat down on the table to wait for the doctor. Just as she had settled in with the magazine article, Dr. Simpkins tapped on the door and entered the room.

"Good morning, Dr. Moses," she said.

"Why don't you call me Evie? I would like it if you did."

Dr. Simpkins smiled warmly. "All right, Evie. How are you feeling? Any morning sickness or complaints?"

"No, gratefully, I haven't been sick yet," Evie answered.

"That's good. Now let me get your vitals," she said. She took Evie's blood pressure and listened with her stethoscope. "Sounds good. Still no weight gain, but I'm not worried about that yet."

The word *yet* didn't sit well with Evie. "I'm eating as best as I can," Evie said, growing instantly emotional. "It's just hard. I miss my husband." Her eyes filled with tears, but she quickly managed to compose herself. She showed the doctor the article in the magazine she was reading. "Do you think Eric's and my baby can feel my grief and heartbreak?" she asked.

The doctor had a sad expression on her face as she nodded. "Yes, I do believe your baby feels what you feel. A baby is sensitive to a mother's emotions and state of mind. Some doctors may disagree, but I happen to subscribe to the theory in that article you're reading."

Evie felt profoundly guilty for subjecting Eric's and her baby to any form of discomfort. "I don't know how to change how I feel," she cried. "I don't know how to stop mourning or missing my husband. I don't know how to stop crying for him."

"I understand," Dr. Simpkins said in a sympathetic voice. "Please take that magazine home with you, and finish reading the article. It will offer some suggestions that may help you and your baby. There are a number of things you can do to comfort your baby. Calming music is a simple start." She smiled. "Just read the article and see," she said as she patted Evie's hands. "I could also recommend a counselor for you to talk to about your grieving process."

Evie thought for a moment. "I'll consider that," she said, immediately thinking of her beloved pastor.

"Okay," the doctor said. "On your next appointment, we'll do your eighteen-week ultrasound."

"Would it be all right if my sister and maybe my mom come with me for that?" Evie asked, wishing it could have been Eric coming with her to see their baby for the first time.

"Of course they can," Dr. Simpkins said. "Unless you need me before, I'll see you then." The doctor turned and walked out the door.

It was a nice fall afternoon when Evie walked out her front door. The colorful view of the trees in her yard and in the park across the street was an awe-inspiring sight. The green beech trees were just beginning to turn a blazing gold, which was highlighted by the sunlight shining brightly through the limbs. The beginnings of the burnt-orange-and-red sugar maples provided the perfect accent colors to the green. Evie stood there for a few moments, taking in the picturesque landscape. The artist within her attempted to surface, but Evie quickly squelched it. She had too much on her mind to even think about painting.

With Cloe shut up in her room, apparently still busy with her online studies and her next sewing project, Evie took a seat on the porch with a glass of lemonade and the baby magazine. Because she'd had such a difficult time concentrating on anything since Eric left, she had to read the article twice. It gave her a lot to think about. She made a couple of resolutions as a result of what she had just read.

The opening of the front door startled Evie a bit.

"There you are," Cloe said, seeming concerned. "I couldn't find you. Are you okay? What did the doctor say?" she asked as she took a seat next to Evie.

"I'm okay, sis. I was just sitting here reading this article about babies. The doctor said we're doing great." Evie fibbed a little. She didn't want to worry her sister.

"Mom just called and invited us over for dinner—again," Cloe said, laughing. "I don't mind going if you don't."

Evie shook her head. "No, I don't mind. I would like that. I'm going to try to start eating better for the sake of the baby, and I can't think of a better way than with Mom's tasty food."

Cloe grinned. "I'm glad to hear you say that."

"And I'm going to start jogging again." She looked over at Cloe, who appeared delighted. "I'm going to start tomorrow."

Cloe reached over and gave Evie a hug. "That makes me so happy, sis. The fresh air and exercise are going to be excellent for you and the baby."

Evie nodded as a tear rolled down her face. "If you still want to, you can come with me next month to see the doctor. We'll be able to hear the baby's heartbeat and maybe see if it's a boy or a girl."

Cloe squealed and clapped her hands. "Of course I'm still coming. You promised me I could."

Evie smiled through her tears at her precious sister. After releasing an audible deep breath, she said, "Now, let's head over to Mom and Dad's for dinner. This baby is hungry."

While sitting down to plates of open-faced roast beef sandwiches and a fresh garden salad, Evie told her inquisitive parents about her doctor visit and what Dr. Simpkins had said. As she had with

Cloe, Evie gave them an optimistic version of the visit. She didn't want to cause them any undue worry.

"Evie's going to start jogging again," Cloe announced, as if it were the best news ever.

"Good for you, sweetheart," her mother said, seeming pleased. "It will do you and the baby good to get out in the fresh fall air. Just make sure to bundle up if it's chilly out."

Evie smiled at her doting mother. "I will, Mom."

"I've got some news too," Lorretta said.

"It's big news," Dan said, beaming.

Cloe almost came out of her chair. "Well, what is it? Tell us!"

Their mother glanced at the two of them and announced happily, "I've decided to retire. Actually, I've already sold my practice. My last day at work will be in just two short months."

Evie was shocked. She'd had no idea her mother was thinking of retiring. She hoped it wasn't because of her. "What made you decide to do that?" Evie asked.

"Yeah," Cloe said, "this seems awfully sudden. You're still so young."

Lorretta smiled pleasantly. "To be honest, I'm just tired of working as a physician. I've been a doctor, and now I want to try my hand at a new profession."

"What?" Evie and Cloe asked at the same time.

"I want to try my hand at writing. I would like to write a novel," Lorretta said. She seemed somewhat timid about her announcement.

Cloe and Evie started to talk at the same time. Laughing, Cloe said, "You go first, sis."

Evie spoke up. "That's a wonderful ambition, Mom. Do you have any ideas for what you'll write?"

"I've been thinking about it for years. I have several ideas in my head, but I think my first one will be a novel about a dubious friendship between a young woman with breast cancer and an older Christian woman who shares a hospital room with her. It's kind of an unlikely kinship sort of story."

"That sounds great and very interesting, Mom," Evie said. "I'm so excited that you'll get to pursue your dream. I had no idea you had a desire to become a novelist."

"Me either," Cloe said.

With tears in her eyes, Lorretta said, "And besides that, I want to be a full-time grandma to my first grandbaby."

Evie's eyes began to sting. "Thank you, Mom. Eric's and my baby will be blessed to have you and Daddy as grandparents."

28
COMFORT

Evie sat down in the inviting office of her pastor, Dr. Charles Andrews. The room looked more like a quaint library than an office. The walls were forest green, with two sides covered in bookshelves loaded with books and tastefully accented with photographs and other religious paraphernalia. Evie imagined that many of the pieces were gifts from his parishioners, as he was greatly loved.

Dr. Andrews offered her a seat and then sat down across from her. Evie sank into the soft chair covered in green fabric.

"I'm so glad you called me, Evie. I pray I can help bring you some comfort," he said quietly.

She could see the deep empathy on her dear pastor's face. "Thank you for agreeing to talk with me," she said, already becoming emotional. Her eyes burned with the threat of tears. "Do you think you can help me?"

"Oh, Evie, I'm not sure if I can, but I know someone who can," he said, wearing a comforting smile. "God can—and will—help you through this unimaginable heartbreak if only you'll let Him."

"I want to," Evie said as the threatened tears rolled down her cheeks. "I just don't know how."

"Well, that I can help you with," he said, appearing eager. "Some people believe there are definitive stages of grief, and I suppose there is some merit to that notion. But when I'm counseling someone during the grieving process, I don't try to figure out which stage he or she is in. I simply pray and ask God to give me the right words to say—the words that the heartbroken individual in front of me needs to hear." He looked at Evie and smiled again. "Would you mind if I take your hands to pray and ask for God's guidance this morning?"

Evie responded quietly, "I wouldn't mind at all."

The elderly pastor came to Evie's chair and knelt down before her. Clasping her hands, he began to pray. "Dear heavenly Father, we come before You this morning with shattered hearts. My beloved friend Evie is in grievous pain, Father, and she needs Your help. I need Your help too, Father. Please give me guidance as Evie and I speak this morning. Please let my heart hear Your words, Father, so that I may, in turn, speak them to Evie. It is in Your Son's precious and holy name, Jesus, that we ask these things. Amen."

Evie repeated the pastor's "Amen." As soon as he let go of her hands, she took a tissue out of her pocket and wiped away her tears.

After he returned to his chair, Dr. Andrews sat quietly for a moment before speaking. "Evie, are you able to talk about your feelings?"

Evie didn't readily respond. For one thing, she was so emotional that she didn't know if she could speak coherently. She put her face in her hands and sobbed. "I miss Eric!" she cried. "I miss him so much."

"I know you do, Evie," Dr. Andrews said softly.

In desperation, she looked up at him. "Will this pain ever go away? It's so very heavy. I feel like it's crushing the life out of me."

He nodded. "I don't know if your pain will ever go away completely, but in time, it will lessen significantly. I can't tell you how long it will take. That varies from person to person. As you know, I lost my dear wife of forty-nine years a while back, so I can tell you from my own personal experience that God will help ease your pain. Scripture teaches in First Corinthians that God will not put more upon us than we can bear."

"He's coming awfully close, Dr. Andrews," Evie said. She looked down at her lap, ashamed of what she was about to reveal. "There was a time when Eric first passed that I considered taking my own life." Tears began to flow again. A few silent moments passed before she could bring herself to look her pastor in the eye again. She glanced up to see his eyes pooled with tears.

"It breaks my heart to think of you in such pain and desperation," he said. His words were wrought with emotion. "I thank God that He stopped your hands from hurting yourself. He has more for you to do down here, sweet Evie."

Sighing and shaking her head, she responded, "I can't imagine that I could be of any use to God or anyone else down here."

Dr. Andrews smiled knowingly. "You'd be surprised at what God can do in and through you, Evie."

Per her pastor's suggestion, Evie wandered around the bookstore, looking for the perfect diary in which to put down her innermost thoughts.

Most of the selection of journals had daisies and colorful patterns on them. They didn't appeal to Evie. Just as she was about to give up and move on to another store, she spotted it—the perfect journal. It was crème-colored, with a gold-embossed replica of the Eiffel Tower on it. Evie picked it up and held it close to her chest, knowing it was the perfect vehicle in which to write down her thoughts and talk to her Eric.

Evie felt slightly better after her first session with Dr. Andrews. They scheduled another time to talk the following week.

Cloe and Evie had just returned from a southern-style dinner of pinto beans, fried potatoes, sautéed greens, and cornbread at their parents' home.

"Well, that sure was a good dinner, wasn't it?" Cloe asked as Evie unlocked the front door.

"It sure was. I'm full," Evie answered while rubbing her tummy. She hoped she would gain a pound or two before her next doctor visit. If her parents and Cloe had anything to say about it, she would.

"Would you like some chocolate ice cream or dill pickles or anything, sis?" Cloe asked, smiling as she touched Evie's tummy.

Evie grinned back at her silly sister. "Not right now, thank you. Are you all finished up with your design homework?"

Cloe's smile transformed into an exaggerated frown. "No. I have at least two more hours of work to do."

"I'm sorry, sis," Evie said as she gave Cloe a good-night hug. "I'm going to get the baby a glass of milk, and then I'm going to my room to start my journaling."

"Okay, I'll see you in the morning," Cloe said as she disappeared into her bedroom.

With her glass in hand, Evie went upstairs to Eric's and her bedroom. There was a chill in the air, so she put on a pair of pajamas and climbed into bed. She looked over at Eric's empty side of the bed. Oh, how she wished he were lying next to her. She closed her eyes and smoothed her hand over his pillow. In her mind's eye, she could see his alluring dark brown eyes and his captivating smile. She would have given anything in the world to see that smile again.

Determined not to cry—but certain she would once she started writing—she piled some pillows behind her back and picked up her journal off the bedside table. With a pen in hand, she began to write.

My dearest Eric,

Oh, how much I miss you. How I wish you were here right now to wrap me in your strong arms and hold me close to your warm body. Oh, how I miss your sweet embrace and beautiful smile.

I wish I could awaken tomorrow to find that losing you was all a horrible nightmare, because that's exactly what it is, Eric. It's a horrific nightmare I can't wake up from.

I don't know how to live in a world without you in it. I'm not even sure I want to learn how. But I know I have to. I have to because of our baby. We're going to have a baby, Eric. I was going to tell you on the night I lost you.

Sometimes I wonder if you somehow know I'm carrying our child. I like to think you do.

When you first left, I wanted to die. To be honest, there are moments when I still do. I'm ashamed to admit this, but I remember vividly the night I was so distraught and emotionally exhausted that I sat on this bed with a handful of pills in one hand and our wedding picture in the other. The only thing that stopped me from swallowing those pills was you, Eric. I looked into your smiling, happy face, and I just couldn't do it. I couldn't let you down. I couldn't disappoint you like that.

I'm sure God had a hand in stopping me as well—as did our baby.

I wonder how you would have reacted if I had gotten to tell you that you were going to be a daddy. I wonder if you would have flashed me one of your trademark smiles and joyfully wrapped me in your arms. I like to think you would have. I like to think you're smiling down on us right now. I wish you could give me some kind of sign—anything to let me know you are there and are watching over us.

I know you're in heaven and are happy. Knowing that helps me make it through one more day of my life here without you. That's the only way I can survive losing you, Eric—one day at a time. I try to look ahead and smile, but I can't. I try, for the sake of our baby, not to mourn too deeply for you, but I find that almost impossible as well.

I'm doing the best I can, and I promise you I will keep on trying. And I will also keep the last promise I made to you: to love you forever and for always.

Until tomorrow. Good night, my sweet husband.

I love you.
Evie

29
WHAT IF

E vie and Cloe sat in the waiting area of Dr. Simpkins's office. They were there for her eighteen-week appointment and ultrasound. Their mom had had a last-minute office emergency and been unable to come along.

Evie watched Cloe's right leg bounce up and down with obvious anticipation. She reached out and pressed on her sister's knee.

"I'm excited," Cloe said apologetically.

"I can see that," Evie said, smiling.

Just then, Nurse Caroline called out Evie's name.

"You wait right here, and they'll come get you when they start the ultrasound," Evie told Cloe.

"Okay," Cloe said. "Don't forget me."

"How could I forget you?" Evie asked.

Stepping onto the scale, Evie was pleased to see she had gained two and a half pounds. That meant their baby was growing.

After Evie gave a urine specimen, Caroline showed her to an examination room. "You won't need to get completely undressed for this visit. The technician can just lift up your top and undo your jeans to do the ultrasound. But first, the doctor will come in to see you."

"Okay," Evie said as she took a seat on the exam table.

Sighing deeply, Evie wished Eric were there with her. Alone with her thoughts, she began to nervously wring her hands. What if they couldn't find the baby's heartbeat? What if her grief had harmed their baby?

Dr. Simpkins tapped lightly on the door and walked into the room with a smile on her face and her tablet in her hand. Looking down, she said, "I don't see any issues with your urine. Your glucose levels are normal, so that's good. I see you've put on a couple of pounds too. I'm happy to see that." Looking back up at Evie, she said, still smiling, "Now, let's give a listen to your heart and lungs and get your blood pressure."

"Okay," Evie replied.

After conducting her examination, the doctor put her hand on Evie's shoulder and asked, "How are you doing, Evie? Have you given any thought to me referring you to a grief counselor?"

Evie teared up a little. "I'm doing okay. I've been getting counseling from my pastor at my church once a week. He's been a great help."

"That's so good to hear," the doctor said, "but if you need anything at all from me, all you have to do is call."

"I appreciate that, Dr. Simpkins."

"How are you feeling physically? Any complaints that you need to tell me about?" the doctor asked.

Evie thought for a moment before replying. "No, ma'am, no complaints. As far as how I feel physically, I'm doing okay. I have my morning walks or slow jogs, and I'm trying to eat healthy. I'm doing my best for the baby."

"I know you are, Evie," the doctor said, appearing pleased. "So are you ready for your ultrasound?"

"Yes, Doctor, I think I'm ready," Evie answered, still feeling somewhat emotional and apprehensive. "Would someone please bring my sister back? Her name is Cloe, and she's out in the waiting room."

"Of course. You just hold tight, and the technician will be right with you, and then someone will get your sister."

No sooner had the doctor left the room than a young woman entered. She extended her hand. "Hi. I'm Cindy, and I'll be doing your ultrasound for you today," she said pleasantly.

"Hi, Cindy. I'm Evie."

"Well, Evie, let's get you ready, shall we?"

After Cindy got her into position on the table, placing her on her back with her shirt pulled up and her jeans undone, Cloe entered the room.

"I'm just in time for the show, I see," she said as she took hold of Evie's outstretched hand.

"Yes, you are. We're just about to start," Cindy said as she squirted warm gel onto Evie's stomach and began to move the ultrasound wand around her belly. "First, let's listen to the heartbeat," she said.

Evie listened intently, but all she could hear was a static sound. Gripping Cloe's hand, she began to panic as the technician continued to explore her stomach with the wand. Looking to her sister, Evie felt her eyes fill with tears. Cloe appeared frightened as well. But then Evie heard it: the sound of the baby's heartbeat filled the small room. It was a rapid, swooshing sound that Evie had heard before as a doctor, but now she was hearing it as a mother. Motherhood became real to her at that moment. She began to cry.

"Your baby's heart rate is one hundred forty-five beats per minute, which is perfectly normal. It sounds very strong and healthy."

"Did you hear that, sis?" Cloe asked.

Evie couldn't speak, but she nodded.

"Now let's have a look at your baby," Cindy said cheerfully.

When Evie turned her head toward the monitor, she gasped in awe at the sight of Eric's and her baby. It rendered her speechless.

"Oh my gosh!" Cloe exclaimed. "It's a tiny baby." Pointing to the screen, she said, "Look at how much it's moving around."

Cindy laughed. "It sure is. That's good. That means the baby is healthy and active."

The technician continued her exam, measuring the tiny arms and legs and just about every other aspect of the little being growing inside Evie. As she worked, she described to Evie and Cloe what she was doing. "Based on my measurements, I can tell that your baby weighs about six ounces and is about five inches long. Also, I don't see anything that would make me change its expected due date. Rather than calling the baby *it*, would you like to know the gender, or would you rather be surprised?"

Finally finding her voice, Evie answered softly, "We would like to know now if you can tell us."

"I sure can," Cindy said as she pointed to the screen. "It's an honor for me to get to tell you that you're having a baby daughter. It's a little girl."

Evie began to cry again, and Cloe squealed and bounced up and down.

"It's a little girl!" Cloe repeated loudly. "I'm going to have a baby niece. I'm so excited!"

Evie could feel Cloe's eyes upon her. She turned her head to look at her enthusiastic sister. Evie felt blessed to have her by her side, but she wished Eric could have been there too. Missing him must have shown on her face. Evie watched as Cloe's zeal began to dampen.

"Are you okay, sis?" Cloe asked.

"Yes—yes, I'm all right," Evie answered. Trying desperately to push her grief aside in order to allow herself to absorb this thrilling moment in her life, she was finally able to smile softly. "I got my wish, Cloe. We're having a little girl."

Cloe's passion returned with a vengeance. "Yes, we are!" she exclaimed.

Cindy had been sitting quietly by while Evie and Cloe celebrated the gender announcement. "Would you like some pictures of your baby girl?" She pointed to the screen. "Look," she said, smiling. "She's sucking her thumb."

"Oh my gosh! That's the sweetest thing I've ever seen," Cloe said.

Evie could see that her sister was about to cry. Cloe was going to make a devoted and wonderful aunt. Their baby would be blessed to have her.

"We would love some pictures," Evie answered.

Evie had never seen Cloe so excited. "Let's stop off at the bakery to get a celebratory cake to take home," Cloe said. "We can get one with pink flowers and have them write, 'It's a girl,' on it. Everyone will be so surprised and happy."

Eric's parents were at Evie's parents' home, waiting to hear how Evie and the baby were doing and hoping to learn if she was carrying a boy or a girl.

Evie grinned at her precious sister. "I think that's a fantastic idea."

"Me too!" Cloe exclaimed. "I'm so glad you're getting the little girl you wanted."

"I am too," Evie said. "Eric would have loved having a baby girl. He would have loved a son too, but I can just see him doting on his daughter." Evie dropped her head and sniffed.

"Aw, sis, don't cry. Please don't cry," Cloe said from the driver's seat. "Look. We're at the grocery store," she said, as though trying to distract a distressed child.

Evie cleared her throat. "Okay. I'm sorry. Let's go get that pink cake."

"With chocolate ice cream," Cloe added.

When Evie and Cloe walked into their parents' home, everyone was seated around the living room, looking anxiously at Evie. Cloe was carrying the cake. Without saying a word, she set the box down on the coffee table and then removed the lid. Evie watched as all eyes fell upon the cake. Seconds later, cheers and smiles ensued. Everyone stood and rushed Evie. Smothered by hugs and kisses, Evie was overwhelmed by the outpouring of love and support for her and the baby.

Finally, everyone sat back down in the living room to chat while Evie and her mother took the cake to the kitchen to get it plated and served.

"I'm glad to have a moment alone with you, Evie," her mother said with tears in her eyes. "I wanted to congratulate you on having a baby girl. Motherhood will be the greatest challenge of your life, but it also comes with the greatest joy—especially from a delicate yet strong and precious little girl."

Evie hugged her mother and sighed. "This is a lot to take in," she said. "I'm scared, Mom. What if I can't do this alone—without Eric?"

Her mother turned from the cake to face her. Placing her hands gently on Evie's shoulders, she replied, "You are a lot of wonderful things, my sweet daughter, but you are not alone. You have all of us to help you in any way we can. Do you understand?"

Gratefully, Evie nodded.

As they headed back to the living room, they met Cloe. She had an excited expression on her face. "May I show the others the ultrasound pictures?" she asked. "Or would you rather show them?"

Evie smiled at her sister's anxiousness. "The pictures are in my purse in the hallway. You can go get it and show them if you want."

"Yea!" Cloe exclaimed as she bounded to the foyer.

After everyone had enjoyed the cake and ice cream and marveled over the ultrasound pictures, Katherine spoke softly, "I know it's soon. I mean, you just found out, but do you have a name picked out yet?"

All eyes were on Evie. "As a matter of fact, I do have a name picked out already," she answered as she looked around the room. "Eric's and my baby will be named after her father and my mom and sisters. I'm going to name her Erica Ann." Evie couldn't help it, nor did she try; she let the tears flow down her cheeks as she spoke their baby's name for the first time. She couldn't wait to tell Eric about it in her journal.

30
CHANGES

F all had turned into winter, so the air felt cold on Evie's face as she stepped out the door for her daily jog. She was bundled up good and warm. Cloe had seen to that. She hovered over Evie like a loving mother bird. The attention Cloe paid her warmed Evie's heart.

"Okay, Erica," Evie said as she massaged her growing baby bump, "let's get us some exercise."

The baby was active and kicked a lot. That morning was no different.

Evie had outgrown her regular clothes and was wearing maternity outfits now—fashionable ones that Cloe meticulously helped her pick out.

Evie had hired a contractor to create an opening in the wall that would connect her and Eric's bedroom to the new nursery. The contractor's name was Joey Leadford. He seemed to be about Evie's age and was shy and accommodating.

As she walked, she thought about the design for the baby's room. With Cloe's input, she had settled on an antique light crème gold for the walls. The window treatments were horizontal blinds with baby-pink shears and light crème curtains that would be draped and tied back. She and Cloe had found the perfect furniture for the room. The crib was ivory wood with an antique feel to it. Evie had purchased a matching changing table, chest of drawers, bookshelf, and floor lamp. She had found some lovely muted paintings and a beautiful pink-and-crème wall hanging that would grace the walls of the nursery. One painting would go above the bookshelf, and one would go above the changing table, while the wall hanging would go next to the window.

Of course, the crib would be the focal point of the room and would be centered on a crème-and-pink area rug on the wood floor. Over the crib would hang a tasteful chandelier, and in the corner would be a comfy crème-colored rocking chair.

Evie smiled as she thought about holding and rocking Eric's and her baby.

"You're going to have a beautiful room, Erica Ann," she said as she massaged her belly. "I can't wait to see it finished, which should be any day now, and I can't wait to see you either."

Evie continued to walk through the park in the chilly air. Even though all the trees were bare, Ritter Park was still lovely. As she turned for home, Evie sighed, missing Eric.

Christmas was just around the corner. This would be her first Christmas without her husband. Evie wasn't sure how she was going to get through it. With a lot of counseling, prayer, and journaling, she supposed. Thanksgiving had been bad enough, but Christmas would be even worse.

She returned home and took off her coat, scarf, and gloves. As she headed for the kitchen for a cup of hot tea, Cloe caught her in the hallway. "Joey's been waiting for you," she said teasingly.

"He has?" Evie asked. "What for?"

Cloe grinned and shrugged.

"Cloe Ann, you are such a troublemaker," Evie said, smiling as she headed toward the stairs.

"After you finish with Joey, we are going out to purchase a Christmas tree," Cloe told her.

Evie raised her hand to acknowledge her sister but said nothing.

As Evie opened the door and stepped into the nursery, it took her breath away. The adjoining doorway's wood trim was completed. The walls were painted, and the window treatments were hung. The chandelier was hanging, and the furniture was in place, except for the crib.

She clapped her hand over her mouth as tears filled her eyes. After she gained her composure, she said, "It's positively lovely, Joey. You did a fantastic job."

He grinned, apparently pleased with her praise. "Thank you, Dr. Moses."

"I told you, Joey: please call me Evie."

"Okay, Evie," he said, sounding reluctant. "I saved assembling the crib for you."

"I'm so happy," she said. "I wanted to help put my baby's bed together."

"It won't be a hard job," Joey said. "I'll do all the heavy parts."

Evie smiled at him, and he smiled back.

As they worked together in constructing the crib, Evie tried to pull Joey out of his shell. "So tell me about yourself, Joey," she said.

"Not much to tell," he said shyly. "I was born and raised here in Huntington. I graduated high school and college here. Guess I'll be here all my life."

"Is that what you want, Joey? You seem a bit reluctant."

"Yes, ma'am. I love it here. It just doesn't seem like much of a dream life, though, does it?"

Evie thought before answering him. "Dreams are what we make of them, Joey. There was a time when I dreamed of becoming an artist, but that dream changed. Actually, it was changed for me, but that doesn't matter. I became a doctor, and if I hadn't, I never would have met my husband and been building this fantasy nursery now."

He looked at her, a bit confused.

"What I'm trying to say is to follow your heart, Joey, but also be open to suggestions from people who love you and want what's best for you." She looked around her. "You do amazing work with your hands, Joey. You create beautiful things. That must be very fulfilling."

"Thank you. It is," he said as he knelt down and screwed in the headboard that Evie was holding in place. "I love my work. It's very rewarding, especially when it makes other people happy. My parents wanted me to become a lawyer, but I followed my heart, like you said."

"Then congratulations, my friend. You have realized your dream."

"Thank you, Dr.—Evie," he said with a bashful smile.

By the time they had finished chatting, the crib was complete, and Evie was pleased. "It looks so pretty. Thank you, Joey," she said. She couldn't help but feel a pang in her heart. She wished she and Eric had been able to build their baby's crib together.

Joey offered her his right hand. "You're welcome, and thank you for the opportunity to work for you."

Taking his hand, she said, "I'm so glad I chose you. I'm blessed that I saw your ad online. I couldn't have asked for a better man for the job."

After putting the finishing touches on the crib and doing one final inspection of the nursery, Joey offered to put up the paintings and wall hanging, but Evie declined. She wanted to do that herself.

They walked downstairs, and Evie paid him the balance due on the job, plus a hefty tip. Joey deserved it. She liked him.

After they said their goodbyes at the door, Evie turned around to find Cloe standing there. She was grinning. "That poor boy is smitten and smitten good," she said.

Evie grinned at her silly sister. "You're crazy, Cloe. Look at me," she said with her arms spread wide. "I'm a fat pregnant lady." Her smile quickly faded. "Besides, my heart belongs to Eric, and it always will."

"I'm sorry for teasing you, Evie. I was only trying to make you smile," Cloe said softly. "But to clarify, you're a beautiful, fat pregnant lady," she said, smiling. "Now, put on your coat. We're going out for an early dinner, and then we're going to go pick out our Christmas tree."

Standing in the kitchen on Christmas morning, Evie was having a cup of herbal tea. She looked in her living room at the glimmering crystal lights and the red and green ornaments on the tree she and Cloe had decorated. She had been dreading the holidays and hoped they soon would be over. She missed Eric so much that her heart actually ached inside her chest. She remembered celebrating last Christmas and New Year's with him as if it had been only yesterday. Mostly, she remembered his surprise proposal after all the hoopla of their first holiday together was over. She would never forget those wonderful days.

Sighing deeply, she took another sip of tea. Her baby moved and kicked inside her. Evie had gained ten pounds, and it was all baby bump. She placed her hand on her protruding tummy as her child made her presence known. She grinned at her rowdy baby.

"Merry Christmas!" Cloe exclaimed as she entered the kitchen, startling Evie a bit.

Looking at Evie's hand on her tummy, Cloe asked, "Is Erica kicking? Can I feel?" Cloe's enthusiasm about the baby was obvious. She insisted on being part of every aspect of the pregnancy.

"She sure is," Evie answered. "She wants to wish you a merry Christmas."

Cloe placed her hand on Evie's tummy. To Cloe's obvious delight, the baby gave her several good kicks. "Does that hurt?" she asked.

"Not really," Evie answered. "It feels uncomfortable when she's kicking my bladder or my ribs, but for the most part, I like to feel her moving. It sort of scares me when she's sleeping."

"I wonder if I'll ever get married and have a baby," Cloe said, appearing contemplative.

"You're just twenty-one, my little sister. You have plenty of time before your biological clock starts ticking," Evie said teasingly. "Do you want to have breakfast, or should we head home to help Mom prepare dinner?"

"You gotta give Erica a glass of milk and a piece of toast, but then I say we go on over to give Mom a hand."

The place settings for the Edwards family Christmas dinner table had increased by two. Eric's parents, Joseph and Katherine, had been invited and seemed pleased to accept the invitation to celebrate the holiday.

As usual, Evie's mother had outdone herself with the food. She had prepared a golden roasted turkey and a pineapple-covered, brown-sugar-glazed ham as the main course, with plenty of her specialty side dishes to go along with it. Her candied yams, whipping-cream mashed potatoes, green beans almondine, corn pudding, glazed brussels sprouts, and macaroni and cheese rounded out the meal.

Evie set the table with the red-and-white Christmas china, while Cloe helped their mother in the kitchen. Just as Evie finished with the place settings, the doorbell rang. "I'll get it," she said, knowing it would be Eric's parents on the other side.

"Hello, you two. Come on in out of the cold," Evie said as she opened the door wide for them to enter. The chilly blast of air that greeted Evie from the outside caused her to shiver.

She took her in-laws' coats and scarves, hung them on the coatrack, and invited them into the living room.

"First, let's have a look at you, my dear," Katherine said. "You look so pretty sweetheart, especially in your red sweater." She looked down at Evie's little baby bump. "May I?" she asked timidly.

"Of course," Evie replied.

Katherine gently placed her hand on Evie's stomach. Evie watched as Katherine closed her eyes and smiled as the baby kicked. Evie could only imagine what was going through the grieving mother's mind, but she assumed they were both thinking about the same thing: Eric and how excited he would have been at the prospects of becoming a daddy.

When Katherine opened her eyes, Evie could see that she was on the verge of crying. Apparently, her husband saw it too. He spoke up.

"I agree with Katherine. You look beautiful, Evie," Joseph said.

"Thank you both. Now, come on in, and make yourselves at home."

The Edwards family greeted their guests warmly with smiles and hugs and offered seats.

"Dinner's almost ready," Lorretta said with a sigh as she wiped her hands on a dish towel. "Would either of you care for something to drink before I head back to the kitchen?"

Katherine and Joseph both declined a beverage and sat down on the sofa next to Evie.

"So how are you and the baby doing today?" Katherine asked.

Evie stayed in constant touch with Katherine and Joseph. She felt Eric would have wanted her to; besides, she genuinely liked her in-laws. They had never been anything but kind and accepting of her. The couple was even considering moving closer to Huntington so they could be nearer to their granddaughter.

"We're doing well," Evie replied as she reached out and patted Katherine's hand. "Don't worry." By the troubled look on Katherine's face, it seemed that not worrying didn't come easily for her.

Lorretta and Cloe emerged from the kitchen. "I'm happy to say that dinner is ready to be served," Lorretta said.

"It's about time," Dan said jokingly. "We're about to starve to death in here."

Everyone laughed as they made their way to the dining room.

Her mom and dad took their seats at either end of the table, with Evie and Cloe on one side and Katherine and Joseph on the other.

"Everything looks so delicious," Katherine said. "We're so glad you all invited us down."

"Of course," Lorretta said. "You and Joseph are family. You're always welcome here."

"Well, let's get this show on the road," Dan said, smiling. "But first, let's bow our heads and thank our Maker."

Everyone bowed his or her head as Dan said the prayer. "Thank You, heavenly Father, for this bountiful table of food and for the precious hands that prepared it. Thank You for this beautiful Christmas Day and, most of all, for the reason we celebrate this season: our Lord and Savior, Jesus Christ. Please comfort our hearts, and give us peace this day. In Jesus's name we pray. Amen."

"Amen" was recited by all.

"Dan, if you'll carve the turkey and the ham, we'll get some food into our bellies," Lorretta said, laughing.

After filling their plates, they began to eat. Sounds of enjoyment of the food, words of praise for the cook, and laughter were abundant while they enjoyed the meal. Evie joined in as best as she could without Eric.

"How in the world did you learn to cook so well?" Katherine asked Lorretta as she took another bite of the candied yams.

"I was never really taught," Lorretta answered. "I suppose I just have a love for it, and it comes out in my cooking."

"You're a gifted doctor, an amazing cook, and a soon-to-be famous novelist," Dan said.

"What?" Katherine asked, appearing pleasantly shocked. "I didn't know you were a writer as well as a phenomenal cook."

Lorretta seemed embarrassed by the attention. "We'll have to see how good of a writer I am. I'm just a beginner." While looking around at the empty plates on the table, as if anxious to change the subject, she said, "Now, who wants dessert? We have pumpkin mousse pie, pecan pie, and lemon curd coconut cake."

Just then, the baby gave Evie a stout kick to the ribs. "Ouch," she said, and Cloe's hand went immediately to her prominent little belly.

"Erica says she wants some cake," Cloe said.

Laughter from around the table filled Evie's ears.

Exhausted from the day's events, Evie noticed that her calves and ankles were swollen, which was not uncommon for her or any other pregnant woman.

Happy to be retired to her room, Evie slipped into her pajamas, got into bed, and picked up her journal. She glanced into the adjoining nursery. It was perfect and beautiful, just as Eric's and her baby was going to be.

She picked up a pen and began to write.

My dearest Eric,

It's Christmas, and I miss you so much, my sweet husband. I would give anything if you could be here with me and the baby right now. We need you so much. I'm doing the best I can without you, but it's hard, my love.

Our little girl is kicking me right now. She's making her presence known and saying hello to her daddy. I can almost see the excitement and awe on your face, with your gentle hands on my belly, feeling your baby move inside me. Oh, how I long to experience that moment with you. I mourn the loss of the moments we won't be able to share—the birth of our baby, watching her grow, and every little milestone in her life. I will miss you during every single one, but you will be with me in spirit. You will live on in my heart, and I will make sure Erica grows up knowing all about her remarkable daddy. I have a framed picture of you on her bookshelf, overlooking her crib. You are smiling your spectacular smile and looking so happy. I will make sure she sees your smile every single day of her life.

I've been thinking about a very important decision I needed to make. I've decided I'm going to take a five-year leave from practicing medicine. Daddy and his partners have been very understanding and kind to me and are willing to let me take an extended sabbatical in order to raise our baby until she starts school. I don't want to leave her in the hands of a babysitter, Eric. I want the hands our baby feels on her tiny body to be her mother's loving hands. I want to witness every milestone in her life with my own eyes. I want to watch her roll over for the very first time, say her very first word, and take her very first step. I don't want to miss those things. I want to experience them all so that I can share them with you.

I want you to know I'm doing all I can for your parents. They are so heartbroken, and I can feel their pain. I know their pain. I'm doing my best to include them in the baby's life. I think that helps. I hope so. I love them, Eric. I love them for you and for me and for the baby.

I'm looking into the nursery right now. Soon our little baby will be sleeping in her picturesque room with her daddy watching over her. I can't wait to hold her. I hope she looks like you. I hope she has your caring dark eyes and captivating smile. I pray she does.

It's snowing outside. Oh, how I wish you were here to hold me like you did that first night we were in bed together—the night you proposed to me. I will never forget that night. I will never forget how it felt to be held by you for the very first time while I slept. I have never felt such comfort, assurance, safety, and love as I did that night and every night thereafter that I was blessed to be in your arms.

I miss you, Eric, and I love you—forever and for always.

Good night, my love.
Evie

31

TIMING

February brought with it blustery days and even colder nights. Evie couldn't wait for warmer weather to come.

Cuddled up under a blanket, she and Cloe had just finished watching a movie on television. Evie shifted restlessly, struggling to find a comfortable position. Her lower back ached, and it seemed as though she spent more time in the bathroom than she did out.

"Are you okay, sis?" Cloe asked as she clicked off the television. She had a concerned expression on her face.

"Yeah, I'm all right," Evie replied. "Just tired, I guess."

"Well, it's probably time for both of us to head to bed anyway," Cloe said as she stood and reached out her hand to help Evie up off the sofa. "Do you and the baby need anything before we go—something to eat or drink?"

Evie smiled at her caring little sister. She didn't know what she would have done without her. Cloe was a godsend. "No, thank you, Cloe. I think the baby and I just need to get some rest."

"Okay then. I'll walk you upstairs," she said.

Evie accepted her sister's kind offer.

Once she was in her bedroom and changed into her pajamas, she climbed into bed and covered up. With pillows at her back and her journal resting on her baby bump, she began writing. She wrote page after page to Eric. She had a lot of things to tell him, especially about the baby.

After placing her journal on the nightstand, she flipped off the bedside lamp.

Despite the mounds of pillows for added support, Evie found it difficult to get comfortable. Even lying down, her lower back continued to ache. Massaging her tummy, she closed her eyes, hoping a good night's sleep was what she needed. After a few moments, she felt herself slipping into unconsciousness.

Evie's eyes popped open as a sharp cramp in her lower belly awakened her. She looked at the clock. It was three in the morning. Feeling the need to urinate, she sat up on the side of the bed. The discomfort in her lower back that she had fallen asleep with was still there.

After going to the bathroom, she lay back down on the bed. Her eyes were heavy, but she couldn't seem to go back to sleep. She was concerned. Something was wrong, and she knew it.

Fifteen minutes later, another cramp in her lower abdomen gripped her. Her heart began to pound. "Not now, baby. It's not time," she whispered as she stroked her stomach.

Watching the clock, Evie waited. Sure enough, fifteen minutes later, another pain hit. It lasted about forty seconds. It felt like an intense menstrual cramp. After the pain subsided, Evie went to the restroom again. Her heart skipped a beat when she saw stains of bright red blood in her underwear.

"Please, God, help me," she prayed tearfully. "Please don't let me be having a miscarriage. I can't lose my baby."

She went downstairs and awakened Cloe.

"What's the matter?" Cloe asked as she shot up in bed. "Are you all right?"

"No, something is wrong, Cloe." Evie felt a tear roll down her cheek. "I'm scared. I think I'm in labor."

"But it's not time for the baby to come yet," Cloe said, as if Evie didn't already know. "You've got almost seven weeks to go."

"Will you come sit with me in the living room while I call Dr. Simpkins?"

"Of course I will."

They sat side by side on the sofa while Evie dialed the doctor's number. She explained what was happening to the answering service and was assured her doctor would receive her message immediately. As she pressed the disconnect button, another cramp gripped her. She bent over and whimpered.

Cloe jumped up off the sofa. "We'd better call Mom and Dad," she said as she began to pace back and forth.

Evie could hear the fear in her sister's voice. "No, not yet. Let's see what the doctor says first," Evie said as the pain subsided.

Moments later, her phone rang. She put the call on speaker so Cloe could hear as well.

"Hello," Evie said tearfully.

"Hi, Evie," Dr. Simpkins said. "Tell me what's going on."

Evie told the doctor about the cramps and lower back pain and spotting.

"How often are the pains coming?" Dr. Simpkins asked.

"About every fifteen minutes. I'm scared, Doctor!" Evie cried. She despised this feeling of being weak and helpless, but she couldn't seem to overpower it.

The doctor spoke in a calm and reassuring voice. "Don't be frightened, Evie. It may only be Braxton Hicks, but because of the bleeding and early gestation, I'm going to have you go to the emergency room at Cabell Huntington Hospital to be checked out."

Evie was worried and speechless. Even though she was a doctor herself, she was a surgeon, not an obstetrician. "Okay, Doctor," she finally said. "Do you think …" She paused. "What if the baby's coming now?"

"Then we'll handle it together. Now, prepare an overnight bag, and go to the ER."

"Okay," Evie said.

Cloe was already up and offering her help. "I'll go upstairs and pack you a suitcase and bring you some clothes down. I don't want you climbing the stairs." Cloe was talking so fast that Evie could barely understand her. "Then I'll get dressed, and we'll get you to the hospital. Don't worry. Everything's going to be okay."

"All right. Thank you, Cloe."

Cloe returned hurriedly with clothes for Evie. While sitting on the sofa, Evie dressed as quickly as she could. As she was putting her arm into her sweater, another pain hit, causing her to double over.

Cloe sat down beside her on the sofa. She massaged Evie's back. "Just breathe. It's going to be okay," she said, sounding as if she were about to start crying.

Once the pain had passed, Cloe jumped up and hit the automatic start button on her car's key fob. "Let's get your coat on and get you to the hospital."

Appreciative of her sister's help, Evie put on her coat and walked to the car. It was dark and cold outside. The wind was blowing, and she shivered all over. Cloe opened the passenger door and helped her into the car.

"It's okay, sis," Cloe whispered.

The hospital was only ten minutes away. As soon as Cloe pulled into a parking space, another pain came. Evie groaned and held on to her stomach. She rocked back and forth in her seat for the duration of the cramp. Leaning back, she breathed deeply.

"Is it over?" Cloe asked, sounding worried.

"Yes. Let's get inside," Evie answered, anxious to get help for her baby.

With Cloe clinging to her arm, the two walked into the hospital.

"We think my sister's in labor," Cloe told the receptionist behind the desk.

"I'm not due for almost seven more weeks," Evie said. "But I'm having cramps every fifteen minutes, and I'm spotting. My doctor, Dr. Sally Simpkins, told me to come to the ER." Evie's eyes filled with tears. She was frightened.

The receptionist smiled kindly. "I remember you, Dr. Moses. We met briefly once before, but I'll need your full name and birth date, please."

Evie gave the woman the information she requested and presented her medical insurance card and driver's license.

"You just have a seat, Dr. Moses, and a nurse will be out to get you momentarily."

No sooner had Cloe and Evie sat down in the sparsely filled room than a nurse called her name. Both Evie and Cloe stood. The nurse introduced herself as Diana and extended her hand to Evie.

"Don't worry," she said soothingly. "We're going to take good care of you and your baby."

After telling Cloe she would have to wait in the waiting room until Evie was settled in, Diana led Evie to an examination room.

"I'll need you to get undressed and into this gown for me," Diana said. "Then I'll come back and start an IV and get your vitals. Do you need my help in getting undressed?" she asked.

Evie shook her head. "No, thank you. I can do it."

"Okay," Diana said. "I'll be back in just a minute."

True to her word, Diana returned shortly after Evie changed and lay down on the examination table. As Evie stretched out her arm for Diana to take her blood pressure, another cramp gripped her. Evie grabbed her abdomen and pulled her knees up. She groaned as the pain intensified. Finally, it let up, and Evie was able to regain her composure. Looking into Diana's eyes, she said, "I'm scared. I'm not due for seven more weeks." She began to cry. She was an emotional mess, and she knew it.

Diana stroked Evie's outstretched arm. "Try not to worry," she said. "Dr. Hatch will be in to see you in just a minute to check you out. He's a fantastic doctor. You'll like him. First, let me quickly get your blood pressure and start an IV before another contraction comes. I'm also going to put a fetal heart rate monitor on your tummy to keep a check on the baby too. Then I'll go get your sister so she can come back and be with you."

"Thank you so very much for your kindness," Evie said.

"No thanks necessary," Diana replied.

After completing her tasks and readying Evie to be seen by the doctor, the nurse left the room with the promise to return with Cloe.

No sooner had Diana closed the door than the doctor entered. "Hello, Evie," Dr. Hatch said quietly as he walked up to the side of her bed. "What's going on?"

Evie knew Dr. Hatch through Eric. They had been close coworkers and friends.

"Hi, David," she said. "I don't know what's happening. I'm not due for seven more weeks."

Looking at the tablet in his hand, he said, "Your vitals and blood pressure are good—one hundred fifteen over seventy-five—and the baby's heart tracing looks good too. I'll need to do a pelvic exam if that's okay."

"Whatever you need to do is fine with me," Evie said. "Just help my baby."

After examining her, Dr. Hatch said, "You seem to be in early preterm labor. Your cervix has begun to soften and dilate as well. You're at four centimeters right now. I'm going to call Dr. Simpkins and recommend that you be admitted to the hospital. She'll examine you and do everything she can to slow down your labor, but only time will tell. We'll have to wait and see."

"Okay," Evie whispered. She stared helplessly at the doctor. "Is my baby going to be all right, David?"

He looked at her sympathetically. Placing a hand on her shoulder, he said, "Try not to worry, Evie. We're going to do all we can for you and your baby."

After Evie thanked him, he turned and walked out the door. Sobbing, she covered her face with her hands. *Please, God, don't take my baby away*, she prayed silently.

She heard the door open again. As she lowered her hands and tried to compose herself, Cloe and her parents entered the room. They immediately surrounded her bed. Unconditional love and deep concern were written all over their faces.

"The doctor said I'm in preterm labor. They're going to admit me to the hospital," she told them while doing her best to stop crying.

Everyone seemed hesitant, as if choosing the right words to say. Before anyone could say anything, another labor pain came. The contractions were becoming stronger and lasting longer. Evie groaned as the pain enveloped her. She felt her mother's hand on hers.

"Just breathe, sweetheart. Just breathe through the pain."

After the cramping subsided, Evie looked up to see Dr. Hatch entering the room again. He walked up next to her bed. "We have a room ready for you in the maternity wing. I spoke with Dr. Simpkins on the phone and gave her an update on your condition. She's on her way to the hospital. She'll examine you and decide if she can stop your labor or if you're going to deliver early." He smiled at her. "Like I said before, Evie, try not to worry."

Thinking that was easier said than done, Evie thanked him for his kindness, and he left the room.

Evie lay on her back in the immaculate and brightly lit birthing room, which would serve as her labor, delivery, and recovery suite. Dr. Simpkins had told her she was too far along to stop her labor. Her baby was coming that day. Evie was in active labor and was dilated to six centimeters. The contractions were coming every two to three minutes.

Cloe and her mother were sitting in the birthing room with her. Her father had gone home and was calling Katherine and Joseph to tell them Evie was in labor.

Rolling onto her side, Evie sat up on the side of the bed. "I need to walk around," she said. "My back hurts."

Cloe immediately stood up from her chair. "Do you need any help?"

Evie forced a smile. "No, thanks, sis. I'm okay."

She paced the femininely decorated room, hoping that movement would speed up the dilation process. She felt another contraction coming on. Groaning and bending over, she grabbed her stomach. Her mom came to her side and began massaging her back.

The cramps were getting more and more intense. This one was stronger than the last. They were worse than Evie had anticipated. Her face and back were beaded with perspiration. She glanced over at the beeping monitor attached to her stomach. It indicated the baby's heart rate was normal at one hundred and twenty beats per minute. Evie's vitals were stable as well.

Dr. Simpkins entered the room just as the contraction eased. "Evie, would you like to reconsider and have an epidural?" she asked.

"No. Not yet," Evie replied. "I think I want to try to do it without medication. I can change my mind later if I want to, can't I?"

"You can get an epidural all the way up until you're fully dilated," the doctor answered reassuringly. "If you'll get back in bed, I'll check to see how far along you are."

After examining her, Dr. Simpkins said, "You're at eight now, Evie, so it won't be long. The contractions will start getting stronger and more frequent."

With that, Lorretta and Cloe came to stand by her bed.

"How much longer will it be?" Evie asked as Cloe patted her face with a damp washcloth.

The doctor shook her head. "There's no way to tell, but without medication, it should move more quickly."

Five torturous hours later, Evie was lying on her back in the bed. Both of her legs were supported by stirrups from her knees down. Cloe and her mom were at her side. She could feel Cloe's hand clamped down on her arm. Dr. Simpkins was fully gowned and sitting at the foot of her bed. The neonatologist from the NICU was standing by, waiting for the baby.

The pain in Evie's body was consuming. She hurt all over. She felt incredible pressure and cramps in her lower body, and her legs were shaking violently.

"What's wrong with her?" Cloe cried. "Why is she shaking like that?"

"It's absolutely normal," the doctor said calmly. "Maybe you should sit down and let your mother take over for a while."

Evie felt Cloe's hand being replaced by her mother's as Cloe stepped aside.

"It's okay, Evie. Everything is fine," her mother told her. "It won't be much longer, and you'll have your baby girl."

"She's crowning!" the doctor announced loudly. "When you feel the next contraction, give me another good push, Evie."

Evie was exhausted. She had never felt so weak. Her long hair was wet with perspiration and was stuck to her body. She could barely lift her arms, and the pain in her lower body was so bad that she could hardly stand it. Although she knew it was irrational, she cried out, "I don't think I can do this!"

"Of course you can, sweetheart," her mother said encouragingly. "You're almost done."

Evie felt the next contraction and heard the doctor tell her to push. Dr. Simpkins began counting. Taking a deep breath, Evie gripped the sides of the bed and bore down as hard as she could. She cried out in pain as she grunted and pushed. For a few seconds, she felt the worst physical pain she had ever felt in her life. She could hardly wait for the doctor to reach ten so she could breathe. When she finally heard "Ten," Evie gasped for air. With tears streaming down her face, she heard the doctor announce, "Her head is out, Evie, and she has a head full of black hair." The doctor sounded emotional. "She's absolutely beautiful."

Cloe crept back up to the bedside. Evie looked up at her obviously frightened sister. "It's going to be okay, Cloe," she said breathlessly.

The doctor told Evie to push again.

"She's almost out. Just one more good push, and you'll have yourself a daughter."

Crying and trembling all over, Evie took a deep breath, gripped the bedrails again, and pushed down as hard as she could while the doctor counted.

"There she is! She's out!" the doctor exclaimed. Evie heard the doctor release a deep sigh as she watched her quickly pass the baby to the neonatologist, who then placed the tiny infant on Evie's chest. He worked quickly on the quiet baby as she lay on Evie's body. He suctioned out the squirming baby's mouth and nose and wiped her back and head with a white towel.

"Oh my God!" Evie cried as she looked into the face of Eric's and her child for the very first time. Words could not describe what she felt. She fell instantly in love with her baby. Overcome with emotion, she sobbed happily as she touched and caressed her tiny baby with the tip of her finger.

As soon as Dr. Simpkins had clamped and cut the umbilical cord, the nurse told Evie tenderly, "The neonatologist needs to take her now. She needs to go to the NICU so she can be checked out."

Evie knew she had to let her baby go, but it broke her heart to do so.

"You can come see her in the nursery in about an hour," the nurse told her as they took her baby away.

Still sobbing, Evie looked up to see that Cloe and her mother were crying as well. The birth of baby Erica had been an emotional time for all involved but especially Evie. It was the most rewarding thing she had ever experienced; she only wished Eric could have been there with her.

Evie, her parents, Cloe, and Eric's parents stood outside the nursery, staring through the window at tiny baby Erica in her incubator. She was moving her little arms and legs, but she wasn't crying. She weighed four pounds and six ounces and was sixteen inches long.

The smiling nurse came out and got Evie. "Come in, and spend some time with your amazing little newborn, Dr. Moses."

As she gazed in awe at her baby girl, tears streamed down Evie's face. "She looks like her daddy," she whispered as she put her hand through one of the slats in the incubator and tenderly touched their child. The baby had Eric's thick black hair.

As Evie gently stroked her tiny daughter's body with her fingertip, the infant appeared to smile. Evie gazed at the semblance of a smile on her tiny baby girl's face. She continued to weep happily as she closed her eyes and thanked God for a safe delivery and a healthy baby. Mostly, she thanked Him for giving her a cherished and living reminder of her beloved Eric.

32

MOTHERHOOD

Five Years Later

While sitting on the side of her bed and stroking her daughter's hair, Evie couldn't believe how quickly time had slipped by. It seemed to have passed in the blink of an eye.

The upcoming month would be an epic one for the Edwards and Moses families. Cloe would be having the grand opening of her new bridal design and formal shop in downtown Huntington. Lorretta would be having a book signing for her first published novel. Evie would be joining her father's surgical group, and little Erica would be starting kindergarten.

After reading her daughter a bedtime story and tucking her in for the night, Evie settled in to write in her journal.

My dearest Eric,

Tomorrow is a big day for your girls. Our little angel is starting school in the morning. I can't believe it. It seems like only yesterday I was bringing her home from the hospital. She was so tiny and helpless. What a priceless blessing she was—and is.

Her first five years of life have gone by way too quickly. As if only yesterday, I can still see her tiny body when the doctor laid her on my chest for the very first time. I can still see the first time she raised her little head and smiled her daddy's smile at me. Her very first words, her first steps, and every milestone in between are burned into my memory and will never be dulled by time. Just like my precious moments with you, my love. They will never be forgotten.

I'm so blessed that I was able to stay at home with our baby and raise her these past five years. That was a dream come true made possible by you, Eric. Thank you.

Now that your parents have moved to town, they and my mother will be the perfect babysitters for Erica after school, making it possible for me to focus on beginning my surgical career.

I need you to watch over Erica and me tomorrow. I have to admit I'm nervous about sending our baby off to school, and I'm a bit anxious about getting back to surgery after a five-year sabbatical.

Our lives are changing quickly, Eric—so very quickly. I wish I could slow down time or, better yet, turn it back. Oh, how I would love to turn back to a time when you were still here. It's been so long ago, but I still remember how it felt to be in your loving arms. I remember how it felt when you kissed me and held me. You made me feel so secure and cherished. My entire being yearns desperately for you, and I think it always will.

With that, I'll close tonight's entry as I always do: with the promise to love you forever and for always.

Good night, my love.
Evie

The following morning, Evie showered and dressed in a pair of light blue scrubs. It felt odd but good to be back in scrubs again. She put on one of her new monogrammed white lab coats. Running her fingers over the black embossed thread spelling out *Dr. Evie Moses*, she smiled softly.

In front of her bathroom mirror, she took stock of her new haircut. As she turned her head from side to side, it felt strange not to have her long locks following the movement of her head. Instead of being halfway down her back, her thick blonde hair now fell softly onto her shoulders. The side-bangs hairstyle was a new look for her too. The change in hairdo had been Cloe's idea. Evie was glad she had taken her fashion-forward sister's advice.

After applying some light makeup consisting of mascara, blush, and lipstick, Evie went into her daughter's room to get her up and ready for her first day of school.

Sitting down on the edge of Erica's bed, Evie slowly stroked her daughter's long black curls. Her hair felt like spun silk beneath Evie's fingers.

Erica began to stir. Slowly, she opened her eyes to reveal large circles of dark brown irises in pools of white. She had her daddy's incredible eyes.

"Is it time to go to school, Mommy?" she asked eagerly as she sat up in bed.

"It sure is, princess. Are you excited?" Evie asked, still stroking her daughter's hair.

"Yeah, I wanna go to school! I'm a big girl!" she exclaimed as she hopped out of bed. "Can I get dressed now?"

"You sure can," Evie answered. "Do you need help?"

"Nope, I can do it myself."

They had picked out her outfit together the night before, so with instructions to get dressed and come downstairs for breakfast, Evie left the room to allow her big-girl daughter to get ready alone. Standing outside the door, she could hear Erica talking to Eric's picture on the nightstand beside her bed.

"Thank you for watching over me from heaven while I slept, Daddy. I love you," Erica said.

Her precious daughter's innocent words caused a lump to form in Evie's throat. It saddened her that their baby had to grow up without the physical presence of her father, but Evie had kept her vow to Eric that their daughter would know who her daddy was and that he loved her all the way from heaven.

While preparing bowls of oatmeal with bananas and slices of toast, Evie heard her rambunctious daughter bound down the stairs and into the kitchen. The little girl grinned and twirled with her arms outstretched.

Evie looked at her lovable daughter. She was dressed in striped leggings with a pink bear-print T-shirt. Erica had an obsession with bears.

Bending down and giving her a hug, Evie said, "You look absolutely adorable. Now, let's go in and have our breakfast."

"Then we can go to school?" Erica asked.

"Then we can go," Evie answered, laughing, as she stroked her daughter's hair.

Evie parked the car and walked her little girl into Meadows Elementary School for the first time. She fought back tears as, hand in hand, they walked into the colorfully decorated classroom and met her teacher, Mrs. Keyser, a middle-aged woman with light brown hair and a large, welcoming smile.

Erica wasn't frightened or shy, as were some of the other children, who were clinging to their parents and crying. She looked around her with obvious anticipation and youthful enthusiasm.

"Would you like to come and meet some of your classmates?" Mrs. Keyser asked Erica.

"Yes, please," Erica answered.

Evie quickly bent down and gave her daughter one last emotional hug and kiss before letting go of her little hand. She watched as her baby girl walked away into a whole new world.

After Evie was met with handshakes, smiles, and warm welcomes from the staff at the Edwards Surgical Group, Evie's dad took her aside.

"How does it feel to finally be starting your surgical career?" he asked.

Evie grinned. "It feels good. It feels like I'm doing what I'm supposed to be doing."

Her father's face lit up. "Well, I can't tell you how happy I am to finally have you here with me."

"I'm happy to be here, Dad."

"Okay, now go make me proud," he said while pointing behind her.

Evie turned to find a familiar nurse standing a few steps away. With short auburn hair and striking green eyes, Nancy was someone Evie had met on many occasions. Evie liked her.

"Good morning, Dr. Moses." Nancy smiled as she extended her hand. "Welcome."

Evie shook her offered hand. "Thank you, Nancy," she said.

"Your first patient is in room three," the nurse said. "Her records are on your tablet."

After thanking Nancy again, Evie quickly scanned her patient's chart before entering the room.

She found an attractive thirty-six-year-old woman sitting on the examination table. She appeared anxious.

"Good morning," Evie said. "I'm Dr. Moses. It's nice to meet you."

The woman laughed a bit. "Well, to be honest, I wish I wasn't meeting you," she said.

"I can understand that," Evie replied as she laid her tablet down on the counter. "I see that your dermatologist has referred you for surgical removal of a squamous cell carcinoma on the left side of your chest."

"Yes, ma'am," she said.

"Would you mind lying down on your back so I can take a look?"

As Evie put on a pair of examination gloves, the woman lay down on the table. Evie removed the bandage from the woman's chest to find a large lesion that measured about three centimeters across. It evidenced a recent biopsy. Evie wondered to herself why this patient had waited so long to seek medical treatment.

"How does it look?" the woman asked. "Is it going to leave a big scar?"

"I'm sorry," Evie said sympathetically, "but yes, you'll definitely have a scar. I'll do my very best to make it as minimal as possible. You may sit up now, and we'll discuss a plan of treatment."

The young woman sat back up on the table as Evie took a seat on a small black stool.

"The lesion will definitely need to be removed. The good news is that for the most part, squamous cell carcinomas are easily cured by removal of the entire malignant area."

The woman appeared to be about to cry. "I knew I had to have surgery, but this can't kill me, can it?" she asked, sounding frightened.

Evie smiled slightly in an attempt to comfort her patient. "Like I said, the highest percentage of squamous cell carcinomas are most often cured by removal of the cancerous tissue. Try not to worry."

"But what about the other percentage? What can happen to them?" she asked.

Evie paused. Since she was being pressed for an honest prognosis, she felt compelled to deliver one. "A very, very small percentage of squamous cell carcinomas have been known to metastasize to other parts of the body, especially the lymph nodes," Evie said quietly. She quickly added, "However, that is not the norm, so please try not to ponder on that. Let's take this one step at a time, shall we?"

"Okay," the young woman answered as a tear rolled down her cheek. "When will you remove it? I want it gone."

"We'll do the surgery on an out-patient basis as quickly as we can get it scheduled."

The woman nodded. "That's good, but I wish we could do it right now," she said as she wiped the tears from her face. "Will it hurt?"

Evie shook her head. "No, ma'am, it won't. You'll be under anesthesia and won't feel a thing. I promise."

The woman smiled, and Evie walked her to the door.

"We'll call you with a surgery date as soon as it's been scheduled."

"Thank you, Dr. Moses. You're very kind."

Evie smiled and shook the hand of her first patient in her professional career.

33

PROCTORS AND SPECTERS

Over the next three months, Erica and Evie both thrived in their new environments. Erica seemed to adore going to kindergarten, while Evie felt invigorated to be back performing surgeries. The only thing that put a damper on her return was the proctor, Dr. Everett Saunders, who had been assigned to oversee and review her hospital surgeries in order to assure she was a safe surgeon after her five-year sabbatical. Evie found being scrutinized while operating on a patient to be a bit unnerving.

After walking out of the operating room, Evie removed her face mask. Dr. Saunders stood behind her at the sink while she washed her hands.

"I must say, you did an impeccable job, as usual," he said. "That hernia repair was very well executed."

"Thank you so much," Evie said as she grabbed a towel and began drying her hands.

"I'll submit this final surgery observance report to the hospital administration and appropriate other channels, and you should be cleared to go solo from now on," he said while extending his right hand. "I hope I wasn't too annoying to have around." He smiled at her.

Evie smiled back and shook his hand. "No, sir, Dr. Saunders. You weren't too bad," she said jokingly.

"Would you like to go to the cafeteria to grab a cup of coffee?" he asked.

Although slightly surprised by his invitation, she found the thought of a nice, hot cup of coffee enticing. "Sure," she replied as she removed her surgical cap.

Sitting across from Dr. Saunders, her self-labeled antagonist over the past three months, Evie found him to be quite personable. He was an average-looking man who appeared to be a few years older than she. He had sandy-colored hair and light brown eyes.

"So tell me a little bit about yourself outside of the hospital," Dr. Saunders said as he took a sip of coffee.

Evie knew exactly how to answer that question. She was a mother first and foremost. "I'm a mom to the most perfect little girl in the world," she said proudly.

"Well, that's a coincidence, because I happen to be a dad to the most perfect little boy in the world." He laughed. "How old is your little one?"

"She's five years old and just started kindergarten. How about yours?"

"He's nine and in the fourth grade."

Evie watched the doctor's expression change from happiness to sadness.

"I don't get to see him as often as I would like. He lives in Morgantown with his mother."

"I'm sorry," Evie said, wondering how he could stand being separated from his child. She wouldn't survive being apart from Erica.

"That's what happens sometimes when divorce comes into your life." He looked up from his coffee cup. With an obvious forced smile, he said, "I can see your wedding rings. How long have you been married?"

His personal question caught Evie slightly off guard. Apparently, he was one of the few doctors in the hospital who hadn't known Eric.

"I was blissfully married for a short time, but my husband passed away about six years ago." Evie's eyes stung. She looked up to find Dr. Saunders looking at her sympathetically. It made her slightly uncomfortable, mainly because she was starting to get emotional.

"I'm sorry, Dr. Moses. I didn't know."

Evie forced a smile. "It's okay." Looking down at her phone, she said, "I'd better get going. I'm almost late for an appointment." She lied, but she was ready for the conversation to end.

"Sure. Maybe I'll see you around the hospital," Dr. Saunders said as they both stood.

"I'll be here," Evie said. Smiling politely, she walked away.

Evie's afternoon had been busy but fulfilling. Getting to see her father during the day, if only in passing in the hallway, was not something Evie took for granted. If she had learned anything good from Eric's passing, it was to never take loved ones for granted.

Standing outside examination room one, looking down at her tablet to review the records of her last patient of the day, Evie was shocked to see the name Sam Wright appear on the screen. It couldn't be the same Sam Wright she knew—could it?

Without reviewing his medical records beforehand, as was her custom, she opened the door to see that it was indeed the Sam from her past. It was odd to see him sitting there on her examination table, dressed in a gown.

She walked over and extended her hand to him. "Hi, Sam," she said, still feeling surprised to see him. "How are you?"

"Other than for the reason that brings me here, I'm doing good. So how are you? You look great," he said, smiling. "I don't think you've aged a day since you were seventeen, except perhaps to get better looking."

Warmed by his flattery but unwilling to continue that topic of conversation, she smiled and thanked him. Looking down at her tablet, she said, "Now, I see from your chart that your primary physician has referred you for a hepatectomy, which is a liver resection for treatment of a benign neoplasm." She felt relieved as she read further. "I'm happy to see that your preliminary biopsy came back negative for malignancy. That's good news." Looking back up at him, she said, "So what we're looking at here is most likely a benign tumor, but it's a large one—about ten centimeters." She discussed the risks of the surgery—the risk of bleeding and, worse, liver failure. "This is a serious surgery, Sam," she said solemnly.

He sat there staring at her as if listening intently. "Can you remove it?" he asked quietly.

"Yes, I can. But I have to ask you, Sam. I know there are plenty of capable surgeons in Kentucky, so why me?"

He smiled. "Because I wanted the best."

She returned his smile. "I have to tell you, Sam, I'm just three months back from a five-year sabbatical. I would like for you to consider that in making your decision in choosing me. It's not that I doubt my surgical abilities; I just believe in full disclosure."

"Duly noted," he said. "So when do you do it?"

One week later, Sam was on her operating table. Evie made it a point to scrub in early so she could talk to him before he was administered the anesthesia.

"There's my doctor," Sam said, looking up her. He had been given a pre-op shot to relax him. It was obviously working.

"How do you feel, Sam?" Evie asked.

"Great! I feel great, and you look great too!" he exclaimed.

Evie nodded at the anesthesiologist, who then administered an injection into Sam's IV tubing.

"I have to tell you something, Evie," Sam said, sounding suddenly serious. "I—" Before he could continue, the anesthesia stopped him.

Gowned up and ready, with her father across the table from her to assist, Evie made a bilateral subcostal incision, thus beginning the arduous procedure.

Nearly four hours later, Evie and her father emerged from the operating room. Her father was beaming as he tore off his mask. "I couldn't have done a better liver resection myself," he said, sounding proud. "It was an honor to assist you, Dr. Moses."

Evie looked at him and cocked her head disbelievingly.

"Seriously. I couldn't have done better."

"Well, thank you," Evie said as she removed her surgical cap, which was wet with perspiration. It had been a grueling surgery but a successful one. Evie felt proud, fulfilled, and a little bit fatigued. Her lower back ached slightly. Looking at the clock, she saw that it was five in the afternoon.

As she and her father scrubbed their hands, he said, "Let's get home and have us some dinner. I'm sure your mom has fixed us something good."

Eating dinner with her parents had become somewhat of a habit since Evie had to go there to pick up Erica after work. Her parents were gracious and loving, and Evie appreciated them more than words could say.

"I'm ready, Dad," Evie said. "I'll see you there in a few."

It was freezing outside as Evie made her way to her car. Since Christmas was only a few weeks away, lights and decorations were abundant and beautiful. Evie enjoyed the colorful scenery on her drive to her parents' home.

When she walked through the door, she was greeted by the family's eight-foot Christmas tree, the mingled smells of pine and pot roast, and an overly exuberant daughter.

"Hi, Mommy! Guess what I did today?" Erica asked as she leaped into Evie's outstretched arms.

"What, princess? What wonderful thing did you do?" Evie laughed.

"I counted to thirty all by myself at school, and Grandma Lorretta let me help her cook dinner."

"Wow! I'm so proud of you, my sweet girl!" Evie exclaimed as she strained to pick up her daughter. "Gosh! You're getting too big for me to carry," she said as she walked toward the kitchen.

"I'm growing up," Erica said happily.

"I know," Evie replied sadly.

34

OLD FRIENDS

"This is a heck of a way to get reacquainted," Sam said through a noticeably forced smile.

Evie walked up next to his hospital bed. "How are you feeling this morning? How is your pain level?" she asked as she pulled down his covers to examine his incision.

"I'm hanging in there at about a four on the pain scale," Sam answered. He winced when she gently pressed on his abdomen with her gloved fingertips.

"The incision looks good. No signs of infection, but we're giving you post-op antibiotics just in case." She looked down at Sam, who was staring up at her. "I can increase your pain meds a bit if you feel the need," she said as she checked his drain tubes.

"How long will those have to stay in?" he asked, pointing to the tubes.

"About a week to ten days. It depends on how much drainage we're getting. Why? Are they hurting you?" she asked.

"No. They're just uncomfortable when I try to turn and stuff. It's okay, though, Doc."

Evie listened to his heart and lungs. Pleased with what she heard, she removed her stethoscope from her ears and hung it around her neck. She was happy there was no jaundice or indication of post-op bleeding or blood clots. She was also elated that his post-op pathology was benign.

"When can I have something to eat, Doc? I'm starving," Sam said with a hint of a grin on his face. Once again, it appeared he was smiling through the pain.

"I'll order some clear liquids for you for this afternoon," Evie said, speaking more so to the nurse standing beside her than to Sam. "We'll see how you tolerate that and reassess in the morning."

"Okay, Doc. Whatever you say."

Evie grinned at him and walked out of the room.

Sam's condition improved with every day that passed. Every morning, when Evie came through the door, she was greeted by Sam's warm smile. This day was no different.

He had been in the hospital for five days and had made it known he was ready to go home.

"When are you going to spring me from this joint, Doc?" he asked as Evie put her stethoscope's ear tips into her ears.

Laughing, she replied, "If you don't behave yourself, I may just keep you here indefinitely."

"Well, if it means I get to see you every day, I guess that wouldn't be so bad."

Shaking her head, Evie listened to his strong heart and clear lungs. Afterward, she examined his incision and checked the amount of drainage in his drain-tube bulbs. "I think I can let you go home today," she said, smiling. "I'm afraid you'll have to take the drain tubes with you, though. They're still draining quite a bit."

He scrunched his face in obvious disapproval.

"Most likely, I can take them out when you come into my office for your follow-up visit in a few days. The nurse will give you an appointment time and date with your discharge papers."

Evie saw him wince when he tried to reposition himself in bed. "I worry about your long ride home," she said. "You can ask the nurse for some pain meds just before you leave the hospital."

"Oh, it's okay," Sam replied. "Dad's going to stay here in town with me in a hotel for a few days. We'll probably do that until I see you again."

"I'm glad to hear that. I think that's an excellent idea."

"And I think coming here to see you was an excellent idea." He grinned at her.

Evie smiled back and shook her head again. Taking his subtle flirtatious remark as her cue to leave, she turned and walked out the door.

Three days later, Evie checked her patient schedule for the day. She saw that Sam would be her first appointment. She found herself looking forward to seeing her friend.

Tapping on the door, she walked in to find Sam sitting on the examination table. He was smiling at her.

"So how are you feeling this morning?" Evie asked.

"I'm doing pretty good. How about you?"

"I'm fine, thank you," Evie answered. "Would you please lie down on the table so I can take a look at you and hopefully remove those drain tubes you're so fond of?" she asked teasingly.

He groaned slightly as he complied with her request.

After putting on a pair of examination gloves, she opened his gown and inspected his stomach and incision. "When did you last empty the drain-tube bulbs?" she asked.

"About three hours ago," he replied. "Please tell me you're going to take them out today."

"I sure am," she said. "Let me get a nurse in here, and we'll get those right out for you."

Evie returned with Nurse Nancy by her side. "Okay, Sam, let's get this done."

With a pair of tiny scissors, she snipped the stitches holding the tubes in place—one on either end of the incision. "Now take a deep breath, and slowly exhale for me," she said. While Sam was exhaling, she pulled the tube slowly from his body. She heard him groan as she did so. "It's out," she said as she placed the tube and bulb on a tray held by the nurse.

"Well, that certainly wasn't a lot of fun," he said with a grimace.

"I'm sorry," Evie said. "Now one more time. Take in a deep breath, and slowly exhale." She repeated the procedure. "All done."

"Whew! I'm glad," Sam said.

After asking the nurse for two small adhesive bandages, she placed them on Sam's abdomen. "Thank you, Nancy," Evie said.

The nurse nodded before turning and leaving the room.

"You can sit up now, Sam," Evie said. Seeing that he was struggling to get up, she offered him her arm with which to pull himself up. He accepted her help. "Things look great, Sam," she said happily. "I couldn't have asked for a better outcome."

He grinned at her. "I knew I would be in good hands with you."

"Well, I appreciate your confidence in me," she said. "I'd like to see you back in a month, and then we'll talk about when you can go back to light-duty work."

"I'd like to talk with you about other things than just that. I'd like to know how you and your family are doing and stuff."

Evie shook her head. "That wouldn't be appropriate, Sam. I'm your physician."

"Well, how about when you're no longer my physician?"

Evie couldn't stifle a grin. "Maybe then," she said as she turned to go.

"Okay then. You're fired," he said, laughing. "You're no longer my doctor."

Giggling, Evie waved goodbye at her joking patient and friend and walked out the door.

35
AULD LANG SYNE

Another memorable Edwards and Moses blended-family Christmas and New Year's Eve was in the books. Since it was late and snowing outside, Lorretta and Dan had invited everyone to stay the night. Their four-bedroom home was plenty large enough to accommodate Eric's parents; Cloe and her new boyfriend, Stephen; and Evie and Erica.

Cloe, Evie, and Erica were sharing a room. Dan carried a sleeping Erica up the stairs and into Cloe's former bedroom. Laughing softly, he placed his granddaughter on the bed. He stood there smiling. "It's nice having my girls spend the night. It's just like old times," he said, looking nostalgic. "Do you all have everything you need?"

"Of course we do, Dad—we have you and Mom," Cloe replied as she gave him a kiss on the cheek.

"Exactly," Evie said as she gave him a big hug.

"Thank you, girls," he said, appearing content. "We'll see you all in the morning."

After exchanging good nights, he left the room.

"Let me get us pairs of pajamas," Cloe said as she headed toward the chest of drawers.

Once they had changed their clothes, Cloe and Evie climbed into the bed with Erica sound asleep in the middle.

"Are you sleepy, sis?" Cloe asked quietly.

"Kind of but not so much that I can't stay awake long enough for you to tell me all about you and Stephen."

Cloe giggled in the semidarkness. The full moon and streetlights, which shone brightly through the sheer curtains in the windows, provided just enough light for them to see each other. "I was hoping you'd ask," she said. Propping herself up on her elbow, she whispered, "I think Stephen is the one, sis. I'm really head over heels in love with him."

"You are?" Evie asked as she too propped herself up so she could look into her baby sister's glowing face. "How long have you known?"

"Ever since the first time I saw him." Cloe's face was adorned with a brilliant smile. "Was that how it was with you and Eric?"

Evie thought for a second. "Not exactly," she admitted. "I was definitely attracted to him, because it would have been hard not to be, but I think love came as we got to know each other."

Cloe's smile faded. "I'm sorry, sis. I didn't mean to bring up a bad memory."

Evie shook her head. "It's not a bad memory at all, Cloe. I have nothing but good memories about Eric, except for when he ... when he left." Evie felt bad for stealing her sister's joy and, hoping to reignite it, added, "Have you two talked about marriage or anything yet?"

Cloe's face lit up again. "Yes, we have. We've talked about what we want for our future. We've even talked about whether or not we want kids."

"And what did you decide?"

"Well, we both want to pursue our careers before we settle down with children. I want to see my design shop thrive for a couple of stable years before I take a maternity break, and he wants to get his law practice off the ground."

"That makes sense," Evie said. "It's crazy that out of all the attorneys in town, you chose him to help you get your business started."

"I know!" Cloe exclaimed. "It's nuts, but that's how fate works, I guess, huh?"

"It's not fate, Cloe … it's God," Evie said. "Has Stephen hinted as to when he might propose?"

"Not really, but I think it might be soon—maybe my birthday in late spring."

Evie smiled at her joyful baby sister. "I hope so, Cloe. I want nothing but happiness for you, and I can see that Stephen makes you happy."

"Yes, he does." Cloe looked at Evie and cocked her head to one side inquisitively. "Speaking of being happy, what is this I hear about you and Sam?"

"There is no 'me and Sam,' Cloe. I'm his doctor. That's all," Evie answered.

"Yeah, but it's obvious he's been carrying a torch for you all this time. After all, he sought you out for his surgery. That must have meant something."

"It did. It meant he needed surgery," Evie said, laughing. "Now, go to sleep, my dear, nosy little sister. I'll see you in the morning."

Cloe appeared slightly deflated as she said her good night.

Evie rolled over onto her back. Staring up at the ceiling, she wished she had her journal with her. She needed to talk to Eric.

Evie awakened the next morning to the smell of bacon and coffee. Stretching beneath the covers, she discovered that Cloe and Erica were already up and gone. She was in the bed alone.

She got up, got dressed, and was heading downstairs, when her phone in her pocket notified her that she had received a message. It was a text from Sam: "It's me—Sam. I just wanted to wish you and your family a happy New Year. So happy New Year, Evie. And thank you for saving my life."

She thought for a moment before answering. She typed: "Thank you for the New Year's well-wishes. Happy New Year to you too, Sam, and you are welcome. I was pleased to be your surgeon. Evie."

She hit the send button and waited to see if he responded. He didn't.

Evie looked at her schedule for the week following the New Year's holiday. Barring any emergencies that popped up, it appeared to be a fairly easy week. She saw that her last appointment before lunch was Sam. He would be coming in for his second, and hopefully last, appointment following his surgery. Evie found herself looking forward to seeing him again, and she wasn't sure how she felt about that.

After a rewarding morning of patient visits, Evie tapped on the door of the room where Sam sat waiting for her.

"There she is. The greatest surgeon in the world," he said, smiling.

She chuckled. "So I guess that means you're feeling well."

"Yes, I am. I'm feeling really good. My stomach is still a bit sore, but that's to be expected, right?"

"Of course, some tenderness is absolutely normal. Let me have a look," she said as she opened his gown. The incision scar on his rippled abdomen appeared to be healing nicely. There were no signs of redness or swelling. With the tips of her gloved fingers, she pressed around the incision, which caused him to groan slightly.

"That's not fair. You're cheating," he said, laughing.

Evie laughed too. "I expected my examination to be somewhat uncomfortable. I'm sorry."

"It's okay. When can I go back to work, Doc?" he asked, appearing anxious.

Evie thought for a moment. "I can release you for light-duty work only. I know the type of work you typically do, Sam, but you can't go back to that just yet. You had a very serious surgery. Like I said, light-duty only—maybe some supervising work, but that's all. No lifting for at least two more months."

Sam smiled. "I can live with that. I've been about to lose my mind sitting around at home, twiddling my thumbs. When do I come back to see you again?"

"I don't think you'll need to come back unless you're feeling some discomfort at the incision site—or anywhere in your abdomen, for that matter," she answered.

He appeared somewhat disappointed. "Is it your lunchtime? Can I buy your lunch? It's the least I can do for your saving my life." His former expression of disappointment had evolved into a look of hopefulness.

Evie didn't know what to say. Her indecision must have shown on her face.

"It's just lunch between old friends," he said encouragingly.

"Lunch between old friends," Evie repeated. "I guess I can do that, but it'll have to be a brief lunch. I have to be back here in a little over an hour for my next appointment."

Sam appeared happy. "Perfect. You just tell me where to take you, and I'll have you back in time for your next patient."

"Okay," Evie said.

After he opened the passenger-side door of his truck for her, Evie climbed in and then watched as he slowly pulled himself up into the driver's seat. He groaned as he did so.

"You okay?" she asked.

"I'm great," he said. "You just lead the way."

Evie directed him to her favorite restaurant in town, Jim's Steak and Spaghetti House. "I think you'll like it here," she said. "It's practically a local landmark."

"If you like it, I'm sure I will," he replied.

Although the line of waiting patrons was long, it moved quickly. Once seated, they looked at their menus.

"They have a little bit of everything," Sam said. "What do you recommend?"

"Well, it's all delicious, but the haddock sandwich is to die for, and the spaghetti is my daughter's favorite. You can't go wrong choosing either one."

Laying his menu aside, Sam asked, "So you and your husband have children?"

Evie looked down at the wedding rings on her left hand. "Yes, we have a little girl," she said quietly. "She's about to turn six."

Before Sam could respond, the waitress came to take their orders.

"I would like a fish sandwich, please," Evie told her.

"With tartar sauce and coleslaw?" the waitress asked.

"Yes, please."

The waitress turned her attention to Sam.

"I'll have the same, please."

"Good choice," Evie said.

Leaning back against the booth, Sam said, "Well, you know what I've been up to. I've been busy growing a big tumor in my liver." He chuckled. "So how's married life treating you? I hope your husband knows what a lucky guy he is."

Evie touched her wedding rings again. She felt her eyes threaten to tear, but she was able to hold the tears back. Still looking down, she said, "My husband, Eric—he passed away about six and a half years ago."

Evie looked up to find Sam leaning forward. He had a look of profound sympathy on his face. For a moment, she thought he might reach across the table and try to touch her hand. She hoped he didn't.

"Oh! I had no idea, Evie. I'm so sorry! And I'm sorry for bringing it up. I didn't know."

Sighing deeply, Evie told him, "It's okay, Sam. There's no way you could have known." With her head down, she noticed his left hand. She saw that he wasn't wearing a wedding band. "What about you and Martie?" she asked as she looked up at him.

"There is no 'me and Martie,'" he answered. "She called off the wedding two weeks before we were supposed to get married. She knew. She knew what I was afraid to say."

"I'm sorry," Evie said.

Just then, the waitress returned with their lunches. "Is there anything else I can get you?"

Sam looked at Evie. "Do you need anything?"

Evie shook her head and glanced up at the waitress. "No, thank you, ma'am. We're good for now."

Sam looked down at his lunch. "This is the biggest fish sandwich I've ever seen."

Evie grinned. "Yes, and it tastes just as good as it looks."

She watched as Sam took his first big bite. He gave her a thumbs-up as he chewed. Happy that he appeared to be enjoying his lunch, Evie took her first bite as well.

Evie was surprised by the easy conversation they made while they ate. They talked about their careers and their families. Evie was glad to hear that Sam's father was still working and in good health.

"I can't believe Cloe is all grown up and doing so well," Sam said. "She was just a tiny little girl when I last saw her."

Talking about those days made Evie think of sweet Clarissa. She wondered what her little sister would have been like had she lived. Would she still have been the spitting image of Cloe? Evie wondered about what could have been.

"I did it again, didn't I?" Sam asked. "I brought up another sore subject."

Evie looked at him. He seemed saddened by his comment. "No, you didn't, Sam. It's okay." Deciding to change the subject, she looked at his half-eaten sandwich and asked, "So how is your lunch? Did I steer you right or what?"

He grinned. "It's absolutely the best fish sandwich I've ever had, and don't forget: I lived most of my life right next to the sea, so that's a strong testament to this sandwich."

"I remember," Evie said, wondering why he had moved away from the place he loved so much. "What made you and your father relocate to Kentucky?"

"It's a long story," he said. "I'll tell you about it sometime when we have more time."

Looking at the clock on the wall, she replied, "You're right. I've got to be getting back soon."

"I wish we had more time to talk. Would it be all right if I called you sometime—just a friend calling a friend? A friend who just so happened to save my life?" he asked with a hopeful expression on his face.

Evie wasn't sure how to answer. She supposed that having Sam for a friend wouldn't hurt. She could use a friend, she thought. Elizabeth and George had both moved away, and she had lost contact with them, so other than her new friends she was making at work, she didn't have any close confidants. She could see Sam filling that void.

Nodding, Evie replied, "Sure. You can call me sometime if you want."

"Oh, I want," he said, smiling. "I've wanted to call you for a long time."

"Why didn't you?" Evie asked, surprising herself with her boldness.

Sam looked suddenly ashamed—of what, Evie didn't know. "I just …" He shrugged. "I didn't feel like I had the right."

The waitress returned with their checks. Evie reached for hers, but Sam got to it first. "The least I can do is buy your lunch. After all, you did save my life with those miraculous hands of yours."

Evie laughed. "You're being a little overly dramatic, don't you think?"

"Not from where I sit I'm not. Now, come on, you. Let's get you back to work. You have patients to save."

Sam drove Evie back to her office, got out, and opened the truck door for her. He held out his hand to help her, but Evie pretended not to see it.

"Thank you very much for lunch, Sam," she said.

"You're most welcome. Thank you for leading me to the best fish sandwich I've ever had. I'll be wanting to come back for more of those." He looked at her with hesitation. "Would you be willing to go with me again?"

Evie thought for a moment before answering. She smiled. "Just as friends."

He grinned. "Just as friends," he repeated.

36
FRIENDSHIP

It was a cold and snowy February evening. Evie drove slowly and carefully as she and Erica made their way home after having dinner with her parents, Cloe, and Stephen.

Evie's cell phone rang. Glancing briefly at the car's monitor, she saw Sam's name appear. He had called her a couple of times since they had eaten lunch together. For the most part, their conversations had been about insignificant things, and that was the way Evie liked it.

"Who's Sam?" Erica asked. "He's calling you. Who is he?"

"Oh, Sam's just a friend, princess. I met him a long time ago when I was just a young girl."

"Is he your boyfriend?"

"No, Erica." Evie laughed. "He's not my boyfriend. He's just a friend."

"Grandma Lorretta and Aunt Cloe think you should have a boyfriend. I heard them talking." She paused for a moment. "Are you lonely, Mommy?" she asked as Evie pulled into the driveway and parked the car. "Grandma Lorretta and Aunt Cloe said—"

Evie interrupted her adorable and curious daughter. "First of all, my dear, you shouldn't be listening in on grown-ups' conversations, and second of all, no, I am absolutely not lonely." She smiled. "How could I be lonely when I have the best daughter in the whole wide world to keep me company?" She reached over and tweaked Erica's cold nose. "Now, let's get inside before we turn into human icicles out here."

Giggling, they hopped out of the car and trudged through the snow up to the front door.

"If this snow keeps up, I bet school will be canceled tomorrow," Evie said as they walked into the foyer.

Erica's eyes grew wide. "Do you think so? Can you stay home with me?" she asked.

Evie extended her arms and hugged her sweet daughter. "Mommy would love to, princess, but I have to go to work. I have patients coming in who need me, but you can stay with Grandma Lorretta or Grandma Katherine. You can pick which one."

Erica paused for a moment before answering. "I think Grandma Katherine this time. I stayed with Grandma Lorretta the last time, so it's Grandma Katherine's turn. I don't wanna make her feel bad."

"Well, that's very sweet of you to think of her feelings, princess. I'm very proud of you for that. Now, what's say we get your bath and get you ready for bed?"

"Then can I watch some TV?"

"For a little bit, but then it's off to bed."

"Okay, Mommy. Then we'll read a bedtime story together, right?"

"Of course we will. I love sharing a book with you before bed. I couldn't sleep without it."

"Me either," Erica said as she took off her coat and handed it to Evie.

As they started toward the stairs, Evie heard the words she would never tire of hearing: "I love you, Mommy."

After getting her daughter to bed and getting herself out of her scrubs and into her pajamas, Evie opened her journal and wrote to Eric. Glancing at the clock, she saw it was too late in the night to return Sam's call. Just as she was about to click off her bedside lamp, her cell notified her of a text message. She picked up her phone and read: "Are you still up?" It was from Sam.

She returned his text. "Yes, I'm still awake."

"Wanna talk?"

"Sure."

Seconds later, her phone rang.

"Hi, Sam."

"Hey, Evie. I phoned you earlier. I was a little worried about you. I heard on the news that you all were getting quite a bit of snow."

"We're okay, but you're right. We're supposed to get a total of six to eight inches by morning."

"How will you get to work?" He sounded worried.

"My dad will come pick us up in his four-wheel-drive truck. He'll drop Erica off at her grandma's and then take me to work with him. Don't worry about us. Dad lives for a big ole snow like this. He loves it." Evie laughed.

"Good," he said, sounding relieved.

"How about you guys? Are you getting any snow?"

"Not tonight. It's frigid outside but clear as a bell."

There was a moment of silence before Sam spoke up. He sounded hesitant. "Evie, if I drive up on Saturday, would you have lunch at Jim's with me again?"

Evie got quiet. They had already discussed that they were just friends, but she had to make sure. She didn't want to lead him on. She had no intention of dating him or anyone else. Her heart belonged to Eric, and she planned on keeping it that way.

"You mean as friends, right?" she asked.

"Of course," he said, chuckling. "I have a craving to share a fish sandwich with an old friend."

Evie laughed. "Okay then. What time do you want to meet?"

"Let's say one o'clock," he replied.

"All right then. I'll see you there on Saturday."

After they said their goodbyes, Evie returned her phone to the nightstand. Glancing at her wedding picture, she closed her eyes and wished Eric good night.

After taking a good-natured sisterly teasing from Cloe about her lunch "date" with Sam, Evie left Erica with her parents and drove downtown to meet her friend. She saw his red truck parked on the street outside the restaurant. She found a space a few cars in front of him. When she stepped out of her car, he was walking toward her. He had a wide smile on his face.

"Have you been waiting long?" she asked.

"No. Just a few minutes," he answered.

As the cold wind picked up, she pulled her coat tightly around her.

"You're freezing," he said. "Let's get you inside."

After stepping into the warm restaurant, they were taken to a booth and given menus.

Sam helped Evie off with her coat and waited for her to be seated before he sat down.

"It's a good bit colder here than it was when I left home this morning," he said as he laid his menu aside.

"It's been crazy cold here lately," Evie said while rubbing her hands together.

Their waitress came to take their orders. They both ordered fish sandwiches and sodas.

"I'll be right back with your drinks," she said.

"Thanks for agreeing to have lunch with me," Sam said.

Evie nodded. "Thank you for being willing to drive all this way. That's very sweet of you, Sam."

"It's okay. I'm a sweet person," he said with a chuckle.

"I know you are," Evie replied.

The waitress returned with their sodas and set them down in front of them. Evie picked up her straw, placed it in her drink, and took a sip of the cold beverage. "It probably would have been smarter to order a coffee on such a chilly day."

"We can go for coffee after lunch," Sam said. "If you want to, that is," he added quickly.

Evie appreciated his driving more than two hours to spend time with her. She couldn't bring herself to turn down having a cup of coffee with him. "Sure. Coffee would be nice."

The waitress returned with their lunch orders. After they assured her they had everything they needed, they picked up their sandwiches.

Evie smiled as she watched Sam take his first bite. He smiled back at her as he chewed.

"Man, these things are addicting," he said. "I've been craving one of these for days."

Evie nodded. "I know. They're delicious." She glanced down at her plate and took a bite of her coleslaw. When she raised her eyes, she found him looking at her.

"I'm sorry for staring," he said. "You just look very nice today."

Evie wore a raspberry-colored blouse with a black jacket and a pair of black slacks. "Thank you," she said, feeling a bit embarrassed by his gaze.

"I know I've told you this before, but I can't get over how you haven't changed." Reaching behind him, he pulled out his wallet. He opened it up, took out a picture, and showed it to her. It was the picture they had taken on their last night together at Virginia Beach. "See? Here's proof that you haven't changed."

She looked at the weathered picture in his hand. It touched her that he had kept it close for so many years. Smiling softly, she gazed at the image of the young girl she used to be. "I remember that girl," she said quietly.

"I remember that night," Sam replied.

Uncomfortable with where the conversation was going, Evie quickly changed the subject. "If you have room after your sandwich, they have incredible pies here too."

"That sounds like a great idea—with a cup of coffee," he said as he returned his wallet to his pocket.

Sam seemed to be in a talkative mood. He talked about how good it felt to be back to work. He told her that his father's and his company had scored a great inside job for the winter, and it was coming along nicely.

"I'm glad to hear that," Evie said. "You recovered well from such an extensive surgery. I'm so happy for you."

"Well, I had great surgeon," he said.

The waitress came to take away their empty plates and asked if they would like dessert.

Sam looked at Evie. "I'm in your capable hands," he said.

"We'd like two slices of chocolate cream pie and two coffees, please," Evie told the waitress.

"Be right back," she said.

Evie glanced back to find Sam staring at her again.

"I'm enjoying spending some time with you, Evie," he said.

Evie looked at him. Seeing remnants of the younger man she once had thought she loved made her smile. "I'm enjoying myself too, Sam. Thank you for driving all this way."

"My pleasure," he said. "And then there's also the fish sandwich," he added, laughing.

She laughed too. His funny comment reminded her of Eric. Eric always had said witty things to make her laugh. She missed that.

"What are you thinking about?" Sam asked. "You got a serious look on your face all of a sudden."

"Oh, it's nothing. I think my mind was wandering—that's all," she responded.

"It's okay," he said just as the waitress brought their pie and coffee.

Evie grinned at her friend across the table. "You're in for a real treat," she said as she watched Sam pick up his fork and take his first bite of the creamy chocolate confection.

Nodding in approval, he chewed his pie while she took a bite of hers. "This is so good," he said.

It made her happy to see him enjoying his meal and dessert.

They chatted while they ate their pie and drank their coffee.

"I confess that I'm trying to eat slowly," Sam said. "I don't want our lunch to be over." He looked at her hopefully, as if wishing she felt the same.

She didn't know what to say. She was afraid of leading him on, so she chose her words carefully. "I'm enjoying myself too, Sam. I'm glad to call you a friend."

His smile was warm and genuine. "I'm glad too, Evie."

After their meal was finished and their dishes were cleared away, the waitress laid the check down on the table. Sam and Evie reached for it at the same time. Their hands touched briefly. Evie quickly pulled hers back.

"I'm sorry," she whispered.

Sam remained quiet until she looked up and made eye contact with him.

"It's okay, Evie," he said softly. "I know."

With her eyes threatening to tear, Evie replied, "Thank you for understanding, Sam."

"Always," he said.

37

THE UNEXPECTED

As the chill of winter gave way to the warmth of spring, Evie and Sam's long-distance friendship blossomed. His bimonthly trips to Huntington to see her were something she looked forward to. They were growing closer as friends but remained physically distant, not only in miles but also in touch. Evie still couldn't bring herself to welcome any physical contact. They hadn't even hugged.

Evie knew that was irrational. Even friends made physical contact. She was aware, but she couldn't bring herself to touch Sam. She couldn't betray Eric by touching another man, especially not Sam. She could tell he was in love with her. She could see it when she looked into his hazel eyes. It made her feel guilty at times—like she was playing with his heart. Whenever she tried to explain herself or break off their friendship, he would assure her that he was fine with their relationship the way it was. She didn't believe him, but deep down, she didn't want to end their friendship either.

She hadn't introduced him to Erica. Erica was aware that her mommy had a friend named Sam, but that was it. Evie had no intention of confusing her daughter or causing her emotional pain of any kind. Having to grow up without her father was painful enough.

It was a balmy but rainy April afternoon when Evie drove to the restaurant to meet Sam. She saw him coming toward her car with a large black umbrella. Standing next to her door, he waited for her to get out while holding the umbrella over her head.

Side by side, they headed toward the shelter of the restaurant's green awning. Evie's body touched Sam's as they walked. She started to pull away but quickly realized she was being foolish. Sharing an umbrella with another man didn't mean she was betraying Eric.

Sam opened the restaurant door, and Evie ducked inside out of the rain.

After Sam stowed his dripping umbrella in the stand beside the door, the hostess took Evie and Sam to a booth.

"Whew! It's pouring out there," Sam said.

"It sure is," Evie said as she tried to smooth her disheveled hair with her hands.

"Don't bother," he said while watching her. "You can't improve on perfection."

Evie laughed and thanked him for his compliment.

"What'll it be today?" the waitress asked as she set down two glasses of water.

"I'm going for spaghetti today," Sam said. "A large one, as a matter of fact. How about you, Evie?"

"I think I'll join you in that spaghetti. But a small one, please," she told the waitress.

"And what kind of dressing on your salads?" she asked.

They both chose the Thousand Island, and the waitress turned and walked away.

"I'm starving. Are you hungry?" Sam asked.

Evie laughed softly. "You're always hungry when we come here."

"I know! I wish we had a Jim's in Lexington."

"I don't. Then you wouldn't drive all this way ..." She trailed off, stopping herself from saying more.

Sam grinned at her. "I'd still drive all this way—just to see you. Don't you know that?"

Evie didn't answer. She just smiled and shook her head. She was glad when he changed the subject.

"So tell me—how are your parents and Cloe and Erica?"

"They're all just fine. Mom is working on her second book. This one is nonfiction. It's an autobiography titled *The Missing Piece*."

"Oh, that's interesting," he said. "I enjoyed her first book very much. I'll look forward to reading the new one when it's published."

"Me too," Evie said. "She won't let any of us read her work until it's in book form. She wants us to have the experience of holding the book in our hands as we read. She's kind of old school like that."

The waitress returned with their salads and drinks. "Your spaghetti will be right out," she said.

"Thank you," they replied in unison.

"I remember your dad used to say a prayer before dinner all those years ago. Does he still do that?"

Evie bowed her head, slightly embarrassed that she hadn't followed her father's example. "Yes, he still says a blessing. I used to, until ..." She paused.

"Until what?" Sam asked.

Evie raised her eyes to meet his. "Until God took Eric away from me," she replied stoically. "Now it seems I only call on Him when I need something." She was ashamed of her declaration.

"I understand," Sam said. "And I think God understands too."

"I hope He does," Evie replied honestly.

The waitress returned with their plates of spaghetti, but they had yet to take their first bite of salad.

"We'd better get busy eating," Sam said.

They chatted about Sam's latest construction job while they ate. It was nearly finished, and he had submitted a bid on an even bigger project.

"I hope you get it," Evie said. She enjoyed listening to him talk about his work and his father. His love for his dad was obvious and endearing. "I'd like to meet your father sometime. I feel like I already know him."

"I'd like to introduce you to him. He would love to meet you too. I talk about you all the time—well, not all the time," he said, chuckling.

Evie smiled at him.

After they finished their dinner, they ordered coconut cream pie for dessert, along with a cup of coffee. Lingering over a slice of pie and several cups of coffee had become their routine.

Evie was sad when their time together came to an end.

Turning his head and looking out the window, Sam said, "It's still raining out there. I hate for you to have to go out and get wet."

"It's okay," Evie replied. "I won't melt."

"Okay then," Sam said, sounding as reluctant as Evie felt.

Finally, Evie took the initiative and stood up first. Sam followed and helped her on with her jacket.

They stepped out of the restaurant and stood underneath the awning to say their goodbyes. Then, once again, beneath the shared umbrella, Evie felt the warmth of Sam's body next to hers as they walked. Once again, she didn't pull away.

When they reached her car, he opened the door for her. As she turned to get into her car, they were face-to-face—just inches apart. For a split second, she could feel his warm breath on her skin. She looked into his eyes before quickly climbing into her car.

The rain was pouring, so there was no more time for talking. Evie watched as Sam ran to his truck. She waited until he drove away.

Evie returned to her parents' home to pick up her daughter. Apparently, Erica had been watching for her, because she met her at the door with wide-open arms and her daddy's engaging smile.

"Did you miss me?" Evie asked as she hugged her baby girl.

"Yes," Erica answered. "But Grandpa and I've been playing games. Grandma and Aunt Cloe are fixing dinner. Can we stay for dinner? Please, can we, Mommy?"

"I don't see why not," Evie said, smiling at her delightful daughter.

"Yea!" Erica shouted as she released Evie and ran off in the direction of the living room.

Evie followed her nose to the kitchen. Even though she had just eaten, the beginnings of dinner sure smelled good.

"Hi, Mom! Hi, Cloe!"

"Hey, sweetheart," her mother said. "How was your lunch with Sam?"

"Yeah," Cloe said with a sly smile while sitting on the kitchen counter. "How's Sam doing?"

Evie shook her head at her impish sister. "Sam is fine, thank you. Now, what is smelling so good in here?" she asked as she lifted the lid on a large pot on the stove. "Erica invited us to dinner."

"That's because I invited Erica and you to stay and eat with us. I have something I want to talk with the family about."

Her mother sounded serious. Evie couldn't help but assume the worst when her mother used that tone. She looked at Cloe, who shared the same concerning frown. "Is something wrong, Mom?" Evie asked.

"No, sweetheart, nothing is wrong. I've just been thinking about something, and I want to get everyone's opinion on it. That's all. Don't worry."

Evie looked at her sister again. Cloe shrugged her cluelessness.

"We have chicken and potato stew for those who don't like seafood—like my precious granddaughter—and pan-seared scallops and lobster for those who do like delicacies of the sea."

"Gosh, Mom, you sure are outdoing yourself," Evie said.

"Well, what I want to talk with you all about goes with the theme of dinner," Lorretta said mysteriously. "Besides, you know how much I love to cook."

Cloe shrugged again.

"Have you ever thought about writing a cookbook, Mom?" Evie asked.

Lorretta grinned. "As a matter of fact, I have. I think that might be my next writing project."

The doorbell rang, and Cloe's face instantly lit up. "It's Stephen," she squealed gleefully as she hopped down from the counter and ran toward the door.

Evie smiled, remembering how it felt to be that excited over a boyfriend. She remembered those feelings of Eric vividly and fondly.

Greetings from the living room finally made their way into the kitchen as Cloe, clinging to Stephen's arm, entered the room.

"Hi, Stephen. It's good to see you. How are you doing?" Evie asked.

Stephen was a tall and lanky man with blonde hair and blue eyes. He towered over Cloe, but still, they looked as if they belonged together.

"Great! I couldn't be better," he answered, appearing as if he meant it. "And you?"

"The same," Evie replied, wishing it were true.

Evie heard her mother clear her throat. "Before we have an early dinner, I'd like it if you all would come into the living room with me. I have something to discuss with you."

Once again, Evie felt anxiety rise in her chest at her mother's secretiveness.

Silently, they followed Lorretta into the living room, where Erica and her grandpa were on the floor, playing a board game.

Everyone took a seat, except for Lorretta. She stood at the entrance to the living room and waited until she had everyone's undivided attention.

"I have something to talk with you all about, but first, I ask that you let me finish before you respond. Okay?"

Everyone agreed.

"As you know, I've been working on my autobiography, *The Missing Piece*, for quite a while now. I'm happy to say that it's finished and has been submitted to the publisher for the first round of editing."

Everyone appeared pleased but remained quiet, even Erica, who had come to sit on Evie's lap.

"I wrote about my childhood, of course, but mostly, I dwelled on you, the most important part of my life—my family." Teary-eyed, Lorretta bowed her head for a moment as if trying to maintain her composure. "And I wrote about Clarissa."

The room got even quieter. It was as if everyone were holding his or her breath, waiting for Lorretta's next words.

Raising her eyes again, she continued. "And I wrote about her death and how she took a large piece of my heart with her when she left." Lorretta wiped her cheeks with a tissue. "Now, here is the part you may not understand. While writing about our annual trips to Virginia Beach as a complete family, I realized that by blocking out the horrible circumstances of my baby's death and the place where it happened, I was blocking out all the good times we had there as well. We had so many wonderful times there at the ocean."

Evie glanced over at her father, who was in tears. Her heart broke for him. She knew the depths of his pain and loss all too well.

"I don't know how you all would feel about this, but I was thinking that when summer comes, we might go back there as a family again. I think—I hope—each of us can find some peace and closure that we all need," Lorretta said as she wiped away her tears again. "That's all I have to say."

Everyone remained quiet for a moment, as if absorbing what Lorretta had just said. Evie, for one, had vowed years ago never to go back to the ocean again. She wondered if the rest of her family had sworn the same.

Erica was the first to speak. She turned and faced Evie. "Are we going to go to the beach, Mommy?" she asked anxiously.

Evie smiled softly as she looked around at the rest of her family. She found them smiling through their tears as well.

"It looks like we are, princess," Evie answered.

38
RETURNING

The eve of the day Erica had been talking incessantly about for three months finally arrived. The Edwards family was returning to Virginia Beach the next morning.

Evie had her hands full with trying to get her excited daughter to go to bed.

"If you don't go to sleep, you're going to be too tired to enjoy the trip, and you'll be asleep while the rest of us are having fun," Evie told her wide-eyed daughter. "Now, close your beautiful brown eyes, and go to sleep," she said while tweaking her daughter's nose.

"Okay, Mommy," Erica said as Evie tucked her in, and they said their good nights.

Contentedly, Evie went to the living room and sat down on the sofa. She dialed Sam on the phone. She and Sam had fallen into the habit of talking daily on the phone after Erica went to bed.

He had been shocked when Evie told him they were going back to Virginia Beach. The night she had told him about her mother's tearful request, he couldn't seem to understand. He still didn't.

"I don't get it," he said. "I've never told you this before, Evie, but the main reason my father and I moved our business to Kentucky was because of what happened to your baby sister. I just couldn't look at the ocean without thinking of what happened to her." He paused for a moment. "I felt responsible. I told you the ocean was safe. I downplayed the fact that you yourself were wounded by one of them—by one of those monsters."

Evie was slightly taken aback by his confession. She'd had no idea he had been carrying around that guilt for so long. So much guilt had been shared by all concerned.

"It wasn't your fault, Sam. All of us have been burdened by guilt for what happened to Clarissa. Some of us have blamed ourselves—and God and the ocean and the creatures in it—but the truth is, none of us were to blame. It was a freak accident that no one could have predicted or prevented." She paused for a moment. "Are you getting what I'm saying, Sam? No one has ever blamed you, so you've got to stop blaming yourself."

"I'll try," he said quietly. "But that's easier said than done."

"I know," Evie replied.

"You all drive safely tomorrow," Sam said. "If you don't mind, shoot me a text when you get there to let me know you arrived safely."

"I will," Evie said. "Dad rented a van so we could all ride together. It's gonna be fun riding with everyone."

"How do you really feel about being back at the ocean? Are you going to go swimming?"

"No. Neither I nor Erica will be swimming in the ocean. We might get our feet wet, but we'll do our swimming in the pool."

"That's good to hear," he said, sounding relieved. "I'm glad."

Evie heard him release an audible breath.

"I'm going to miss our nightly conversations," he said.

"I will too," Evie replied honestly. "I'll try to call you, but I'm not sure how much privacy I'm going to have with a houseful of people."

"Don't worry about it. I understand. And you know that old saying: 'Absence makes the heart grow fonder.'" He laughed.

Evie liked the sound of his laughter. It made her laugh too. "I've heard that before. We'll see, I guess. Won't we?" she asked.

"Yes, we will," he replied.

The day had finally arrived. The family was in the van and were just moments away from their destination in Virginia Beach. Erica was bouncing up and down in her seat excitedly.

"I can't wait, Grandpa. Are we almost there?" Erica squealed. She was sitting in the smallest seat, in the very back of the van, with Cloe and Evie in the seats in front of her.

"We're almost there, pumpkin!" Dan shouted back to Erica. "In just a few more minutes, we'll be at the beach."

Evie turned and looked back at Erica, who was gazing at her with such innocent anticipation that it touched Evie's heart. Erica looked so much like her father, and Evie was glad for that. Her thoughts were interrupted by the sound of her father's booming voice announcing their arrival at the two-bedroom oceanfront beach house that would become their home for the next week.

"Can I unbuckle now?" Erica asked excitedly.

"Yes, you can unbuckle, but wait for me before you get out of the van."

"Okay, Mommy."

As Evie and Erica stepped out of the vehicle, the ocean was in plain view. Evie watched her daughter's face light up when she saw the majestic beauty of the sea for the first time.

"Oh my gosh!" Erica exclaimed, jumping up and down eagerly. "It's so pretty. Can we walk down there, Mommy?"

Now that they were there, Evie wasn't sure how she felt about being back at the ocean, the place that had taken her baby sister away. Suddenly flooded with the familiar but unsettling sights and smells around her, she wasn't sure she wanted to be there. Part of her wanted to turn and run away.

Looking down at her daughter's anxious face, Evie swallowed hard and shoved aside her own feelings, replacing them with those of her innocent little girl.

"Of course we can," Evie answered. "Let's take off our sandals and go squish our toes in the sand."

After asking if anyone else wanted to come along, Evie and Erica made their way to the ocean.

"I love the sound of the waves," Erica said.

"I do too, princess." Evie had always adored the sound of the water crashing against the shore.

As they stepped into the foam of the water, Evie felt an overwhelming apprehension. She held tightly to Erica's hand.

Erica squealed as wave after wave rolled in. She tugged on Evie's arm, clearly wanting to go out farther into the water.

Evie hadn't told Erica the details of what had happened to Clarissa. She still had no intention of telling her daughter the horrific truth, but she had to explain why they couldn't walk out deeper into the sea.

She knelt down beside her enamored daughter. "The ocean is beautiful to look at, Erica, but it is a dangerous place for us to swim. Very large animals live in the ocean. We've talked about that before, remember? The ocean is their home, not ours. Do you understand?"

"I understand, Mommy," Erica answered. "I won't go swimming in the ocean. I promise."

Evie smiled at her sweet little girl's assurance. Standing up, she squeezed her daughter's tiny hand, and they waded respectfully at the edge of the vast and mysterious sea.

Early the next morning, while the rest of the family was sleeping, Evie got up for an early morning jog on the beach. While getting dressed, she grinned at Erica and Cloe, who were in the same bed, sleeping. Erica clearly treasured her aunt, and her adoration was plainly reciprocated by Cloe. They made their love for each other evident not only in words but also in deeds.

After successfully dressing and exiting out the back door without waking anyone, Evie stood and stared out at the vast ocean. She was still uncertain how she felt about being back there.

It was slightly dark outside, but the impending sun, along with lights from the boardwalk, lit the way for a promising, slow eastbound jog.

Evie had gotten out of the habit of jogging, but her love of it came rushing back with the first pound of her shoe against the wet sand.

It had been many years since she had jogged along the surf line, and she had a plethora of things running through her mind. The scenery, the ocean, Clarissa, Eric, and Sam all seemed to be clamoring for her attention at once. She felt guilty for thinking about Eric and Sam at the same time, so she pushed thoughts of Sam aside.

As the sun began to peek over the horizon, the rich, warm colors seemed to envelope her. They reminded her of her youthful desire to become an artist. She smiled as she thought of her teenage self, so full of lofty dreams and ambitions, ready to take Paris and the art world by storm, but there was not a molecule of Evie's being that regretted the path she had taken in life. Any other path, which would have excluded Eric and Erica, held no regret or wonder for her whatsoever.

Her jog felt invigorating. She had missed the mixture of exercise-induced endorphins and fresh air in her lungs, but with getting Erica ready for school and herself ready for work, she didn't have time for her morning runs anymore. This week was different, though. She looked forward to her early morning jogs for the rest of the week.

While stretching her body after her run, she admired the awesome beauty of the landscape around her. As she did, she felt the old familiar artistic desire to create and paint come over her again. She hadn't felt that in a long time. It was like embracing an old friend—one she planned on becoming reacquainted with. She felt eager at the thought of putting paint on canvas again—just for the sheer joy of it.

Walking up to the open back door of the house, Evie could smell fresh coffee and the beginnings of breakfast.

She came in to find her mother and Erica busy in the kitchen.

When Erica looked up, she ran to Evie and wrapped her arms tightly around her waist. "Did you have fun, Mommy?"

"Yes, princess, I did. Are you having fun helping Grandma Lorretta make breakfast? It smells delicious."

"Yeah, Mommy. We're making pancakes and lots of other stuff. Do you wanna help?"

"Of course I do, but first, I have to wash my hands."

Evie watched as Erica went back to the chair she had pulled up next to the counter. She was slicing fresh fruit with a plastic knife.

"Now, what can I do to help, Mom?" Evie asked.

Her mother appeared grateful for the offer. "You can set the table if you wouldn't mind. Breakfast is almost ready. And then you can go drag Cloe out of bed." She laughed.

Evie set the table and then went to get Cloe. She tapped on the bedroom door before entering. She found Cloe awake and dressed and just hanging up from a call to Stephen. Evie could tell whom she had been talking to by the enormous smile on her face. It did Evie's heart good to see her sister in love.

"So how is lover boy this morning?" Evie asked, giggling. "It's too bad Stephen couldn't come with us."

"He's great, but he misses me," Cloe answered. With an ornery smile on her face, she added, "I bet Sam misses you too."

Evie grinned. "I think Sam—*my friend*—might miss me a little."

Cloe patted the bed, an obvious invitation for Evie to sit down beside her. "You know that man's in love with you, don't you?"

"No, I don't know for sure that he is. We don't talk about love, Cloe. We're only friends. That's all I want to be. I can't be anything more—not right now," Evie said solemnly. She felt Cloe's arms envelope her.

"I wish there was something I could do to help you get past Eric," Cloe said.

Evie pulled away and looked into Cloe's face. Evie's eyes were stinging. "That's just it, Cloe. I don't want to get past Eric. I can't ..." She paused. "I won't leave him behind. I love him," she said tearfully.

Cloe pulled her into her arms again. "I'm sorry, sis. Of course you can never leave Eric behind."

Evie cried in her sister's embrace. When her breath became steadier, she felt Cloe pull away.

"But, sis," Cloe said, sounding cautious, "I feel I need to say this, even though it may not be what you want to hear." After a pause, she continued. "What you went through with losing Eric was unimaginable and could break even the strongest person, and I'm so proud of you for finding the fortitude to keep going all these years."

"Why do I hear a *but* coming?" Evie asked.

"But," Cloe replied softly, "Eric has been gone for nearly seven years now, Evie. In those seven years, the only one of us who hasn't changed is Eric. He's in the same place, but you're not, Erica's not, and Sam's not."

Just then, their mother yelled down the hallway that they were starting without them.

"I wish you'd leave Sam out of this," Evie said, twirling the edge of the bedspread into a tight knot.

"It's not about Sam, Evie. It's about you. You're letting your life pass you by, and I don't want you to be old and alone and realize you made some grave misjudgments."

"I am not alone, Cloe. I have Erica," Evie said defiantly.

"Erica is such a blessing and a joy, but you know as well as I do that she will grow up, and if you've raised her right, she will go on with her own life." Quietly, Cloe continued. "Your heart has amazing capabilities, Evie. When you found Eric, you didn't love me and Mom and Dad any less, and I know that when Erica came along, she didn't replace how you felt about Eric. You have room in your heart to love and cherish Eric and open it up to someone new."

Evie stared into her sister's eyes. The two were clearly at a stalemate. Finally, she responded, "I'm sorry, Cloe, but you don't know what you're talking about."

Before her sister could respond, Evie pulled away and started down the hall. She had just reached the edge of the dining area, when she heard her father's voice. She bowed her head.

"Father, we come to You this morning with heavy but happy hearts, sad for those who are no longer with us and grateful for those who are.

Please be with us and watch over us every day but especially this week. Help us to appreciate our time here together as a family. Help us to heal and to forgive. Help us to make peace with the tragedies we have suffered by embracing the peace we can find in You, if only we will seek it. Thank You, Father. And finally, please bless this food and the precious hands of Lorretta and Erica, who prepared it for us. Amen."

It was their fourth day at the beach, and Evie had to admit she missed talking with Sam. After tucking her phone into the side pocket of her jogging shorts, she snuck out of the house for her morning run and alone time.

She knew Sam would be awake, so she sat down on the boardwalk and dialed his number.

"Well, hello, stranger," he said when he answered the phone.

Evie could hear the smile in his voice. She smiled too. "Hi, Sam. How are you doing?"

"Other than missing my friend, I'm doing good. How are you? How's the family doing?"

"We're doing surprisingly well," she answered. "I have to admit it feels odd being back here, but at the same time, I think it's been good for us. I hope and pray that Mom and Dad are finding some closure here."

"How about you, Evie?" he asked seriously. "Are you finding any closure for yourself?"

Evie wasn't sure what he meant. Was he talking about Clarissa or Eric? It didn't matter because what she had to say applied to both. "I'm trying to find some closure and peace, Sam," she said. "I'm trying really hard." Turning her head in the direction of the surf, she said, "I look out at the ocean, and I can still see the beauty of it, but it kind of mirrors life, you know? It's beautiful, but it can swallow you up in an instant. Just when you're at your happiest, it can roll in and devastate you."

Sam was quiet for a moment. "To be honest, I don't know how to respond to that analogy, Evie. As you know, I've known loss too. I lost my mother to breast cancer all those years ago. I still miss my mom, and God knows I still love her, but I realized I had to move on. Mom would have wanted me to move on." He paused for a moment. "I get what you're saying, Evie. I do. But just because life deals us a tragedy that brings us to our knees doesn't mean we must stay down there. We can get back up if we choose to, but we have to want to. We have to fight to."

Now Evie knew for sure he was talking about Eric, and she didn't like it. He had no right to judge her grief or determine how long it should last. She had already put up with this from Cloe, and now Sam. She didn't know what to say to him, so she didn't say anything.

"Evie? Are you still there?" he asked.

"Yes, but I gotta go," she said, on the verge of angry tears.

"Please, Evie, talk to me. Don't shut me out," he said.

Evie disconnected the call.

Evie tried her best to enjoy the remaining three days of their family vacation. She and Cloe had come to an unapologetic truce and were back to their old selves, although they hadn't spoken more about their conversation. Evie managed all right until she thought about Sam. During her run the morning after their last telephone conversation, she decided it would be best to end their friendship. Friendship was apparently not enough for Sam, but it was all Evie was capable of giving for now. She planned on telling him when she got back home that their friendship had to end.

The morning of their last day at the beach house arrived. They had just finished breakfast, and Evie and Cloe were clearing the table.

Erica's usually smiling face was scrunched into an adorable frown. "I don't wanna go home," she whined. "I like it here."

"We like it here too, princess, but this is not our home. Don't you want to go home and see your friends?" Evie asked in an effort to cheer up her child. "School will be starting back soon. Don't you want to go back to school?"

Erica perked up a bit. "I guess," she said. "But can we take another walk down to the pier and ride the Ferris wheel again tonight? Can Aunt Cloe come too?"

"You just try to stop me, peanut," Cloe said as she bent down and tickled Erica on her sides. Erica let out a squeal and laughed as Cloe played with her.

Evie continued to clear the table while watching her unusually solemn parents. They hadn't walked down to the ocean yet. They had been outside and in the pool with Erica, but they had yet to walk to the edge of the sea that had taken away their baby daughter.

Evie's father cleared his throat. "Your mom and I are going to go take a walk on the beach," he said as they both stood.

Erica's face lit up. "Can I come too, Grandpa Dan?"

Evie went to Erica. "Not this time, princess. Grandma and Grandpa need some alone time."

Erica wrinkled up her nose. "Why?"

"Sometimes adults need to be alone to think about things. Understand?"

Erica shrugged. "I guess."

"Hey, peanut, how about if you and I play a game while your mother does the dishes?" Cloe asked, laughing.

"Very smooth, Cloe," Evie replied while Erica ran and picked up a board game.

While standing at the kitchen sink, Evie watched her parents walk hand in hand down to the beach. They walked slowly together until they reached the surf. She watched as they stood there holding each other, obviously distraught. Evie could feel their heartache. She knew their pain. She prayed they could find the healing and peace they had come there for.

39
BETWIXT

The Edwards family had returned home from an enjoyable and, hopefully, healing trip to Virginia Beach.

It had been two weeks, and their routines were almost returning to normal. Just as planned, Evie had broken things off with Sam the night they returned home, and she had not heard from him since. She found herself missing him; she missed her friend. It saddened and even angered her that Sam had expected more from her than she could give. If he had just been content, this wouldn't have had to happen. Why couldn't he just understand?

After an exhausting day at work, Evie put Erica to bed with a story and her usual tuck-in. Just as Evie was about to turn off the bedside lamp, she heard, "I love you, Mommy." Erica's voice was soft and genuine.

Evie stared into the dark brown eyes of her precious little girl. "I love you too, my princess—more than you will ever know."

Erica grinned. "I know, Mommy."

They smiled at each other, and Evie turned out the light.

After putting on a nightshirt, she climbed into bed with her journal. She needed to talk to her husband.

My dearest Eric,

I just put our baby girl to bed. I'm so blessed to be her mother. We created the most loving child I have ever met. Watching her grow is such a privilege. Every day is magical with her.

I'm so glad she has your eyes and your smile. You would be so proud of her. I know I am.

I've been through a trying few weeks, Eric— confusing weeks. I don't know how to feel. My thoughts and emotions are sometimes scattered and conflicted, and I don't know how to make sense of them. I need your help.

I have … I had a friend. His name was Sam. At one time, many years ago—way before I met you—I thought I was in love with Sam, but after loving you and being loved by you, I think maybe it was just infatuation.

I broke off my friendship with Sam a few weeks ago. I'm glad I did, because it was for his good. I was hurting him, and I didn't want to do that anymore. The thing is, I miss him. Not in the way that I miss you, of course. I miss you more than words can describe. You are in my heart, and you always will be.

Sometimes I wonder if my deep and abiding love for you has destined me to be alone for the rest of my life. I think it has, Eric, and the funny thing is, I'm not bitter about it. I have my memories of you and of loving and being loved by you, which will sustain me until my dying day. I consider that a blessing. But sometimes, like tonight, I miss being held and cherished. For the life of me, I can't even fathom being with anyone but you, my love. I can't imagine another man's touch. Even if I loved him, it would feel like such a betrayal to you. I couldn't—I won't do that to you. I just won't.

People tell me I need to move on. That's easy for them to say but impossible for me to do. When people tell me that, I have to wonder if they have ever been truly in love. If they had, they wouldn't say that to me. And if you wanted me to move on with Sam or anyone else, you would send me a sign. I know you would. You would find a way to help me. I know that because I know how deeply you loved me.

I love you too, Eric, and I will love you forever and for always.

Good night, my love.
Evie

The following day was one of Evie's scheduled surgery days. She spent the majority of it on her feet. Her back ached, and her feet were sore as she climbed into her car. It was a sweltering late-August evening, so Evie turned the air-conditioning on full blast. She sat there relaxing for a moment with the cool air blowing in her face. She felt tired but relieved. Having people's lives in her hands on a daily basis was terrifying at times but also rewarding and humbling. Thankfully, all of her surgeries had gone without incident that day. They were all successful, and for that, Evie was grateful.

As she was about to pull out of the parking space, her cell rang. Looking at the screen, she saw it was her mother calling.

"Hi, Mom," Evie said. "I know I'm late, but I'm on my way."

"That's okay, sweetheart. Actually, I'm calling for Erica. She wants to speak to you."

"Hi, Mommy." Erica's sweet voice came over the speakers in her car, causing Evie to giggle.

"Hey, princess. I'm in the car and on my way."

"Grandma Lorretta made pork chops for dinner. I don't like pork chops," Erica said, as if it were the end of the world.

"I know you don't like pork chops. What would you like for dinner?" Evie asked, knowing the answer before she asked it.

"Chicken nuggets!" Erica replied excitedly. "Will you bring me some?"

Laughing, Evie said, "Of course I will, princess. Chicken nuggets coming right up."

"Thank you, Mommy!" Erica shouted.

"You're welcome, princess. I'll be there in a few minutes."

"Bye, Mommy."

Evie relished the sound of her delightful baby's voice as she pulled out of the parking lot.

In an effort to relax from such a tiring day, Evie turned on the radio, tuning in to some soft classical music instead of her usual oldies.

As she pulled into the extensive line of drive-through patrons to get Erica's chicken nuggets, her phone rang again. Looking at the screen, she saw that it was Sam calling. She turned off the music and froze—unsure what to do. Seeing his name on the screen, she realized how badly she wanted to talk to him, but she wasn't sure if she could bring herself to answer the phone.

Confusing emotions overcame her. Suddenly, she felt divided, as if she were living with one foot in the past with Eric and the other hoping desperately to step into the future with Sam. Having never felt this way before, she didn't know what to do.

With every ring of the phone, her heart beat faster, until finally, the ringing stopped, and her heart sank. Feeling conflicted and sad, she couldn't stop the tears from forming in her eyes.

Knowing that only one person could understand, she began talking out loud. "Please, Eric, help me," she pleaded. "Tell me what to do. I need your help. Please give me a sign. I need you to let me know somehow that it's okay for me to move on." Sobs racked her body at the thought of moving on without Eric. It felt wrong; still, she continued. "I don't know what to do, Eric. I feel so torn. I need you to help me, my love."

Looking down at her hands, she said, "I can still feel your hand in mine. I can still feel the warmth, love, and strength I felt when you held my hand." She was sobbing so hard she could barely speak. "I can't open my hand to release you, Eric. I just can't let you go. You'll have to do it for me. You'll have to be the one to let go."

Desperate for an answer from her beloved, Evie waited until it was her turn to place her order. After she did so, the line moved slowly forward. As she pulled up to the open window, she could hear the music from inside the restaurant playing over the speakers. She heard the beginning notes of an old familiar song. Tears streamed down her face again as a flood of pure love and emotion washed over her. Eric's and her song, "How Deep Is Your Love," was playing. He was answering her request. He was letting her go, and it was breaking her heart all over again.

The young woman handing Evie her order looked at her with a concerned expression on her face. "Ma'am, are you all right?"

"Yes, I'm okay," Evie answered while still crying. "Thank you."

Overcome with emotion, Evie drove down the hill and pulled off to the side of the road. She wiped her tears and spoke to her Eric. "I know now that you can hear me, my love. You have heard me all along. I have felt you with me, and I will always feel you with me. I hope you know that. My heart is broken, but thank you, my love, for your blessing on my life. I couldn't let go, Eric. I just wasn't strong enough to release you on my own. Thank you for helping me."

She took a deep breath. With a feeling of resolve, she continued as tears streamed down her face. "I want you to know that as I move forward, Eric, no matter where this life may take me or with whom, you will always be in my heart, my love. You will never be forgotten, and no one will ever take your place."

Smiling softly, with both feet planted firmly in the present, she whispered the words it had taken her nearly seven years to utter. "I have to say goodbye to you now, my sweet Eric," she said tearfully.

Those words caused her pain as they came out of her mouth, but at the same time, she could feel them setting her free.

She sighed deeply. "Thank you, Eric. Thank you for loving me," she whispered as she wiped away her tears. "I have faith that I'll see you again someday. I love you so much. And I will love you forever and for always."

Feeling the need, Evie bowed her head and thanked God for all His abundant blessings and tender mercies on her. Mostly, she thanked Him for the privilege of having had Eric in her life, even if only for a short while.

After raising her head, Evie exhaled a deep breath and wiped away the remainder of her tears. She felt a relief she didn't fully understand yet. That would take some time, but her heart felt lighter somehow.

As she was about to put her car in gear, her phone rang. She looked at the screen. It was Sam calling again. Wanting to talk to her friend, Evie answered his call. As soon as she said hello, he began speaking.

"Please don't hang up, Evie," he said urgently. "Please give me time to apologize for overstepping my bounds during our last conversation. I had no right—"

Evie interrupted him. "It's okay, Sam," she said softly.

"No. No, it's not okay," he said. "I cornered you, and I'm sorry. I wouldn't hurt you for anything in the world. I—"

Evie interrupted him again. Surprising herself, she asked, "Sam, would you like to go to lunch with me on Saturday?"

He didn't readily respond. "Am I hearing you right?" he finally asked, sounding stunned.

Evie spoke quietly. "Sam, you're not the only one who needs to apologize. I've been so focused on my own needs that I haven't given thought as to how difficult this has been for you. I'm so sorry. All I can tell you is that I'm trying to find my way, Sam. It's impossible to put into words how difficult it has been, but I'm trying. I just need a little more time to adjust. I need you to be patient with me." She stopped and summoned her courage. "So to that end, I'll ask you again. Would you like to go to lunch with me on Saturday?"

"You mean as friends?" he asked. "Or are you asking me out on a date?" He chuckled.

Evie smiled. "How about as friends for now, and we'll see where that takes us?" she asked softly. She heard Sam laugh on the other end of the line.

"I would love that," he replied. "Sounds like the perfect plan to me."

His unselfish response warmed Evie's heart. It made her happy that he was open to wherever their friendship might lead.

You may visit the author's website at
www.writingsbyclaudia.com.

CPSIA information can be obtained
at www.ICGtesting.com
Printed in the USA
FSHW011851230321
79792FS